DAY 7

BOOKS BY KERRY DREWERY

Cell 7
Day 7

A Brighter Fear
A Dream of Lights

DAY 7

KERRY DREWERY

HOT
KEY
BOOKS

First published in Great Britain in 2017 by
HOT KEY BOOKS
80–81 Wimpole St, London W1G 9RE
www.hotkeybooks.com

ISBN: 978-1-4714-0569-3
also available as an ebook

1

This book is typeset using Atomik ePublisher
Printed and bound by Clays Ltd, St Ives Plc

Hot Key Books is an imprint of Bonnier Zaffre Ltd,
a Bonnier Publishing company
www.bonnierpublishing.com

For the Barons
Janet, Jack, Helen and Paul
and also remembering
Edward, Prince and 'beef it' Rocky

During times of universal deceit, telling the truth
becomes a revolutionary act.

Unknown

Prologue

I should be dead.
I
should
be
dead.
I feel cold air in my lungs.
I feel somebody's hand holding mine.
I hear shouting.
'Martha, what . . . ?'
'Martha, when . . . ?'
'Martha, how . . . ?'
Too loud.
Too loud.
Shut up. *Please.*
I can see lights –
white.
Dots of phone eyes watching me.
Massive TV cameras blinding me.
Photographs.
Bam, bam, bam.
I have no comment for them.
I'm walking.
Holding the ring you gave me, I keep walking.

Away from you, and I'm sorry.
So sorry.
I'm in pieces.
Part of me stays with you.
And if you die, that part of me will die with you.

DAY 1

TV STUDIO

10.30 a.m. Credits roll for *Buzz for Justice* – the latest popular TV show

A wide studio. At the rear, stepped seating is filled with the waiting audience. At the front, on the right of the stage is a black, glossy witness box on a raised platform, security glazing around the top half. On the wall to the left is a large screen.

Between the stage and the audience is a long desk with three panellists. In front of each panellist is an oversized blue buzzer, and hanging above each is a 3D representation of the *Buzz for Justice* eye logo – faintly illuminated and blinking slowly.

A lively, fast-paced theme tune fades out and the host, Kristina – wearing a fitted grey pinstripe trouser suit with pale blue low-cut blouse – strides onto the stage. She smiles and flicks her blonde wavy hair to the side. The audience's applause quietens.

KRISTINA: Hello, and welcome to today's episode of *Buzz for Justice*, where we will have, I promise you, exclusive coverage of crimes, lies and jail terms, quiet innocence versus angry guilt. We will have tears, we will have truths, and most probably we will have tantrums!

The audience applaud and a murmured 'oooh' can be heard.

KRISTINA: Yes indeed, we have plenty to come, believe me, so let's move quickly on and welcome our judging panel, who have this incredible opportunity to dispense justice. Don't forget, ladies and gents, only a majority is needed: two buzzers pressed, two guilty votes cast, and our accused is going down!

She pauses, the lighting above the panellists increases and Kristina turns to them.

KRISTINA: A big *Buzz for Justice* welcome to panellist number one – Ava, a pensioner from Camden whose lifelong ambition is to appear on television.

The camera focuses on an ebullient Ava, waving madly, before moving to the next panellist.

KRISTINA: Hello to Sadiq, panellist number two. From a small village in Derbyshire, he dreams of a future in the music industry.

Sadiq smiles warmly.

KRISTINA: And last but by no means least, panellist number three – our wannabe actress, Candice from Birmingham. Hello, Candice.

The camera moves to Candice. She strikes a pose, tosses her head back and smiles widely.

KRISTINA: What an inspiring group of justice seekers we have in charge of decision-making today! Let's bring out our first criminal, someone who may already be familiar to many of you. He certainly is to me – it's former death row prisoner and recent *Death is Justice* guest, yes, the one and only . . . Gus Evans!

Music plays as spotlights zip around the studio, highlighting Gus: a thin, dishevelled man, in faded and torn jeans and a crumpled T-shirt, as he steps out from backstage. Escorted by a security guard, he walks to the witness box with his head down, and takes his place. The guard turns the lock. The music fades and the lights steady.

KRISTINA: Gus, how wonderful to see you again. Let's think, it's been all of a . . . a week?

She laughs at him. Gus nods slowly.

KRISTINA: Well, I for one cannot wait to hear what you've
been getting up to these past seven days and to
discover what exactly has brought you here for
judging. Without more ado, let's take a look.

She turns to the screen behind them, filled with the previous
day's CCTV footage of the renowned death row building.
Grand and imposing, a facade for a justice system that knows
no remorse, the pain of the prisoners travelling along its death
row cells – one for each day of the week – hidden by its sleek
doors and shiny frontage. The reality of the sentence given
by public vote on the seventh day obscured by its neon eye
logo above and its promises of entertainment for all who
tune in to watch.

The feed focuses on Gus, standing a little apart from a mass
of demonstrators holding placards reading 'A Life For A Life'
or 'We Demand Safe Streets'. The placard Gus holds says
'One Person, One Vote', and his mouth moves as he chants,
shifting his weight from foot to foot to keep warm before
punching the air with a fist.

A car pulls up; Gus throws down his placard and charges
forward. As the crowd descends on the car, rocking it and
pushing it, the camera pulls back. Gus is lost among the mob.
The car tips onto its side then over to its roof. Glass shatters
across the road and the picture cuts before zooming close
on a grainier image: a young woman crying on the ground,
then an elderly man sitting at the roadside with a cloth held

8

to his bleeding forehead. It shifts again, freeze-framing on Gus, his face contorted in anger and his hands resting on the upside-down car.

Kristina turns to Gus and shakes her head.

KRISTINA: I think I speak for us all when I say we are somewhat shocked to see your behaviour. Behaviour that clearly led to the injuries of innocent civilians, that young woman and that frail senior citizen among many others.

She turns back to the screen.

KRISTINA: But let's see what your actual charge is.

The image of Gus slides to the right side of the screen while on the left the word 'CRIME' illuminates in large blue lettering. Underneath it rows of LEDs flash and the tension builds. The lights stop with a bang; formed by them is a list: 'PUBLIC AFFRAY, CAUSING A NUISANCE, INCITING RIOTS'.

The audience murmur.

In the witness box Gus raises his hands in the air and his mouth opens and closes but no sound can be heard. The security guard unclips his baton from his belt and taps it on the glass in warning.

KRISTINA: *Three* public-order offences. *Three.* How do we feel about that, ladies and gentlemen?

Tutting ripples through the audience.

KRISTINA: Is this the type of man we wish to see on our streets? Someone who we've previously given the benefit of the doubt, but has thrown it back in our faces? Someone who has pretended to be an ally to our sister programme, *Death is Justice*, but has continued to associate with criminals? Someone from the impoverished Rises who we've befriended and supported, yet is unappreciative of our kindness? Do we want him on our streets?

The audience jeer.

KRISTINA: Not on my watch, I say. But this is not my decision to make. It's yours: the people's. Your land, your rules, your democracy – in your hands. The decision is with the three representatives who've bravely put themselves forward for the task, who've paid their own good money for that honour and for the responsibility of representing the thoughts and opinions of you, the public. But first, let's find out what Gus Evans's sentence would be if our panellists do find him guilty.

Again she turns to the screen. Beneath the list of crimes, the word 'TOTAL' appears and next to it a row of LEDs flash and flicker and again stop with a bang. It reads '7 YEARS'. Kristina gives a low whistle.

KRISTINA: Quite some prison term you've racked up there, Gus. Don't you think so, viewers? My word. But, I have to say, much deserved. And, of course, a vital message and deterrent to any others with thoughts of upsetting the status quo.

She strides across the studio floor towards Gus.

KRISTINA: But of course, in this true democracy of ours we couldn't ask the panellists to deliver a verdict without first hearing from our defendant.

She stops at the witness box. Spotlights above her and Gus brighten.

KRISTINA: Gus Evans, you have thirty seconds to make your statement, starting from . . .

On the screen behind them, the image of Gus at the crime scene is replaced with a large, digital :30. The sound crackles as Gus's microphone is turned on.

KRISTINA: Now!

The display reads :29 immediately.

GUS: Errr . . .

KRISTINA: These precious seconds are yours to persuade
us of your innocence, Gus. Don't waste them!

GUS: I . . . er . . . all I did –

KRISTINA: Perhaps you feel honesty is your best policy here.
Although I do have to point out that – unlike
the past justice system – *we* do not make deals!

She laughs.

KRISTINA: We believe in proper and fair punishments
for crimes, not leniency for admitting you're a
criminal when the fact is already plain to see!

The display reads :16.

GUS: I didn't do nothing! I held a placard, that's all! I didn't
start no *affray*! Didn't cause no riots or nothing! This
is bullcr—

His voice is cut off. The display reads :00. His mouth moves
as he shouts unheard, spit flecking onto the glass, his palms
slamming against it, everything smeared and steamed up.

The camera moves to a smiling Kristina.

KRISTINA: Time's up, I'm afraid, Gus. Let's turn our attention to our panellists. Do they think justice as important as we do, viewers? Audience?

Her high heels click along the studio floor as she strides towards the panellists. The lighting changes, spotlights on Ava, Sadiq and Candice. Above them the 3D eye logos crackle like static as each iris glows an ice blue.

On the screen the timer reverts to :30.

KRISTINA: Panellist number one, Ava, we come to you first. You've seen the video clip, you've heard Gus's defence, you now have thirty seconds to make your decision.

A timer ticks loudly as the numbers count down. Ava's elderly hand hovers over the button in front of her.

KRISTINA: Ava, I shall have to hurry you. If you wish to vote Gus guilty and send him to prison for the seven years, then you have –

She glances to the screen.

KRISTINA: – ten seconds to decide. Remember, press the button for guilty, don't press if you think him inno—

13

Ava slams both hands onto the buzzer. Above her the eye brightens, crackles louder and brighter blue shines down on her.

KRISTINA: One down, two to go. A majority needed. Gus, if Sadiq votes you guilty, you'll be heading off immediately to begin your sentence. Sadiq, your decision, please.

The display begins its countdown again. Sadiq's hands lie flat on the desk, one either side of the buzzer. He stares at it. Blue from the eye above shines down on him. His hands tremble.

KRISTINA: Fifteen seconds, Sadiq.

He lifts both hands and they hover over the buzzer.

KRISTINA: Ten.

The display pulses with every second. The audience chant the countdown. Sadiq looks to Gus, folds his arms across his chest and shakes his head.

KRISTINA: Five. Still time, Sadiq. Three. Two. One.

The eye above Sadiq closes and fades to black. He's drowned in darkness.

KRISTINA: Well, ladies and gentlemen, viewers at home, what a surprise! I, for one, thought this an open-and-shut case. It seems, Gus, that you've been given a lifeline – but maybe not for long!

Kristina steps towards the next person.

KRISTINA: Panellist number three – Candice – the decision is all yours. Gus's fate lies in your hands. But are they hands ready to deliver justice? Let's hope so. It's all down to you. Press that buzzer and Gus Evans, former death row inmate and now accused of three – yes, *three* – public-order offences that resulted in the injuries of hundreds of innocent civilians, will serve his seven years in prison. Candice, follow your heart. Your thirty seconds start . . . now.

The timer begins again. Every second flashes blue over the darkened studio.

Candice places her hands on her cheeks in mock horror. The audience shout advice; she spins around to see them. Some give a thumbs down, a few shake their heads.

CANDICE (shouting): I don't know what to do!

She shrugs, reaches across the desk and rests both hands on the buzzer. They shake. The audience cheer, but as she glances up to Gus their eyes catch. He flicks a smile and she pulls her hands back again.

The audience boo and jeer.

KRISTINA: Fifteen seconds, Candice. Ask yourself – would you want to be caught up in an affray with this man? What about your mother? Your grandmother perhaps? What is your heart telling you to do? Twelve seconds.

CANDICE (shouting): I don't know!

The display flashes down to ten . . . nine . . .

Candice looks back to the audience. One man is staring intently at her.

KRISTINA: Seven seconds, Candice, six . . . You need to act now.

The man mouths something to her and she reaches into a pocket. Unseen to camera, she glances down to a business card. An address is scrawled across it and the words 'Audition tomorrow if he goes down'.

KRISTINA: Three . . . two . . .

Candice glances to the man and back to the buzzer.

KRISTINA: One . . .

Candice slams her hands down and above her the eye glows brighter, bathing her in iridescent blue.

On stage Gus sways in the witness box and rubs a hand through his messy hair. His mouth forms the shape of words that can't be heard. The audience cheer. Kristina smiles.

KRISTINA (loud, over the audience): Well, ladies and gents, viewers, audience, a good result, I believe. One I'm certain makes us all feel safer. Gus Evans, despite your pleas of innocence, justice has prevailed. The people have spoken. *You* are going down!

Spotlights come up and dance across the stage as a victory tune blasts. The security officer unlocks the witness box.

KRISTINA: Gus Evans, you will now begin your sentence with immediate effect. Your crimes, as severe as they are, mean the full term of your incarceration – seven years – will be served with no eligibility for parole or early release.

Some of the audience stand and slow clap as Gus is taken across the stage, his hands cuffed behind his back but his head still up.

GUS (shouting): This is a joke! A sham! All I did was tell the truth, but nobody wants to hear it. So they stitch me up! Wake up, you morons. Wake up!

KRISTINA: Thank you for joining us, viewers, and thank you panellists for ensuring justice is served.

The guard drags Gus across the stage, but as he nears the panellists' desk, away from the eye of the camera, the man who looked at Candice leans from the shadows.

MAN (whispering): We warned you, Gus; you didn't comply. This is the result. This is how powerful we are. You shouldn't have forgotten.

The man blends back into the darkness. Now with his head down, Gus is led away.

Isaac

I've never known silence like this. It's so quiet I can hear my eyelids making a noise when I blink and the saliva against my teeth when I swallow. My own breathing is almost deafening.

They didn't let me make a statement; they told me what I said in my victim speech yesterday would serve for that.

They asked me if I'm stupid.

'Why the hell did you take the rap for that? Especially for that piece of shit Honeydew girl.'

I didn't reply. I kept my mouth shut and tried to block them out as they shaved my head, stripped me naked and watched me dress in white prison garb.

'Don't rise to it,' I told myself.

And now here I am in Cell 1.

Six more cells and six more days ahead of me. A system I don't believe in, that promotes lies and sensationalism, headlines and hearsay over honesty and truth. A deluded and tricked public deciding whether someone lives or dies on a basis of propaganda and misinformation.

It's black or white. Guilty or not guilty. No grey, no reasons. Yes or no, without explanation.

The law states an eye for an eye.

I knew that. I knew it when I pulled the trigger and shot my so-called father.

That Martha would've died if I hadn't done so serves no reason in a system where reason isn't allowed.

Fact: I killed him.

Fact: I'm guilty.

Fact: I will die.

Martha

I want to eat the food in front of me because they told me it would help. Eve and Cicero and Max, that is.

But I can't.

And I lie down on the bed because they told me I'd feel better for sleep and we can sort it all out in the morning.

But how can I sleep?

Your face, Isaac, is in front of my eyes.

Your hand, Isaac, is touching mine.

And your words are whispering in my ears.

I

cannot

sleep.

Cannot

eat.

Cannot

accept a world without you.

My head's spinning.

Can't breathe.

I push out of the bedroom door and into the hallway, through the kitchen and living room, gasping for breath, tears I don't want falling down my face.

I feel sick.

Hands are tingling.

I fumble with the lock and push the French doors open.

The cold hits me like a brick.

Wakes me.

Forces me to suck in icy air.

My feet crunch through frost as I tear across the garden and I collapse onto the grass.

God, I miss you, Isaac.

I'm sorry.

So damn sorry.

I roll on my back.

The wind blows. I shiver. I stare up at the pale sky, wishing it was night and I could see the stars.

Our stars, Isaac.

That don't know guilt or innocence.

Are you looking out of that tiny window right now, staring up at the sky just as I am?

I blot out everything and imagine you're here next to me, and I'm sure I feel your hand take mine.

Isaac

'Deny, deny, deny,' my so-called father Jackson told me once.

I had told him I cheated on the exam, copied from a boy sitting next to me. Told him, my cheeks burning with shame, that I panicked and couldn't remember how to do the graph and explained that the boy saw me and reported me to the teacher.

He laughed at me. 'Just grow a pair,' he sneered.

My stepmother Patty came in and saw us standing in the kitchen together, an unusual sight. I remember Jackson shaking his head as he explained what had happened.

'I told him,' he said, pointing to me, 'they can't prove anything. Deny. It's nothing to worry about.'

But I wanted to be punished; I deserved to be. Cheating had got me an A and would get me into top set when I didn't deserve it. Yet I saw something like pride in Jackson's eyes rather than disappointment.

'You took the opportunity presented,' he said. 'Good on you.'

'They can't prove anything,' Patty agreed. 'It's your word against his. The teacher didn't see you, right? Only the boy.'

'She's right,' Jackson said. 'You want to get somewhere in this life, then look after number one and climb over people to get there. All you did was use your initiative.'

'No,' I whispered, 'I cheated.'

Patty looked at me as if I was stupid. 'Just about as naive as you were when we met,' she threw at Jackson, then she took a step towards me. 'Nobody in this life is going to help you but yourself. Look at your father – how do you think he got where he is today? By taking advantage of situations offered,' she said. 'I taught him that.'

Jackson didn't reply; he was already walking out the room.

At school the next day, standing in front of the head of year while he accused me of cheating, I couldn't bring myself to deny it, so I told the truth. When Patty heard I had a week's detention she called me a fool, but all Jackson did was lift his newspaper to read. The headline 'Isaac Paige Named Teen Crime Ambassador' obscured his face and my own photo leered back at me.

I had no argument then; I was guilty – I knew that when I looked at the other boy's work. And I have no argument now; I am guilty – and I knew *that* when I pulled the trigger. Yet still I did it.

An eye for an eye.

I drag the bed over to the window, it scrapes loudly on the floor but no one comes at the noise. The sky is a crisp, winter blue. Our sky, Martha, and our stars are still there, although hidden by daylight now.

If I twist my head at an uncomfortable angle I can see the path I took to the viewing area. There's a tree down there. It looks out of place, as if someone's planted it far too close to the building.

The branches are bare, waiting for life to come back to it in the spring.

Huh, there *is* life though, there's a bird and a nest. I wonder if it will survive the winter. Maybe someone's feeding it and helping it. I hope so.

Did you see it while you were in here, Martha?

I wish we could've at least spoken after your Cell 7.

I wish I could've stayed with you for longer, held you in my arms and told you I love you, and that I am so proud to be your friend.

Seven days ago you were in here, lying on this bed, within these white walls.

Time moves so fast. Waits for nothing and no one.

Me and you, Martha, have fought to change the justice system, to rid it of the corruption and to make it fair, and we are still fighting. But even if we *do* succeed, will there still be the death penalty? Is that what the people of this country want?

And just because they want it, does that make it right?

The Prime Minister

A private jet stands on the runway underneath a crisp, blue November sky.

The door swings open and, flanked by two security officers, the Prime Minister emerges from the plane. At the top of the metal stairs he pauses to adjust his mirrored sunglasses and they glint as they catch the winter sun. With a smile, his white teeth dazzling, he skips down the steps and takes a few strides across the runway towards the waiting press and public.

Raising both hands for silence, he scans the faces and the cameras, waiting for quiet and full attention before he speaks.

'Ladies and gentlemen, thank you for welcoming me back to the country so warmly, especially on a day that is far from warm itself.'

The audience titter and he smiles again.

'Unlike the blue above us, however, it seems that we have been under somewhat stormy skies of late. I have been watching the unfolding events concerning our justice system while I have been overseas, and in particular watching certain inmates housed on death row with intensity, interest and the utmost concern.'

He pauses, pushes out his chest and lifts up his chin.

'It is imperative we remember that ours is a world-leading, innovative and inspirational justice system. It is vital that we

26

resist any knee-jerk reaction to recent developments. And it is our duty as citizens to protect our system from those unfairly manipulated by fantastical claims of others.

'Let me ask you this – what other country in the world allows each and every one of its people to be a juror in each and every case? Can you answer me that?'

Steadily and calmly, he looks over his audience.

They're silent.

'Do you know why you can't answer that? Because there isn't one. We are iconic, we are pioneers, we are the power to which others aspire. Let us never lose focus of that. Thank you.'

He begins walking away.

'But, Prime Minister,' a journalist shouts, 'what about Martha Honeydew? She was innocent. What if she'd been executed? How would that reflect on our justice system?'

The PM stops.

For a moment he pauses, then turns and nods. 'Often in life, and indeed in leadership, there is the necessity to question the meaning, and society's expectations of, such things as innocence. One must ask such questions here.'

'PM!' another shouts. 'She made a fool of the system, didn't she?'

The Prime Minister smiles and shakes his head. 'Believe that and you are a fool yourself,' he replies. 'Indeed, if those who make such accusations were to stop and examine the way in which the justice system works, it would be apparent to them that the possibility of influencing the decisions made in regards to innocence or guilt on death row is entirely negligible.'

Again he tries to move away, but a barrage of questions hits him, microphones and voice recorders aimed into his face. He takes a nonchalant step backwards and smiles at the crowd.

One of the questions comes louder than the others.

'What about corruption?'

He lifts his sunglasses off. 'What about it?' he replies.

'There were a lot of accusations made yesterday. The Paige lad had a lot of evidence; he made a lot of substantial claims. Claims that it was his father, Jackson, who killed Martha Honeydew's mother. If that were true, it would mean the young man executed for it was innocent, and there was the video –'

The PM raises his hand. 'Let me stop you just there. Unsubstantiated claims such as this are nothing more than ugly and unprofessional attempts to undermine what we in this country stand for. I cannot abide –'

'But they weren't unsubstantiated. He had evidence. And the documents he'd taken from his father's –'

The PM laughs. 'This is precisely what I'm afraid of for our country and what we must stand united against. People casting such aspersions do nothing more than undermine what so many of you, the public, have fought for over the years, and what you all deserve. That is: peace, security, safety.

'Let us not forget how dramatically the statistics for violent crimes have fallen since the introduction of Votes for All. Do you want to throw that safety and security out of the window? I doubt it. These accusations are just that – accusations – and are not worthy of our concern. Indeed, one of the many reasons the courts were dismantled was the constant threat of corruption that could, and *did*, stop the guilty from being brought to justice. Drug dealers given less time if they could name associates, murderers charged for manslaughter instead if they pleaded guilty and thus saved the courts money, police officers let off if they agreed to turn a blind eye to something else.

'This had to stop!' He raises a palm to the audience. 'And it did. Thanks to you, the public. And I beg you, be proud of what we have achieved together. Do not risk throwing it away on winds of gossip and hearsay. We – you and I, and the cabinet behind me – have pledged that we will not stand for corruption in any form, that we will fight it and, ladies and gentlemen, I am proud to say that that is still our stance.

'We took the Paige allegations seriously and, following instructions I gave while on holiday, the police and the serious crime squad thoroughly investigated them, analysed them meticulously and found them to be false. The documents supposedly taken from Jackson Paige's office – and the so-called CCTV footage – were nothing more than cleverly fabricated lies.'

He pauses and looks over his public.

'Together, let's be proud of our moral standing, and together let's stand strong. Do not let the whims of those weaker than ourselves discredit what we hold so dear.'

Cameras flash, microphones are thrust in his face and rowdy questions are thrown in the air, but a young woman walks calmly up to his side.

'We should go, sir,' she whispers.

With a nod and a smile still on his lips, he waves to the audience and strides to the terminal building.

Sofia, quiet heels, trousers and a neat sweater, follows behind, a bunch of files in her arms and a clipboard balanced on top. She blends into the background, yet her eyes are everywhere and everything is on her radar.

Across the concrete, they step inside the building, away from prying eyes and listening ears, and the Prime Minister's smile is gone. His face contorts in anger and he turns on the spot, his hands on his hips as he marches up and down.

'Bloody hell!' he shouts. 'That girl's made a *bloody* mess. This needs quashing now!' He stops walking and shakes his head. 'Bloody hell,' he says again, and blows out his cheeks. 'Sofia, what's my schedule today?'

'There are lots of people asking to speak to you, sir,' she replies as she reads down a list on her clipboard. 'The *National News* would like to interview you, *Death is Justice* have asked if you'll go on as a special guest or perhaps a live link-up, a chat show has invited you along, *Celebrity Now!* magazine would like to do a feature . . .'

He lifts a hand to silence her. 'None of those,' he says. 'I want to speak to Patty Paige. Get her.'

Outside the death row building

Martha sits in the back seat of the car, drumming her fingers on the dusty plastic of the door.

Eve turns the key and the engine falls silent. Her tired blue eyes look into the rear-view mirror.

'I don't think this is a good idea,' she says to Martha.

'Tell me a better one,' Martha replies. 'You've been full of such good ideas since I met you, what . . . a week ago?'

In the passenger seat, Cicero turns round, eyebrows raised as he looks at Martha. 'You're alive, aren't you?' he snaps. 'What do you think would've happened if Eve hadn't been your death row counsellor?'

Eve shakes her head. 'It doesn't matter,' she replies.

'It *does* matter!' He slams his fist on the seat. 'We put ourselves in danger for you, Martha! And Max did. What do you think would've happened if the authorities found out it was Max who hacked into the system at your Cell 7 and showed people that you didn't kill Jackson? Or if they worked out it was me on the phone-in, with my voice disguised so I could fight your corner? Or if they knew Eve passed messages between you and Isaac?' His face tightens as he shakes his head.

In the rear of the car, Martha shrinks into her seat.

'Hey?' His voice quietens. 'Have you stopped to think what the consequences could've been?'

31

Eve rests a hand on his knee. 'Not now,' she whispers.

Cicero sighs and turns around again.

For a moment they sit in silence.

Martha lifts an arm, wipes the mist from the window and peers out. Across the street, reporters look towards the car.

'Sorry,' she mutters. 'You're right. You all helped me get out of there. Thank you.'

'Team effort,' Eve replies. 'We weren't the ones stuck in there.'

Martha shrugs. 'I need the public to hear me,' she says quietly.

Eve unclips her seatbelt, turns to Martha and watches her for a moment.

Eventually Martha glances up at her. 'I get you,' she says. 'But I want them to know I'm not a monster. And how much . . .' She pauses, swallows hard and takes a deep breath. 'Isaac . . . how much . . . what he . . .' She looks away, wiping her sleeve across her face.

'You want me to come in with you?' Eve asks.

Martha shakes her head. 'I'll be fine,' she says. 'But –' she pauses and sucks in a deep breath – 'you'll still be here when I come out, right?'

Eve gives a thin smile and nods. 'Of course,' she replies.

6.30 p.m. The programme –
Death is Justice – is beginning.

On a dark blue screen, flecks of white buzz and crackle like electricity. An oversized eye with an ice-blue iris appears in the middle. It blinks and the words 'An Eye For An Eye For' spin in a circle around the black pupil.

MALE VOICEOVER: An Eye For An Eye Productions brings you . . .

The words stop spinning. The sound of electricity fizzes again and the style of the words goes from smooth to jagged. The eye reddens and closes.

MALE VOICEOVER: . . . tonight's show *Death is Justice* with our host . . .

The blue fades and lights come up on a glitzy studio. The large floor reflects the many studio lights from its silver-blue surface. To the right is an oversized screen filled with the eye logo – the words slowly spinning and the eye blinking – while left of centre is a shiny curved desk with high, glossy stools placed around the back and sides, facing out to the studio audience, who are hidden in shadow.

MALE VOICEOVER: . . . Joshua Decker!

Lights come up on Joshua standing in front of the desk. He wears a midnight blue, slim-cut suit with a crisp white dress shirt. His patterned tie reflects the lights and his shoes click as he strides across the studio floor. He winks to the cheering and clapping audience.

JOSHUA: Ladies and gentlemen, viewers, audience, what a welcome! Thank you! It is an absolute pleasure to be here with you again on this iconic programme.

The audience applaud louder.

JOSHUA: Yes, our dear Kristina Albright has moved on to pastures new. She is now the host of our daytime show, *Buzz for Justice*. If you've yet to see it, then I *implore* you to tune in. What a veritable cascade of entertainment it is! Justice served live, verdicts handed out by a panel consisting of people just like you. Keep a hand over those big blue buzzers, think someone's guilty and *bang*, press your buzzer and wait to see if the majority decision tips in your favour! You want to be part of it?

The audience are quiet.

JOSHUA: I said, you want to be part of it?

AUDIENCE: Yeah!

JOSHUA: Then take yourselves over to the website
www.aneyeforaneyeproductions.com, click on the
Buzz for Justice tab at the top, and apply to buy your
tickets! An absolute bargain at £99 for audience
members, £499 to be one of those all-important,
all-powerful panellists, who judge not just one case,
but all the cases for that session. In what other
society can you be at the absolute cutting edge
of justice? What a thrill! We're already racking
up quite a waiting list, so take yourself over there
today and get your application in. But back to
this show . . .

He pauses for a moment, the lights dim and he strolls
towards the audience.

JOSHUA: Yes, I can barely believe that I am your host, and
I thank you for your enthusiasm and your warm
welcome. I feel honoured and privileged.

Applause roars again.

JOSHUA: And talking about privilege . . . how much more
privilege could someone have had in life than our
latest addition to death row – Isaac Paige. What a

35

future he had laid out for him, yet he threw it all away on a whim. Or did he? What do you think?

A murmur ripples through the crowd.

JOSHUA: Many believe it a waste. Yet perhaps his intentions were pure. Maybe he did it for love? A crime of passion. If so, then I ask you, viewers, what would *you* do for the person you love most in the world?

The audience are quiet. Joshua appears to wince a little and lifts a hand briefly and suddenly to his ear. Collecting himself, he continues.

JOSHUA (offhand): Or perhaps, as some have suggested, he was manipulated into the situation, and into falsifying what he called *evidence* of corruption. A difficult question to ponder on.

Close to the audience he stops and smiles at a woman in the front. She giggles and a murmur drifts around. With a wink, he turns back to camera.

JOSHUA: Perhaps our guest today can shed some light on the situation. Yes, ladies and gentlemen, viewers at home, this evening we have a *very* special guest for you indeed. Perhaps the only person able to explain all of this. Yes, I'm certain you thought it would never happen, but today, following her release, we are speaking to death row evictee herself. Please welcome to the stage . . . Martha Honeydew!

Music thuds across the studio, the lights dip and jive, and Martha steps out from backstage. The audience applause is subdued as she walks over to Joshua, standing next to the desk. He smiles and moves to hug her, but she stiffens and backs away, and the moment is awkward.

As the music dies down and the lights settle, he and Martha take their seats.

JOSHUA: Martha, so good to see you. So good. We're all *so* relieved to see you freed.

MARTHA: Thank you.

JOSHUA: Reports are saying that at the moment you're staying with the counsellor – ex-counsellor, I should say – Eve Stanton. Is that right?

MARTHA (nodding): Yes, that's right.

JOSHUA: For now.

MARTHA: Sorry?

JOSHUA: Eve is allowing you to stay with her *for now*.

MARTHA: I . . . I don't get you.

Joshua laughs, glances to the frosty audience and back.

JOSHUA: Are you aware of what Detective Inspector Hart
from the serious crime squad said last night after
you were released?

Martha stares at him.

MARTHA: I . . . No . . .

The studio falls silent. He looks to the audience.

JOSHUA: Oh dear. Well, it seems, ladies and gentlemen, that we
are going to have to drop a bombshell on our poor
Miss Martha here. Martha, if you'd like to watch . . .

The eye logo moves to the right-hand side of the screen,
while on the left is a freeze-frame image of DI Hart, the row
of medals on his uniform reflecting the spotlights.

It begins to play. Martha is transfixed.

DI HART (video feed): The whole affair has been an utter
sham. I said from the beginning that there was more
to this than met the eye and, unfortunately, I've
been proved correct again. Honeydew has made
fools of the authorities, the victim, Isaac Paige,

the police and you, the public. As a vote-casting member of society myself, I am outraged that she took advantage of ordinary, innocent and vulnerable people and I personally promise you all that this will never happen again. Although she will not be tried for wasting police time, I can assure you that, even as we speak, plans are being drawn up to take her into a care institution to assess her psychological needs as soon as possible, and she will remain continuously supervised until that time comes. She may be innocent of the particular crime she was on death row for, but that does not mean she is fit to be walking the streets as a free citizen. As always, the public's safety is our priority.

The screen freezes on his contorted face. Martha stares at it.

JOSHUA (gently): How does that make you feel?

Martha sways in her seat, closes her eyes and grabs onto the desk.

JOSHUA: Martha, how does that make you *feel*?

She opens her eyes again and stares at the screen.

MARTHA: Sick.

JOSHUA: I'm sorry to hear that. I truly am. You had a very tough time last week on death row, didn't you?

MARTHA: No tougher than anyone else, but what did DI Hart mean when he said –

JOSHUA: Well, yes, but you –

MARTHA: Can they play that back again? I want to know what he meant when he said I'd made a fool of Isaac.

JOSHUA (with concern): We'll come back to that, Martha. As I said, you had a very tough time in there. You *were* innocent after all.

She looks from the screen to Joshua.

MARTHA: Yes, but others were, *are*, too. Oliver Barkova, for example.

JOSHUA: You say that, but –

MARTHA: You know that now, right?

She turns to the audience.

MARTHA: You know he didn't kill my mother. You know that bastard Jackson Paige did, right?

The audience don't respond.

JOSHUA: Martha, I have to ask you to mind your language.

MARTHA: You know he was guilty though? Jackson Paige? I mean, everyone knows that now, right? You saw the video feed, heard that recording, read all that stuff Isaac found –

Murmurs and comments ripple through the audience. A few shakes of heads and tuts of disbelief. Martha frowns, glances at them and back to Joshua.

Joshua's jaw clenches. He pauses as if about to say something else, then continues.

JOSHUA (quietly): You mean this recording?

The screen changes again, DI Hart replaced with a grainy CCTV image. It's zoomed so close onto Isaac pointing the gun at Jackson that Martha isn't visible. The gun bangs, white flashes, Jackson falls. It loops, plays again, loops again. Over and over.

The audience flinch. The feed pauses on Jackson as he falls. In the studio the camera moves back to Joshua and Martha.

MARTHA: It's not showing all of it! It's not showing Jackson threatening me! Someone's cut it. That's misleading! And what about –

AUDIENCE MEMBER (shouting): Isaac deserves to die! An eye for an eye!

41

The rest of the audience cheer.

MARTHA: But . . . that's not right . . . You can't see what was
happening . . . He did it to save me!

AUDIENCE MEMBER (shouting): He did it because he's an
ungrateful, selfish bastard. Jackson
gave him a chance, took him from
the slums, and what did he do?
Threw it back in his face!

Martha stands up. The chair falls over behind her.

MARTHA (shouting): No, that's not right!

She moves around the desk and jabs at the air.

MARTHA: What about the folk Jackson had in his pocket?
The bribes! The crimes they'd committed
that'd been covered up! You saw all that? And
that recording – Jackson had a belt around my
neck, for Christ's sake! He was going to kill me!
Isaac saved –

JOSHUA: Martha, I'm sorry to tell you but the authorities
are claiming you falsified –

AUDIENCE MEMBER: You lying, manipulating bitch!

MARTHA: No! You saw it. You all *saw* it when I was in Cell 7! It was on the TV!

She turns to Joshua, sitting quietly at the desk.

MARTHA: Didn't they? Didn't you? It was on the bloody programme! It was . . . wasn't it?

Her eyes fill with tears.

JOSHUA (quietly): Sit down . . . There is no record of that footage, Martha.

AUDIENCE MEMBER: Liar! Attention seeker! You made it up. You're deluded! There's something wrong with your head! You should be locked away!

JOSHUA: Please, let's be calm –

MARTHA (shouting): Fuck calm! He killed my mum. He deliberately ran her over. We had CCTV evidence of it! Isaac showed it on live TV!

Martha's voice cracks. The audience laugh at her.

MARTHA (crying and shouting): We had evidence of his corruption – lists, documents. The police he'd paid off. The lies. Everything!

They laugh more. Martha stares at them. Tears fall down her face. The camera pans back. Joshua is now at her side. He rests a hand on her arm, but she pulls away.

JOSHUA (quietly): Martha, come and sit down, this isn't helping.

Martha ignores Joshua and lurches towards the audience.

MARTHA: Open your eyes! Open your goddamned eyes! Are you stupid? You seriously think –

Some of the audience stand and shout. Two security officers move onto the stage, one on either side of Martha. They pull her back. Joshua takes a handkerchief from his pocket and dabs his brow.

The audience keep shouting, more are standing, a shoe flies past Joshua and hits Martha. Joshua ducks and turns as another skims past.

As Martha is pulled away from the audience Joshua touches his ear, regroups, turns to camera and smiles.

JOSHUA: Always, *always* the scandal here on *Death is Justice*, emotions running as high as the drama itself! Strong opinions from our studio audience and from our Miss Martha. But what are your thoughts on this case? What are your thoughts

44

on the incarceration of Isaac Paige? Lines are now open for you to phone in. Let's get the discussion going, ladies and gents! And don't forget voting lines are also open. Dial 0909 87 97 77 and add 7 at the end for *guilty* or a 0 at the end for *not guilty*. You can also vote by texting DIE or LIVE to 7997. To vote online visit our website www.aneyeforaneyeproductions.com, click on the 'Isaac Paige Teen Murderer' tab at the top and log your vote. Calls are charged at premium rate, please seek bill payer's permission, texts cost £5 plus your network provider's standard fee, voting online is also £5 after an initial registration fee of £20. For full Ts and Cs visit our website. Join us back here again after this short message from our sponsor, Cyber Secure.

The camera moves back to the screen, filled now with the fluffy cloud logo of Cyber Secure, a golden padlock clicking onto the bottom left corner as streams of information – names, addresses, emails, documents – flow into the cloud.

FEMALE VOICEOVER: Cyber Secure – keeping a lock on all the country's most important data.

Patty and the Prime Minister

With a long, padded coat pulled around her and a faux-fur hat perched carefully on her head, Patty stands in a neat rear garden under a dark, heavy sky.

She stamps her feet and stuffs her hands into the armpits of her coat.

'I don't see why we couldn't have this conversation inside,' she says, her warm breath making temporary clouds in the air.

The old-fashioned street lamp next to her glows gently over the perfect borders and the light twinkles on the frosty path leading across the manicured lawn. To the side of it, seated on a wooden bench under a large oak tree, the PM looks up at her.

'You know why,' he says. His leather gloves creak as he leans back and rests his elbows on the rear of the bench, and as he crosses his legs his perfectly ironed trousers stick out from under his long coat.

'I don't see why you keep our relationship a secret,' she replies.

He laughs. 'Because your interpretation of the word *relationship* is barely comparable to the general public's interpretation of the word.'

'I don't get what you mean.'

'Quite,' he says.

'You think I'll embarr—'

'The arrangement you and I have is not up for debate right now. What is, is your son and that girl.'

'*Arrangement?*' she replies.

Ignoring her, he carries on. 'How could you have let it happen, Patty? It's unacceptable; you know that. Quite honestly, I'm disappointed in you; I expected more. The clean-up operation I've had to implement has been frankly ridiculous.'

Looking away from him, she reaches into her coat pocket and takes a cigarette from a packet. Resting one between her lips, she flicks a lighter and the flame casts shadows onto her face, playing at the lines and wrinkles.

The PM lifts his eyes to her. 'Not in my garden,' he says.

She moves her thumb and the flame disappears.

'Who died and made you boss?' she drawls.

He laughs and stands up. 'I knew there was a reason I kept you around, Patty. You do make me laugh.' He loosens the scarf around his neck and pulls it off. 'But back to this son of yours.'

Shivering, she stares at him. 'He's sixteen, for Christ's sake. I can't watch him all the time!'

'Seems you couldn't watch him at all.'

'It wasn't like that –'

'Or your husband . . .'

'Well, at least that isn't an issue any more.'

She stiffens as he leans forward, and as he loops his scarf around her neck she stares at him.

'I think,' he says, his left hand tightening on the scarf, 'that you need to remember who you're talking to. I could end you just –' he brings his right hand up towards her face, and despite his leather gloves he clicks his fingers – 'like that.'

Somewhere in the distance a siren wails in the night air. A police car or an ambulance.

'The girl,' he continues, 'Martha Honeydew, she's troublesome. She needs containing. If we're not careful she'll end up with a following. I've done my part. Now you.'

'Trust me,' Patty says. 'I'm on it.'

'Are you? It was my people who took down all links to that debacle that was your son's statement, who destroyed footage, corrupted any necessary videos, intercepted phone records from people who were there, and now have the media dragging Martha Honeydew's name through the mud and discrediting everything she and your son said. What are *you* doing?'

'I said trust me. I'll fix her.'

He loosens his grip on the scarf. 'I hope so,' he whispers. 'For your sake, I do hope so.'

Martha

Same sky.

Same stars.

Same world down here. Just a bunch of shit in a different order.

Me out here, you in there. I miss you, Isaac.

It sucks.

It sucks a great big fat one.

Every so often I think I did die and I am dead, and I have to talk to Eve and Max, watch Cicero nibbling the end of his ridiculous moustache, to convince myself. Remind myself again what they all did in their own way to get me off death row.

I watched the live feed of you in Cell 1 for a while, but I couldn't handle seeing you suffer.

I tried to eat the food Max made, sitting around the table with them all, but my stomach refused.

And I listened to them – Eve, Cicero and Max – as they explained to me that all you fought for, everything you showed on the TV, was for nothing, that it either disappeared down some black hole where all missing information seems to go, or the police and the government have managed to convince everyone that we made it up.

Then I realised, once and for all, that I must be alive, because I sure as hell couldn't make that crap up.

'Martha can stay here with us, can't she, Mum?' Max asked when he was offloading lasagne onto my plate.

'Of course,' she replied, but I didn't dare look at her because I knew what I'd see in her eyes.

Lies.

Lies to make me feel better; I know damn well what will happen tomorrow.

We're back to square one, Isaac.

I won't give up on you though.

I'll do whatever it takes.

But the fact is, I don't know what that is.

Be with me, in my head, next to me, and help me find it.

DAY 2

Isaac

I'm sitting on a white swivel chair in the middle of the white virtual counselling room. My bare feet are cold on the tiled white floor. I fold my arms across my chest; the prison overalls are white too, or at least I imagine they began life white but are now more of a dirty shade of grey.

'Isaac Paige,' the computer says. A staccato, metallic female voice. 'Welcome to day two on death row. I am your virtual counsellor, here to serve your psychological and emotional well-being. How are you today?'

I lean forward and peer into the tiny camera mounted at the top of the display. 'Martha,' I say. My voice is croaky from not being used. I cough. 'Are you watching?'

'We ask that you refrain from speaking of things which do not directly refer to the question asked. How are you today, Mr Paige?'

I ignore it and continue. 'I hope you are.'

There's a distinct whirr and a dull thud.

'Shortly we will show you images of your past. You are instructed to share your thoughts on them and memories of them, which will be informative for the viewers and aid our monitoring of your well-being. Here is the first.'

A photo of a young woman in a hospital gown comes on the screen. She's holding a baby wrapped in a blue blanket.

Her face glows with sweat and her dark hair is unkempt; yet she smiles so happily.

My mum. My real mum.

I feel an urge to smile back, but I don't want to give them the pleasure of any reaction.

I carry on speaking to Martha. 'I hope you're safe,' I say.

The photo of Mum is replaced by one of a toddler with a chubby face and unruly hair. Me. On my T-shirt is a badge with a large number two, and on the table in front of me is a small chocolate birthday cake. I wish I could remember that day. She's sitting next to me, watching me, smiling at me – Mum.

My eyes flicker and my face frowns before I can stop myself.

'I hope the press are listening to the facts now,' I say, trying to keep myself distracted.

That photo fades away.

Now there's one of a boy in a school uniform – me again – standing at the front door of some flats, next to a sign saying 'Bluebell House'; it must've been my first day of school. I stare at it longer than I want them to notice; the trousers seem a bit worn at the knees and there are bobbles on the jumper. The shirt looks greyish too. But look at me – clean and tidy, hair washed and brushed, standing upright with my chest out and a huge smile.

She did everything she could for me.

'I hope people are taking notice of that list of crimes I put up,' I continue. 'I hope justice will be served now and I hope everyone realises how these people with power and money have been manipulating the system.'

'We would remind you, Isaac Paige,' the computer voice says, 'that it is imperative you comment on the photos. It is vital that the public are informed as to your feelings regarding your birth mother and the situation that befell you.'

I don't move or give a reaction. I just stare at the old photo of me looking out with all that innocence, unaware that in a little over a year my life will have changed irrevocably.

Finally a different image appears – the front page of a newspaper. Blasted across the front is the headline: 'Celebrity Millionaire's Heart Of Gold'.

Words drift up the screen like an autocue and I can't help but read them.

In a world where we're often too busy to stop and help those less fortunate than ourselves, it can often take something extraordinary to make us act. Yesterday was proof, if there was ever any doubt, that celebrity millionaire Jackson Paige is not one of those people who would simply walk on by and ignore people in need.

It is a tragic story, yet not one without a happy ending. Last week saw the shocking suicide of a young mother in the High Rises. Clearly unable to cope with her situation, she took her life by jumping from the balcony of her flat, leaving her six-year-old son, Isaac, alone.

Was it a miracle that one of the country's most generous men happened to be in the vicinity at the time? Or was it fate that he was the first person on the scene? Rather than leave this poor orphaned boy to be brought up in a care institution, Jackson Paige and his glamorous wife, Patty, saved him from this terrible fate and offered him a home with them and thus a future any child could hardly dare wish for . . .

I want to shake my head in disbelief at the stupidity and naivety of these words, but I refuse to give any reaction.

A photo from the newspaper comes up now.

Me. Immaculate black suit and tie, shoes reflecting the grass I'm standing on and my hair combed with military precision. Mum's coffin is next to me. I remember feeling numb, but not crying, yet on that photo there's a single tear on my cheek. Did they put that on for effect?

I clear my throat and lean forward.

'I miss you,' I say into the camera. 'I miss you, Martha Honeydew.'

I miss you too, Mum, but I won't say that to them.

'Isaac Paige,' the virtual counsellor continues, 'we must remind you that this service is offered to help you come to terms with things which may have been troubling you and allow you to safely explore, and potentially put to rest, any traumatic events from your past before you pass from this world. The video feed is to allow the audience to attain a thorough knowledge of you and so vote from an informed position. It is not an opportunity for you to communicate directly with specific individuals.

'Communication with the outside world is strictly forbidden, and any further attempts to do so will result in your immediate and permanent expulsion from the virtual counselling service.'

I look at the photo again; the bare legs next to me must be Patty's, and those on the other side, in grey trousers, Jackson's.

'Martha Honeydew,' I say with a smile, 'I love you.'

The screen flicks off, the lights go down and I'm plunged into darkness.

Martha

'I love you too,' I whisper to the TV, quietly so no one hears.

They're all milling about behind me in the kitchen. Eve's on hold on the phone, standing at the window with Cicero, peering out through the blinds. They think I can't hear them, that I'm not listening, but I am.

'I've never seen so many journalists,' she mutters.

'Vultures,' he replies. 'Hoping for a glimpse. Waiting to plaster her over the front page with more lies.'

'Maybe we should talk to them.' Eve's whispering now. 'We could give her side of the story. Or tell them they can have an interview with her if they agree to print the documents from Jackson?'

'Dangle her like bait? Nice idea, but there's no trusting them. Look what they did on *Death is Justice* today. That CCTV clip made things worse. No, they spin everything into what they want –'

I turn round to answer, argue. To tell them, Yes, I'll do that. I won't let them manipulate me. It could help – but Eve puts a hand up to stop Cicero.

'Yes,' she says into the phone as she walks out of the room, 'this is Eve Stanton, could you put me through to someone who deals with . . .'

Her voice drops real low and I can't hear too well, but I'm pretty certain she says *adoption*.

Something hisses and spits and I turn around – Max is standing at the cooker, reading off his phone in one hand while he's making something in a frying pan with the other.

Don't know what it is but it smells nice.

Nice to have someone cook.

Nice to eat something not out of a packet or a cardboard box.

Nice to be in a warm house.

I turn back to the TV.

The feed of Isaac in the virtual counselling room is gone, replaced by fuzz and static.

Eve's given me a chain so I can hang the puzzle ring Isaac gave me around my neck, seeing as I can't put it together yet, and I fiddle with it as I flick through the different cell options.

No one in Cell 7, some guy in 6, and then a woman – a really old woman – in Cell 5, no one in 4 or 3, and then I flick to 2.

Empty.

Then where the hell is he?

I put the coffee cup down, bite my nails. Can't help it.

And then there he is. The door opens, and some hands shove him in. First thing he does is look to the screen, and it's as if he's staring right at me, like he knows I'm watching him.

Oh God, it'd be easier not to feel this *pain*, this *anguish*. It would be easier to hate him. To be angry that he took my place. It would be easier to be dead.

The screen changes. One of the cameras is filming him from the other side of the room, but he doesn't realise.

All I see now is the back of his shaved head.

Someone touches my arm and I spin around.

'Martha?' Cicero says, his eyes crinkling as he smiles. 'Why don't you eat something? Max has made pancakes.'

I let him lead me over to the table and I sit down.

I'm finding it hard to understand their kindness.

It's overwhelming. In a good way.

'How did they do it?' I ask.

All three of them look at me.

'How did they do what?' Eve asks, turning the phone off as she comes back into the room and sits opposite me.

'Get rid of all the recordings of last night. Millions of folks must've seen it. It should be all over the internet. But it isn't.'

Cicero puts a copy of the *National News* in front of me. Two photographs on the front page.

'You're on the front page of every newspaper. You are more interesting. Some of the headlines are more sensationalist than others.'

There's me from last week, shaved head and a mugshot board.

And next to the photo of me, there's Isaac from yesterday. What a pair we look.

The headline leaps out at me – 'Desperation Of True Love'. I drag the paper over to read.

In a remarkable act of true love, son of celebrity millionaire Jackson Paige stepped forward on Death is Justice *and admitted live to camera that he – not the accused, Martha Honeydew – is guilty of his father's murder.*

Some sources state that Honeydew proclaimed her own guilt from the very beginning of proceedings in an attempt to spare the life of her lover, Isaac Paige.

My cheeks burn at 'lover'.

While at first it seemed that public opinion was swaying towards sympathy for them both, pollsters are now stating that the overwhelming feeling is one of anger, both at being lied to, and at the escalating cost of the case to the taxpayer. When asked today, many of those who voted in the case of the State versus Honeydew said they will be putting in compensation claims against An Eye For An Eye Productions, although the legal team maintain this goes against terms and conditions.

Other sources believe Honeydew may have misled Paige . . .

I can't read any more. I turn the paper over. Can't handle seeing those photos.

Max puts a plate in front of me with a pancake on and pushes some syrup across the table. I glance up and watch as he picks up the newspaper and throws it in the recycle bin.

'Ignore it,' he says.

'But folk read that crap,' I say. 'They believe it.'

'We've still got all the documents,' Cicero blurts, 'copies of the video feeds from all the cameras –'

'But they think it's faked,' I say.

Max's pan hisses as he pours more batter into it. 'It doesn't matter,' he says. 'I'm putting it up on the internet. People can see for themselves that it's not forged . . . And I'll link to it from the newspaper websites, on the comments section where everyone moans. We'll get it out there. It'll be OK.'

I want to believe him, but he doesn't know life like I do.

'It'll go cold,' he says to me, pointing to my plate with his spatula.

I can't remember the last time I had a pancake. Some Shrove Tuesday back God knows when, when Mum was still alive. Can't say I really want one now. Don't really want anything.

'Eat,' he says. 'It'll do you good.'

It feels rude not to, so I pick up the fork.

Eve sits next to me. 'He likes to cook,' she whispers to me. 'Makes him feel helpful. And he is.'

'He'll make someone a good wife one day,' Cicero says from the other side of the table, and he gives a flicker of a smile and a wink and I realise this is some kind of long-standing joke.

'I heard that, Judge,' Max replies. 'Don't eat it if you don't want it.'

'Are there lots of folks outside?' I ask, chasing a piece of pancake around the plate.

Eve nods. 'Yes,' she says, 'a lot. You've made quite an impact.'

I shrug. 'Not the way I wanted to. I didn't expect to be here. I expected . . . I expected it to be Isaac here. I didn't plan for this!'

'There are people out there who agree with you –'

'Then why don't they tell me?' I bang my fork down in frustration. 'I haven't achieved anything. I should let them take me away and save you the grief.'

'Before you do that, you should know that some people sympathise, but at the moment a lot more hate you,' Max says behind me.

My stomach tips.

Eve looks across to him in shock. 'Max –'

'Oh, come on, Martha, what did you expect? You announce to millions of viewers that the people who run this country are corrupt. You tell them that someone they idolised like a god is a murderer, a cheat, a liar, slept with prostitutes and was a drug dealer. Did you think they'd all thank you for showing them how stupid and naive they've been? It's easier to hate you and call you a liar than to face up to the truth!'

'But –'

He slides a pancake onto Eve's plate.

'You back down now, they'll presume you just did it for attention or something. They'll believe what the government's trying to say about you being unstable or whatever. Now's the time to fight harder and stronger and to stand firmer. We put all the evidence out there, the CCTV clips too, and we show them proof that they can't deny. But the truth's uncomfortable. They don't like it. And they'll fight you the whole way.'

The doorbell rings.

Everybody stops moving.

'Maybe a journalist trying their luck?' Cicero suggests.

'Maybe.' Eve shrugs, but I can see worry in her eyes.

I catch the glance between Max and Cicero as Eve heads out of the room, and after a second Cicero nods and follows her. I stand and edge towards the door, peering through the gap.

63

'You can trust them, you know,' Max says from over by the sink.

'I know,' I whisper, but I'm curious, and I'm scared.

I tiptoe down the hallway, a cold draught around my ankles from the open door, but the voices are too quiet. I step further down, quietly, slowly, cautiously, and as I get to the corner the voices are louder.

'It has come to our attention that Martha Elizabeth Honeydew has no legal guardian and is under the age of eighteen. A minor in the eyes of the law . . .' A male voice. Deep and loud.

'Only when it suits you.' Cicero.

'DI Hart has given specific instruction that she be taken to a local care institution where her psychological and emotional needs will be assessed and where she will be looked after until she is of age.'

Shit.

'She's in my care. She can stay here.' Eve.

'Madam, you're not registered by the authorities as being a suitable person for the care of a minor.'

'I've been calling the official number all day but I keep getting cut off! I'm a counsellor – I have all the necessary checks for being alone with children.'

'But you're not registered. It would be a breach of protocol if we were to let her continue staying with you. Last night was an act of goodwill on our part and was only for the one night.'

'But she'd be happier here.' Eve.

'That's not our concern.'

'Then how do I register?'

'There are forms –'

'Fine. Then give me them!'

'Madam, please stay calm. The forms are available at the care institutions. You can collect them or we can arrange for them to be posted to you, but be advised that applications take approximately six months to process. We need to take the fugitive now.'

'*Fugitive?*'

I don't wait to hear any more.

I run back down the hallway, quietly as I can, into the kitchen and close the door.

Max stares at me.

'Quick,' I say. 'Shoes.'

'What?'

'I need shoes. Where are some shoes?'

Cicero's voice booms from the front of the house. 'You are *not* coming in!'

'What's going on?' Max says.

'They've come for me. Quick, shoes. I don't have any shoes.'

He runs out the room, is back within seconds, throwing me a winter coat. 'Take this,' he says. From under the table he grabs a pair of boots. 'She never puts them away.'

'You have *no right* to come into my property!' Eve's voice echoes down the hallway.

I pull the coat and boots on.

'We have every authority, madam. Now please step aside.'

Shit. They're in the house.

'I want to speak to your supervisor.' Eve.

'That would be Detective Inspector Hart. I imagine he's busy right now.'

'I demand to speak to him.'

'You can demand all you like, but this warrant gives us the power to enter your property –'

'Where are you going to go?' Max asks.

I shake my head. 'I don't know,' I reply. 'Listen,' I say, 'buy me some time, hey? Tell them I'm on the loo or something, yeah?'

He nods. 'Sure.'

I turn to head out of the French doors but he grabs my arm.

'You'll need some money,' he says.

'No,' I say, 'I can't –'

He pulls forty pounds from his pocket. 'Take it,' he says.

I stare at him. He doesn't know me. I've caused him so much trouble. I should be nothing to him, but . . .

'Don't touch me!' Eve's voice again.

'Take it!' Max hisses, and shoves it in my pocket. 'And this.' He yanks open a drawer filled with junk and takes out a mobile phone. 'It's my old one, but it's charged. I'll put some credit on it.'

'Max, I –' A door slams and I stop.

'We can try every room, madam, but we will find her.'

'*Go*,' Max says, but I don't need telling.

I nod at him, run through the French doors and into the garden.

The last thing I see before I head across the grass and into the hedgerows is two suits barging into the kitchen and staring at Max as he spoons pancake into his mouth at the table.

Bless you, Max Stanton.

Bless your caring soul.

* * *

Where to go?

I sneak through back gardens, squeeze through hedges, over fences and walls and out onto some busy street, somewhere close to where the City and the Avenues meet.

I could head further in. More crowds. Hide in plain sight.

It's drizzling, that fine drizzle that soaks you through without you realising. Nobody's taking any notice of anything except themselves – staring into their phones, probably thinking of where they're going or what they're going to have for tea or whatever.

What do I do now though?

I have no clue.

What do you want, Martha? I ask myself in my head.

Safety. Home. Comfort. Love. Isaac.

I want Isaac out.

I want to be with him and I want the world to know the truth.

That's a lot to ask.

Shouldn't be.

What would you do for it?

Wrong question.

Right question is, *What wouldn't you do for it?*

I walk some more.

Get wet some more.

Feel lonely and useless a whole lot more.

My legs, my head, my brain, whatever it is, leads me through the streets, down roads I didn't know existed, till I find myself looking at the Rises on the horizon.

'Some sense of direction you've got,' I whisper to myself.

The sun's behind rain clouds today and everything's dark and grey. Grey sky, grey pavements, grey world. And so dark that folks' lights are on in the daytime. Dots of life in the grey.

I keep going towards the Rises, and the spots of light in the flats make them look like robots, glowing like they're on charge, waiting to be set free.

I cut through the underpass and see all those bloody flowers and stuffed toys and crap left for Jackson.

How can a whole society be taken in? Deluded, lied to, not ask questions? Not see the smokescreen around them?

It makes me so angry.

How can so many people be so manipulated?

I think I hear feet. Heels on concrete maybe.

Move, Martha, I tell myself, and I get out from the underpass, walk quickly past the boarded-up shops, onto the scrubby grass and towards the dilapidated park with the broken bench and the swings – places I thought I'd never see again.

The swings where we sat together, Isaac.

My eyes blur. I want to say it's the wind making them water, not the memories, but I don't know.

I wipe my eyes. Focus. There are cars over there – no flashing lights, but I reckon they're police cars.

Do I risk it, or do I move on?

I go a bit further, heading to Daffodil House – my home. There's a few folks milling around. Some kids sitting on a wall, some woman hunched up carrying shopping bags, an old guy pushing a shopping trolley – the usual sort. But not the sort the police would even think about questioning.

Frankly they wouldn't be bothered.

The kids would give them hell, that woman would mutter some nonsense and the old guy'd smell too bad. That's what the police would think anyway, but actually the kids would give them a bit of grief when really they just want a laugh and some attention, the woman would ask if they would be so kind as to help her with her bags, and the guy would try and get arrested so he'd have somewhere warm and dry to sleep for the night.

Stereotyping?

No, just seen it a million times.

I get a bit closer, slow down, edge sideways and slink into the shadows near the communal bins.

Jeez, it smells.

I wonder what the police are up to. I'm guessing they're looking for me. I'd wanted to go up and see Mrs B, or go to my flat and get some clothes and stuff, maybe stay there for the day and think what to do next, but it seems that was a bit naive of me.

I peer out just as white headlights swoop across the area and I lift a hand to shade my eyes and watch as the car pulls up.

Big and shiny, a personalised number plate.

P P41GE

What the hell is Patty doing here?

I duck down and I watch her legs slide out from the car followed by some long, posh-looking coat. The door thuds behind her and her heavy perfume wafts my way.

'Mrs Paige,' a policeman shouts from the front doors of Daffodil House. 'Is it wise for you to be here unaccompanied?'

He strolls across to her.

'I'm perfectly capable of looking after myself, thank you.'

'Strictly speaking, cars aren't allowed to park there, but in your case we'll make an exception,' he says, closer now. 'May I ask what your business is here?'

'I'm here to offer my condolences to Lydia Barkova.'

'Mrs B?'

'Why *does* everyone call her that?'

I could tell you, I think, *but I won't.*

'Yes, anyway,' Patty continues, 'poor woman has been through a lot. I thought it my duty to visit and offer my support. I've brought her some groceries too.'

I hear the rustle of a shopping bag.

'Mrs Paige, your kindness is an inspiration to us all. Your husband's charity will live on in you.'

Is he a suck-up or just plain stupid?

He carries on. 'Let me accompany you to Mrs B's flat. I can wait for you and escort you back to your car again too if you'd like. We wouldn't want anything happening to you.'

What an arse, I think. *And there goes my plan for getting into my flat. There's no way I'm going to be able to sneak past Mrs B's next door.*

I watch him hold the door open for her and them both disappear into Daffodil House.

Only one thing for it then, I think, and, hoping the other officers won't challenge someone coming out of the bins, I step out and head away across the grass.

Mrs B

In her knee-length socks, thick skirt and jumper, Mrs B pads from the kitchen of her flat. Balanced on the tray she's carrying is her old chipped teapot and mismatched crockery, and as she walks through the door of the living room her eyes narrow at her guest and she wrinkles her nose against the overpowering smell of perfume and cosmetics.

The cups rattle in their saucers as she thumps the tray down on the table between the sofa and her upright chair.

'That's really very kind of you,' drawls Patty, perching herself on the edge of the sofa and crossing her legs, a short skirt despite the winter.

Mrs B doesn't answer; she just pours the tea.

'We're all very worried about Martha,' Patty says.

Mrs B glances up to her with her eyes wide.

'And we were hoping you'd know where she is. You do know she's run away, don't you?'

'Who is this *we*?' Mrs B asks.

'I beg your pardon?'

'You said, *we*.'

'Why,' Patty replies, '*everyone*, of course!'

Mrs B lifts her cup of tea and continues staring at Patty.

'Myself, friends, the press, and of course Mrs Stanton and Mr Cicero.'

'You know them? You friends with them?'

'With Mrs Stanton and Mr Cicero? Yes.'

'Cos you not seem their kind of people.'

'Why would you say that?'

'Cos they are nice.'

The air freezes. Silence falls.

Patty lifts her cup and takes a sip, a pink lip print left on the rim. 'I don't quite know what you are insinuating,' she replies.

Mrs B just watches her.

'But regardless, we're all very worried. All we want is for Martha to be safe. And happy.'

'And you can help with that?'

'I believe I can, yes!'

'Is nothing to do with money?' Mrs B asks.

Patty laughs nervously. 'How could it be anything to do with money?'

'Cos if Isaac put to death in five days, then Martha gets all money. You get none. You will have only your . . . what did Jackson say? *Small living allowance.* How much is that?'

'I . . . I . . .'

'No more expensive perfume, make-up, shoes, clothes,' she says with a glimmer in her eyes. 'Shit the bed, you might have to . . . what is that word now . . . let me think . . . oh yes, I remember . . . *work.* You might have to *work.*'

Patty stares at her.

'You know what that is, Mrs Paige? *Work.* I am betting Martha worked more in her sixteen years alive than you worked in . . . How many? Forty-five . . . forty-seven?'

Patty's face turns red. 'Thirty-six!' she splutters. 'I'm thirty-six!'

'I think you need to leave, Mrs Paige.' Mrs B stands up. 'I not know where Martha is, but if I did, I not tell you anyway. You are not good person. You are all for this . . .' She rubs her thumb and fingers together. 'Money. Money, money, money. Like the song, yes?'

Patty stands up. 'You're wrong. This has nothing to do with money. That girl is the only link I have to my son . . .'

'Pah!' Mrs B wafts her hand in the air.

'I . . . I . . . I thought . . .' Patty stammers, a catch in her throat, 'I thought we could . . . support each other . . . comfort . . .' She draws a jagged breath and reaches into her designer handbag for a tissue. 'I'll respect your wishes and leave, but, please –' she dabs at her nose – 'if you do speak to her, ask her to contact me. My number's here.' She places a business card on the table next to the abandoned cups of tea. 'I'll see myself out.'

Mrs B says nothing, but watches her leave through narrowed eyes.

Striding down the corridor to the lift, Patty pulls a small bottle of sanitiser from her bag, her lip curling and her eyebrows lifting as she pumps it into her hands and spreads it carefully and thoroughly down each finger.

Martha

Rain's coming down heavy now. Great big fat drops of it. I like the rain, but, Jesus, is it miserable when you've got nowhere to go.

I took my time heading over to Gus. Cut back and forth, keeping to the shadows, avoiding groups of folk. Not that I don't trust them, but word gets round quick in a place like this, even quiet words and whispers.

Folks like gossip.

I'll tell you a secret, but don't tell no one, they say.

Course not, comes the reply, but with fingers crossed behind backs.

Gus's place is in darkness and the curtains are closed.

Odd.

I tap on the door and wait.

No answer.

I tap on the window, thinking he's most probably asleep on the settee.

Still nothing.

The wind's howling across the grass and the rain's soaking me through.

I bend down and peer through the letter box, but I can't see anything. I shout his name but there's no movement.

'He's not there.'

I spin round on the spot, my breath held, ready to run.

'Din't you see it on the telly?'

I relax; his neighbour. Thank the Lord.

'He's gone down,' he continues.

I frown at him. 'I don't get you.'

'He were on that programme,' he says. 'Din't understand what were going on much. They had them buzzer things.'

My stomach sinks. '*Buzz for Justice*,' I sigh.

'Yeah, I reckon that were it. *Buzz for Justice*. He's gone though. Won't be living here no more.'

'How long did he get?' I ask.

'Oh . . . years. Seven years it were. Shame.'

I look at him, an old guy in slippers and a dressing gown, rain pasting what hair he's got to his head. 'You should go back in,' I say. 'You'll catch your death.' I pull my hood further down to hide my face.

'You an' all,' he replies. 'Here, take this.' He stretches out a skinny hand, a key between his fingers. 'We need more young folk like you, Martha Honeydew,' he says. 'Not less of 'em. Get warm and dry. Don't go dying. An' don't stay too long cos they'll catch you.'

I stare at him for a second, remembering what Max said – some people sympathise – then the old man walks away and the grey swallows him up as fast and easy as it spat him out.

Don't go dying, I think to myself, nearly with a smile. *Yeah, I'll try my best not to. I won't give them the satisfaction, and I won't desert Isaac.*

Gus's flat is cold and damp.

I don't put the lights on just in case – I don't want to draw attention to myself – but there's just enough light so I don't fall over the empty pizza boxes and drinks cans. I head to the kitchen, open the fridge, but all that's in there is half a pint of milk, some ham with hard, curly edges and the left-overs of a Chinese takeaway still in its plastic container.

I think about warming it up, but Lord knows how long it's been there. Instead I root around in the cupboards and find some cornflakes, bags of crisps and instant coffee.

That'll do.

I go back to the fridge, take the milk out and sniff it, but it's so rank I nearly throw up.

It'll be dry cornflakes and black coffee then.

I have to wash a mug and bowl.

The light of the TV flickers around the room. I set the volume low and huddle in front of the electric heater, the bars glowing red as it warms up and there's a weird smell of burning dust.

I grab the duvet off the bed. I don't know when Gus last washed it, but I don't care; it might smell a bit, but it's warm and comforting while I dry off. I watch the rerun of him being sent down, with his duvet and his smell wrapped around me, thinking of how he looked out for me in the Rises, and it makes me so, so sad.

He did nothing wrong. In fact, he tried his best to do everything right.

But they used him to try to get information they wanted. Screwed with him when he didn't agree with the system, and tossed him away when finally he stood up against them.

Seven years. What future will he have left by then?

6.30 p.m. *Death is Justice*

The heartbeat theme tune plays. The eye logo spins on the giant screen and the lights come up. Joshua strides out wearing a light grey shiny suit, trousers tight around his buttocks, a black shirt and a black-and-grey striped tie. His clean-shaven skin is bright and his smile is wide. He stops at the edge of the stage, close to the audience. They applaud and he raises his hands in thanks.

The theme music fades. The applause dies down.

JOSHUA: Hello and good evening, ladies and gentlemen, viewers, audience, and thank you for joining us!

The audience clap again.

JOSHUA: And what delights we have in store for you today! It will be quite a show. You are indeed in for a treat. I can barely *contain* my excitement. You want to know?

AUDIENCE (shouting): YES!

JOSHUA: I bet you do!

He smiles, strides across the studio floor to the curved desk and perches on the high stool at one end, notes spread out in front of him.

JOSHUA (solemn): Well, ladies and gentlemen, last week saw us travel a very bumpy road together, culminating in the truly appalling events in Cell 7 with Martha Honeydew. We were all shocked, some of us traumatised, and I know and understand that the stress of this is far from over as we continue to perch on the edges of our seats, the drama still unfolding as Isaac Paige, the young man Martha was willing to give her life for, makes his week-long journey from Cell 1 to Cell 7. As I'm certain you all remember, we spoke to Miss Martha yesterday, but . . .

He pauses, glances sideways with a finger to his lips and back to the audience again.

JOSHUA: Perhaps it's only me, but I am still pondering over this, thinking about what could have pushed Martha to plead guilty to such a crime, wondering how Isaac could stand by and let the supposed love of *his* life die, debating back and forth in my head my own feelings regarding this tragic story of young love. I'm not ashamed to tell you, I've shed a few tears.

He shakes his head gently, looking sombre.

JOSHUA: And I'm not afraid to tell you that I, for one, am confused; my opinions sway back and forth, and it's at times like these that I seek clarification. And where better to look for clarification than to the top, to our leader, our Prime Minister, the man we voted to lead our country. Yes, we are delighted to welcome to this evening's show none other than our Prime Minister, Stephen Renard.

Vibrant music sounds. Joshua stands and applauds as the PM strolls out onto the stage in a petrol-blue Savile Row suit, crisp white shirt and a blue tie. He pauses for a moment and smiles, his perfect white teeth catching the studio lights.

The audience stand and cheer. The PM raises a hand to them and strides to the desk. As he reaches Joshua the music stops. They shake hands. Once the PM has taken his seat, Joshua sits too.

JOSHUA (smiling): Thank you, sir, for taking time out of your hectic schedule to come on our show. It most certainly is a huge honour to have you as a guest.

The PM sits tall and adjusts his suit.

PM: Thank you very much for inviting me. This programme and *Buzz for Justice* represent all that is most democratic in our society. They are an integral part of the development of our judicial system, reaching all communities as they do, and showing the cases from every angle, thus allowing the public to make informed, intelligent decisions. I feel – we in government feel – very privileged to have such a podium, and one that allows the world to see what innovators we truly are.

JOSHUA: Thank you for your kind words, Prime Minister. I wonder if it would be possible to ask your opinions on recent developments. There has been some controversy. Indeed, some are commenting quite ferociously on the fact that we nearly murdered an innocent teenage girl.

Joshua winces and touches his ear. The PM barely moves.

PM: Joshua . . . May I call you Joshua?

JOSHUA: Please do.

PM: Joshua . . . my view on this . . . well, firstly I have to pick you up on your terminology there. 'Murder' isn't technically correct in the instance of the death penalty –

Joshua frowns and glances down to his notes.

JOSHUA: According to my notes, the definition of murder –

PM (laughing): A triviality, Joshua. Let's continue with what is important here. As I was saying, these dissenters – there will always be people who like to stoke problems and controversy. This is not necessarily a negative as it forces us to look at the decisions we make, our policies, our opinions, and to ensure we are truly representing the wishes of the majority. It is vital that we consider the views of these individuals; they are, after all, one element – however small – of society's big picture. But, as world leaders, as innovators, as protectors of the public, it is our responsibility that, while considering these views, we also have the strength and courage to stand by our own opinions and beliefs, and not lose sight of what is *right* and what will ensure the public's safety.

The audience applaud. The PM waits patiently.

PM: It is my firm belief, and the belief of my cabinet, that many lives are more important than one solitary life. This isn't taking heart away from a decision, it's putting it in it – right at the very centre – where it needs to be. Where it should be.

He turns to the audience.

PM: Think for a moment of the logic here. Let us take Martha Honeydew, accused of shooting Jackson Paige. If she were executed, one life would be lost. She is sixteen, so mathematically speaking, presuming the life expectancy used in the bible – three score years and ten, i.e. seventy – then a loss of fifty-four years. Now, supposing she was found not guilty and freed, but then went on to kill again. Let's not forget that she's already killed a thirty-six-year-old man, which is a loss of thirty-four years. Her next killing could cause the loss of another thirty, forty, perhaps even fifty years. And then factor in the *pain* caused, the damage to families that statistics can't show. The wives, mothers, husbands, fathers, grandparents, but also the children. The *children*. Made orphans, thrust into poverty and misery at the senseless act of one solitary person.

He pauses, sighs and shakes his head.

PM: A person we *chose* to set free. A person who would have been removed from this world and thus unable to cause such pain and suffering, had we not failed to act. That, ladies and gentlemen, would have been *our* failure. Our fault and on our heads. I for one will not take that chance. Let me ask you this . . .

He stands and walks slowly towards the audience, the spotlight following him.

PM: Would you set a tiger free from the zoo, telling people that it may well have teeth but it most probably won't use them? And would you then let that tiger wander the same streets as your family? Would you take a spider from the confines of its vivarium, knowing it to be lethal but trusting it to always be calm even as it crawls over you and your children? No, you would not.

He stops at the edge of the stage.

PM: And the situation is the same here. As I have said countless times, and as I will continue to say for as long as I am able, the safety of the public is paramount, and I will do whatever it takes to ensure that.

The audience stand and applaud. The PM bows his head slightly.

PM (louder): Who wants to live in a society where our children cannot walk home safely from the shops? Where our daughters and sisters are fearful of taking shortcuts down alleyways after nightfall? Where our grandparents are too scared to open their doors? Where gangs of youths sit on street corners terrorising passers-by? Not me, I say. And not on my watch!

The PM strolls back to the desk. Whistles, cheers and applause sound over the audience. Joshua smiles, raising his hands to quieten them. The PM sits down.

JOSHUA: Well indeed, Prime Minister, and thank you. It seems the public feel safer with you at the helm of this ship. There is one further thing, if you don't mind, that has come up this last week, which I wonder if you could clarify for us.

PM: Of course. That's why I'm here. I am at your service.

JOSHUA: I would never wish to give voice to controversy, but in my mind these things are better spoken and dealt with rather than –

PM: Than going underground. Quite. I couldn't agree more.

JOSHUA: Could you tell us where you stand on the issue of the voting price? There have been voices claiming that the current system is unfairly weighted towards those who can afford to vote.

PM: Joshua, I'm so glad you've raised this, and I'm so glad I'm here to allay any fears and concerns. As always we have listened to the voices of our voters, our public, the people we serve, and I am happy to be able to reveal plans that will allow the less fortunate in our society the same rights as everyone else. We have one of the best human-rights records in the world, and this latest development, I believe, will see us top those polls. In order to assure equality, as of today we will be giving every single person within the most deprived area of the country, the High Rises, their own mobile phone, thus allowing them internet access and the opportunity

84

to vote on this iconic programme. Individuals will be able to add their own credit as well as downloading the *Death is Justice* app, which, as you know, Joshua, gives up-to-date information on the cases, the stats, the individuals' histories, as well as one-click voting linked directly to their bank accounts.

Joshua nods, a stretched smile across his face.

JOSHUA: Yet to vote, people still have to pa—

PM (interrupting quickly): We are the first ever country to dissolve the poverty-technology discrimination line in such a way and give the same opportunities to the poorest citizens; I feel honoured and proud to be involved in this latest development.

Again the audience cheer, and the PM dips his head and lifts a hand.

JOSHUA: Well, ladies and gents, viewers, audience members, what do we make of that? Quite an offer from our government there. Very generous indeed, yet what would be more generous, and fairer, would be if the votes were free.

He winces suddenly and touches his ear. The Prime Minister ignores him.

PM: And we are already beginning the roll-out. At this very moment we have staff going door to door as well as attending community centres, GP surgeries and post offices, handing out these phones as a matter of priority.

Joshua smiles again but it's forced and awkward.

JOSHUA: Well, there you go. If you're watching from the Rises, do be sure to pick up your free mobile phone or answer the door when they come knocking. We'll be back after this short break and in the meantime don't forget to log your vote. All the information you need is at the bottom of your screen now.

A blue band with the numbers and details written in silver glides across the bottom of the screen. Joshua's smile slowly fades.

Martha

I mute the TV.

The wind's howling outside, empty tins banging in the road and God knows what skittling down the gutters, but I heard something else.

What was it?

A door?

The wind rattles the letter box and pelts rain against the windows, but it wasn't that either.

Someone's talking.

Sounds like that guy from earlier – the neighbour.

I press the off button on the remote.

The red bars on the electric heater glow, but apart from that it's darkness, just a glimmer through the old net curtains.

There's another voice.

A door shutting.

What did the PM say earlier – handing out phones in the Rises, going door to door . . . I hear a knock, not on Gus's front door, but close by.

I shudder, like ice has been tipped down my back, and pull the duvet tight around me as if it can protect me from everything.

Do I want to wait and find out?

With the duvet still around me I tiptoe to the window and peer through a hole in the net curtain.

There's a man at the door opposite; he looks smart. Someone else is with him and they're talking to whoever lives there.

Is that the postman with his red trolley?

He's taking something out of it, hands it over, gets the guy to sign for it.

The postman turns and looks at the window.

Right at me.

Can he see me?

I'm looking straight into his eyes, but he doesn't give any recognition. I know who he is though; I've seen him around. It's always the same postman here; he always nods.

But this time he winks.

Oh shit.

I step to the side of the window, hoping the shadows hide me. I can still see him though, and the other guy.

Can see their outlines.

The other one turns. 'This is a ball-ache of a job,' he says.

'Don't see why they've got someone of your stature doing it,' the postman replies. 'Any fool could. I could do it by myself.'

'No disrespect,' the first man continues, 'but we're on the lookout for the girl too, remember. You know, the Honeydew girl who's on the run.'

'They don't know where she is then?'

'If they do, nobody's told me. Where are we up to anyway? Which house is next? Let's get this done so we can go home.'

Their shadows move across the window to Gus's front door. It's solid, no glass, and I crouch down behind it. The key's in the lock, but I can't remember if I turned it or not.

Should I check it?

Risk making a noise?

Or just sit and wait?

Suddenly there's a banging like hell, and the door rattles on its hinges. I throw a hand over my mouth to stop myself from screaming out.

'This one's a shithole,' the man says.

'You won't get an answer,' the postman replies. 'This is Gus Evans's place. He went down yesterday. Won't be anyone here.'

'Huh. What about squatters?'

The letter box rattles. Fingers poke through and hold it open. I freeze.

'Shouldn't think so.'

The flap bangs shut again.

'Put it down as undelivered then. I'll ring it in, get someone to come and check. I'm not hanging around in this weather.'

Their feet move away but I stay still.

I hear him knock on the neighbour's door and I hear someone answer it, and I listen to his spiel about the free phone, the government's act of goodwill, promoting equality and all that.

He asks for her name, confirms her address, asks for her date of birth, National Insurance number, next of kin . . . everything . . . The hairs lift on the back of my neck.

This is some weird shit, I think.

I don't know what they're up to, that slimeball Prime Minister, Stephen Renard, and his cronies, but I can't risk staying here.

Can't go back to Eve's.

Can't go to Mrs B's or hide in my old flat either.

Where then? Why is it always so hard for some and so easy for others?

I grab an old rucksack of Gus's and stuff a blanket in it. I root through the cupboards again, find a half-eaten packet of biscuits and shove them in too, and with one last look over the place I slip out of the door, put the key in my pocket just in case and, with my home and my people behind me, I head into the City.

I've walked miles and my feet ache. These boots of Eve's are warm but they don't fit properly and it feels like I've got blisters now. I thought about taking the train or the bus, but I didn't dare risk it.

Max's coat keeps the worst of the weather off, but my face is ice and so are my legs. My hands are shoved up the sleeves.

I'm not sure where I am, just heading for lights and people. Hoping for anonymity in numbers.

I think as I walk, mull things over, ask myself questions.

Would it be that bad in a care institution? Should I just hand myself in? It'd be warm and dry. I'd be fed. I could go back to school. Maybe things might be normal.

Yeah, you reckon? my head says. *They're only interested because they want that stuff off you. They might've destroyed the footage from that night, got rid of any stuff Max or Cicero put on the internet, discredited you, but you've got the originals and they know that.*

To them, you're a danger.

Too many folks on that list with stuff to lose. You hand yourself in now – it's game over.

For once my head thinks sense.

I remember Max's phone in my pocket and think about turning it on. Ringing him and listening to a familiar voice, a kind and friendly one. Asking him what's going on, what he's managed to do. A website maybe, or some video channel.

It's evening on day two, and so far I've done nothing to help Isaac. He has five days left.

There's a TV shop across the road, and I dart between traffic and across to the other side. There are loads of screens showing different channels, and I move up and down, checking them all. Then I see a news channel, the reader mouthing what'll be the headlines, and there it is – Isaac the lead story. I hold my breath as his picture comes up on the screen.

Jesus, he looks awful. Head shaved, little nicks out of it with dried blood, red eyes, a bruise on his cheek I know for damn certain wasn't there before.

God, Isaac, I'm sorry.

Everything blurs in front of me. I'm surrounded by people all getting on with their lives, not bothered or interested.

Tears fall down my cheeks, and when I blink and my vision clears, your face has gone from the screen.

I follow crowds of people and keep my head down.

Loads of folk all of a sudden. Swarms of them.

The woman next to me smells nice and her hair is perfect. Her shoes click on the pavement. How wonderfully *normal*.

She's got something tucked under her arm; she moves and holds it outstretched in her hands, showing her friend with her.

The streetlights shine on it and I gasp.

91

My feet stutter, my heart pounds and my face stings with heat, but I manage to keep walking close to them.

Jesus . . . there aren't the words!

It's Isaac. His face. Smiling out from some glossy page.

Shit . . .

They do souvenir booklets for it?

What the . . . ?

It says *Death is Justice* across the top. The eye logo. Isaac in the middle.

A booklet of those facing the end of their life.

How come I never knew? Is this a new thing?

My legs stop.

People bump into me as they surge forward, but I can't go anywhere. I can't move.

I look around the crowds. The smiling faces, the laughter, the posh clothes, make-up and slick hair. Painted fingernails carrying *those booklets*, Isaac's face on every cover.

I push against the flow, going to wherever they came from. Knowing now where that'll be.

Their chatting voices mingle into each other, but one conversation is louder. With my head down, trying to move to the side, I listen.

'I'm telling you,' says a female voice, 'my mum works for the press and she was at Martha's Cell 7 – she saw what happened and told me.'

'A cover-up?' a man replies.

'Mum said there was a video clip of Jackson holding a gun on her and one of him hitting her mum with a car. And they had documents showing these awful crimes . . .'

'I heard the documents were fakes.'

'Well, the video wasn't! Mum filmed it on her phone, but then, *then,* her boss said that everyone was having their phones upgraded and . . .'

Her voice fades as she moves away.

Hell.

I push through the last of the crowds pouring out and I'm left standing there.

Black railings stretching away to either side, that massive door in front of me, the building towering over me and around me, and above it, way up there, where that beautiful round window used to be, is the eye logo, its ice-blue iris shimmering in the night sky. Almost a planet in itself.

I stare at it; it holds me.

They still call it the Royal Courts of Justice, but there's no justice there any more. Just the *Death is Justice* TV studios and all the offices.

Maybe one day, I think, *it'll be what it used to be: a place for true justice.*

I move to the side and slump into a doorway, looking from the shadows and up the stone walls and arched windows. Outside, apart from that eye, it's all gothic and traditional; inside it's all shiny surfaces, glitz and glamour and everything's all right Jack.

We smile. You clap.

We tell you some scandal and you *oooh* and *ahhh*. Tune in for more.

More viewers, more votes, more money.

There's no smoke without fire, you say.

So we kill a few folks and you cheer.

Crime rates go down. It's working, you say.

Just close your eyes, ignore the facts, don't ask questions.

Easier that way.

It'll never be me, you say. Why would I care?

Apathy.

A gate creaks nearby and I shuffle my head into my jacket and lean back further into the shadows.

'Can I get you a taxi, Mr Decker?' a male voice asks.

'No, thank you, not tonight. The fresh air will be good,' comes the reply.

Decker, I think. *Decker. What?* Joshua *Decker? The presenter?*

I glance out of the shadows and catch a glimpse of him walking towards me.

Bloody hell, it's him.

I hold my breath as he gets closer.

'Rather you than me, Mr Decker,' the first voice calls after him. 'It's a bit cold for my liking.'

I hear Joshua sighing as he walks past me and I watch him pull the collar of his overcoat up against the wind. He passes so close I could reach out and touch him. But I don't.

I stare after him, watching him get further away.

And I think back to being on TV with him in my useless attempt to help Isaac.

I come out of the doorway and fall in step a little way behind. And I follow.

He doesn't walk fast. His route takes him past the Old Bailey, then down to the Millennium Bridge. He stops in the middle, stands to the side and leans on the railings, staring out.

I watch him, wondering what he's thinking about.

I'm a bit of a distance away, but even from here he doesn't look like he does on TV or when I met him. He looks sad.

After a while he sets off again and I follow him some more.

I wait down an alley while he goes into an off-licence, coming out with a bottle in a bag. I slow down as he crosses roads and dodges between traffic. He won't see me. With the dark and the wind, the streetlights that don't work in some places and the headlights and brake lights of cars and buses and everything, and all the people, anyone could be following anyone.

He stops at the kind of house I dream of living in with steps leading up to a big wooden door, large windows either side, and those old-fashioned railings.

As someone opens the front door to him, I move out of the shadows and walk across the road.

Eve

'Max!' Eve slams the door behind her and marches through the house. 'Max, where are you?'

'This came for you,' he says as she enters the kitchen. 'They made me sign to say I'd received it on your behalf.' He passes her a letter.

She trembles slightly as she takes it from him, tears at the flap and pulls out a sheet of paper, and as she scans the words she lifts a hand to her mouth.

'Bad news?' he asks.

'Not good.'

She passes it to him and turns away, breathing out long and heavy.

'"Failure to hand Martha Elizabeth Honeydew over to the authorities by midday tomorrow will be deemed an act against the safety and security of our nation and in direct violation of the requests of the authorities. This would result in your arrest and a subsequent charge of perverting the course of justice",' Max reads out loud.

He looks up. 'They want to *arrest* you? How can not handing Martha over be "perverting the course of justice"?'

'It doesn't matter,' she says. 'They'll make something up. They see Martha, and us, as a threat.'

'Because they know we have the original files and documents? And the CCTV feed? Even though they're doing everything to discredit us already?'

'Why risk it, when they can silence us before anyone can start to listen?' she says.

'Well, it won't work,' he replies. 'I've already scanned everything in. I've emailed it to all the newspaper editors, TV producers, anyone I could find. I've posted them on a website I've set up, with the video clips . . . I won't be intimidated.'

'But, Max, this –' she points to the letter – 'we can't fight it. If we don't tell them where Martha is, they will come for me.'

'You're not thinking about actually handing her over, are you?'

'How could I anyway? I don't know where she is.'

They both fall silent. Max reaches over to turn the kettle on.

'I need wine, not coffee,' she mutters, and as she pulls a bottle from the cupboard, he looks back to the letter in his hand.

'"This serious criminal offence carries the maximum prison sentence of life",' he reads, glancing up as she pours herself a full glass, '"although this is decided on a case-by-case basis within the parameters set out on *Buzz for Justice*."'

Eve pushes the cork back into the bottle. 'Yeah . . . my fate decided by three random people. There's no rigging of that one. Two buzzes and I'm sent down.'

She lifts her glass and looks at him. 'Max,' she says, 'if this happens, if they decide I'm guilty –'

'It's all right,' he reassures her. 'You told me before – if anything ever happens to you, you've got it written with a solicitor that I go and live with –'

'Not that,' she interrupts. 'There's something –'

'Stop it, Mum. It'll be fine. You'll be fine. We'll talk to them, explain.' He wraps his arms around her and hugs her.

'I don't deserve a son like you,' she whispers.

Martha

Whoever lets him in the house stands to the side and I don't see them.

I see Joshua's smile and the relief on his face though. Relief at being with a loved one, letting your guard down. Pleasure at being within those walls you call home, where you can just be yourself and screw the world outside.

What's Joshua like when he's being himself? I get the feeling it's not the guy we see on TV with his perfect hair and clothes and his film-star smile.

I walk up the three stone steps to that impressive front door. Raindrops down the black gloss door, soft light from inside filtering through the glass panels, plants in tubs on either side, one of those things you scrape your muddy boots on.

And a brass knocker.

I touch it.

Lift it.

But I can't drop it.

Gently I put it back down.

What are you doing? I ask myself in my head.

What are you hoping to achieve?

I'm cold.

Hungry, tired and lonely.

I want . . . need . . .

To be found? For Joshua to ring the police and them take you away and you never know freedom again?

If this is freedom, do I want it?

Isaac's face on all those souvenir booklets fills my mind and I don't know the answer, but I know I'm *far* from done.

Stepping down, I head back to the path, but something makes me turn.

This glorious house of Joshua's is four storeys: the level with the front door, two more above that, and a basement below. There's a light on in the basement. I edge backwards, spot a smaller staircase leading down, ivy covering some steps, others broken.

Sticking close to the side and in the darkness of the overhanging plants, I edge down.

Nobody can see me from the road now.

And they won't be able to see me from inside – the light will make it impossible – but I can see them.

There's Joshua. He tosses his keys into a pot on the table and he kicks away his shoes. Then he pulls off his socks too and stands flexing his toes with his eyes closed. Someone else walks into the room, a man, average height, dark hair – I don't recognise him – and he takes Joshua's jacket from him and hangs it from a coat peg near the door.

Joshua sits at the table and puts his head in his hands.

The other man walks up behind him and rests his hands on Joshua's shoulders, then he wraps his arms around him, hugs him and kisses him.

Huh, I think, *he kept that quiet. I wonder why.*

And then I think of *Death is Justice*; he's the new face of the show. The women fawn over him. How many tune in just to see him? Do the programme makers know he's gay? Would it matter to them? Would it matter to the public? The viewers? The voters?

The man moves and sits next to him, and as I watch, I see Joshua's head lift and shake and I see the tears on his face and his partner passing him a tissue.

This is not for my viewing, I think, and I head back up to the street.

What do I do now?

Use this precious forty pounds from Max and see if I can get a room? But where would be safe?

I wish I could press pause on life so I can think and rest. I'm so tired and cold, bone cold, but I can't stop. Every minute, every second, I waste is a second closer to Isaac dying.

You can rest in five days, I tell myself. *Can sleep then. And then you'll be able to look back and know you did everything*, everything, *you could.*

But right now I'm doing nothing. Absolutely nothing. I need some space, need to think and plan what I'm going to do.

The Prime Minister

The PM strides along a long wood-panelled corridor, deep carpets softening his step and paintings of erstwhile leaders staring down at him from the walls.

He's seen them countless times, and as always he walks by without even a glance or a thought. To him they're not history, and nor do they hold any meaning; they are simply paintings.

He pushes through double doors then turns immediately left and presses a thumb to a pad on the wall. The door clicks open and he steps into a room painted blue.

Inside, one wall is taken up by a large central screen, with other smaller ones surrounding it. The smaller screens all show different views: looking down on streets, across roads, focused on the fronts of houses, shops or schools, while on the central screen is a satellite image of the City, the Avenues and the Rises. Red dots pinprick it, some stationary, some moving, at differing speeds and in all directions.

Sitting on one of two leather swivel chairs in front of the screens is Sofia, his aide.

'Sir,' she says, standing up as he enters. 'I've collated it all into one feed for you. It's clearly her.'

The PM sits down.

'I was scanning over the feeds of celebrity houses as I do every evening at this time. Joshua Decker has recently moved up the watch list; otherwise I probably wouldn't have found it for another hour or so.' As she speaks, she presses buttons and clears the smaller screens.

'Then I followed them backwards, plotting the route she must've come by. It gets a bit hazy once we get into Rises territory because of the number of cameras vandalised – you'll notice some are fuzzy and a few skip.'

The same feeds come up on all the smaller screens, various shots of Martha on different streets as the footage flicks from one camera to another.

'But I did manage to follow her all the way back. Seems she was at Gus Evans's place.'

On the main screen all the red dots fade away and it zooms in on the Rises.

'But then, as the mobile phones came online and we began tracking those, I noticed an old signal corresponding with her movements. I believe she must be carrying Max Stanton's mobile. Fortunately, rather than delete those old signals, we'd archived them, so I could still carry them across.'

She presses more buttons; a single red dot comes up on screen.

'And there she is. Or was.'

'Are you certain that's her?' the PM asks.

'Quite certain. As you see, when I cross-reference the CCTV feeds we found her on, with the signal from that phone . . .' She pauses as she presses buttons and the central screen shows the journey of the red dot while the screens around it show CCTV of Martha's progress across the City.

'Astonishing. We can now follow her every movement?'

'Yes, sir. In fact, with your new phones-for-all initiative, you can follow everyone's movements.'

'Exactly what I wanted,' he says with a sideways smile.

'As long as nobody finds out. I think some people may take issue with their every movement being watched.'

He waves a hand in the air. 'Only to be knocked down by those pointing out that they must, therefore, have something to hide. No, that is not an issue. Sofia, you have truly excelled yourself. I trusted you with this, and you have now earned the right to more responsibility in the future. Well done. You can leave now. Have an early night.'

She glances at the clock on the wall – 11.30 p.m.

'Thank you, sir,' she replies, and heads out of the room.

Alone, the PM leans back in the chair; it creaks and groans, and he taps his fingers on his chin as he thinks, his eyes narrowing as he sighs.

He leans forward to the keyboard, brings up the option menu on the screen and in the name box types 'Patty Paige'. The screen blurs for a moment, the feed moves, then refocuses and zooms in on a satellite view of the City, a red dot motionless inside a building.

He takes the phone from the desk and dials.

As it rings, the red dot moves out of the building and into a side street.

'Hello,' Patty says as she answers the phone.

'Patty, darling, how are you?'

There's a pause. A whoosh of traffic noise.

'Stephen?'

'Prime Minister to you, Patty, but yes. How the devil are you?'

'Good, thank you,' she replies.

'Excellent. I was concerned. I thought perhaps you might be struggling with your loss and your son being on death row.'

'He's no son of mine.'

'You're not feeling the need to drown your sorrows, are you?' He zooms further in on the satellite feed, the screen refocuses on the bar she's just come out of, the name – Holly's – in neon letters.

'I remember you like to frequent Holly's . . .'

'That dive? Absolutely not,' she replies. 'I'm in my car. I've just pulled up. You can probably hear the traffic.'

'I don't doubt you for a moment, Patty,' he says, watching the red dot move closer to the road. 'You have my full confidence.'

'Good,' she says. 'I'm completely in control of this situation. As I promised you I would be. It isn't an issue; I'll deal with Honeydew.'

'It would be a terrible thing, Patty, if we didn't have a complete understanding of each other. As I said before, I'd hate to terminate our friendship and agreement. To this point it has been mutually beneficial, but that needs to continue, and for it to be so, there needs to be total cooperation.'

'Absolutely,' she replies.

'So where is Honeydew?' He brings the option box back onto the screen.

'Errrr . . .'

'Because you did say, in fact, multiple times, that you're sorting this.' He types 'Martha Honeydew' into the name box and presses enter.

'I can assure –'

'Where is she *now*, Patty?'

The screen pans out, a red dot appears at the edge, and it zooms back in again.

'I –'

'Shall I tell you?'

'She's . . . She's hiding in the Rises . . .'

'No, she's not.' He gives a huff. 'Obviously you don't know, and if you don't know then you can't be in control of the situation.'

His foot taps against the floor.

Patty doesn't answer.

'She's at the park near Joshua Decker's house, the one with the bandstand. You have twenty-four hours. If the situation isn't sorted by then, your whole public persona will be heading down the toilet. Clear?'

'How –'

'I don't expect to be handling your side of this arrangement as well. Get yourself away from that dump of a bar and get on with it.'

'Are you spying on me?'

He ignores her outrage. 'Sofia will inform you of any updates. Now, get on with it, Patty. Falling from that high pedestal you've put yourself on would make a lot of mess. Tomorrow evening. No excuses.'

He puts the phone down and looks at the bank of screens.

'You, Martha Honeydew, are one troublesome young lady.'

DAY 3

Martha

I'm so cold. It's freezing – even with this blanket and jacket.

Can't remember the last time I slept properly.

Before that night probably – the night you shot Jackson. When we were together, back in my flat.

I sit here and let my eyes get used to the dark. I can see the shapes of trees, branches moving in the wind, can hear them rustling too. I put up with the cold because I have to; the only people I trust are ones I can't go to for help. So here I am.

Some church bells ring; count them – one, two, three, four, five.

Five o'clock. I suppose I must've slept then.

I take the chain off my neck and drop the puzzle ring into my palm. I stare at it. Five bands linked together but in pieces. I fiddle with it, trying to get them all to slot in, but it's useless. I think about what he said – 'I hope you choose to wear it and to remember me, wherever I am right now, and I hope it inspires you to keep trying.'

I try pushing them into place, but they get all jammed and then fall apart again.

Frustrated, I put it back on the chain and around my neck.

I am trying, Isaac, I think, *and I will keep trying.*

One more reason to get you out of there too, so you can show me how it works.

I stare up at the sky, still dark – velvet blue – stars shining. Our sky, Isaac, our stars. Can't imagine how it'll feel to look up at them after you're gone.

I feel like I'm watching a train plummet down the tracks and on the tracks a car is stuck. Everybody else is standing around waiting for the carnage.

I know it's coming.

I realise I might be able to stop the train at some point, slow it down or something, but not in time to save the car.

Jesus, this is some real crazy shit.

If you'd told me this time last year that this was going to happen, I'd have laughed in your face. Told me this time two weeks ago, I could've believed some of it. Told me this time last week, then I wonder if I would've still done what I did in Cell 7.

Isaac

I'm waiting for the sun to break and to be moved into a new cell.

Yesterday, in the moments between being taken out of the last cell and put in this one, I looked down the corridor and saw the door to Cell 7. It looms at the bottom like a gate to heaven. Or hell.

Or a theatre door.

We are backstage and the public, our audience, wait on the other side for our performance.

Will they get what they want?

Will they judge my *performance* worthy of their applause? Maybe even give me a standing ovation?

What a farce.

I feel sick with nerves and with fear.

Martha

Day 3 and I've still not been able to get you out of there or help in any way.

I take the phone Max gave me out of my pocket. I've never used one much, couldn't afford to. Had an old one about as big as a brick that only did calls, but then I didn't have any money and I didn't have anyone to ring anyway.

This looks fancier though.

The time glares at me through the dark – 5.16 a.m. – and a missed call.

Home, it says as well. My stomach tips for a second but it isn't my home. It'll be Max's. He'll have rung from there so I could see who it was. It says 2.30 a.m. – I must've been asleep.

There's a message too.

I manage to get it up on the screen – 'Where are you? I'm worried. Shall we meet? Ring me.'

Later, I think to myself.

I stand up, my legs aching and my arms stiff – *This could've happened in spring or summer*, I think, *but no* . . . – and I stagger down from the bandstand and across the park.

It's quiet, feels calm.

Maybe, Isaac, if I can get you out, then we could come here together. Kick the autumn leaves or walk on the frosted grass. Hold hands through woollen gloves.

I'm out of the park now and the streets are busier than I thought they'd be. It's a weird feeling – a city waking up, coming to life, people going to work. I watch them, wondering what's going on in their worlds – are they happy or sad, is someone they know dying, are they living hand to mouth?

Sometimes it shows on their faces and in their eyes, but most have their shoulders down and they follow the grey pavement forward and forward like robots.

Automatons.

Programmed to go from point A to point B by a certain route.

Programmed to believe what they are told and not to question.

Programmed to read something in a newspaper and believe it as truth.

And programmed to feel sadness one minute for folks suffering, then gratitude it's not them the next, and finally forgetting they ever read or heard it.

Apathy. Ignorance. Cowardice.

I'm ranting. I sound like some crazy activist or something.

Here I am.

The death row building's in front of me.

Looming big and tall and dark.

It scares me. But it's where Isaac is.

Black iron railings, black iron gates, huge wooden doors to the front entrance, and above them that massive eye, blinking and watching, lit up neon ice blue. Every few minutes 'An Eye For An Eye For' spins around the iris, then that fizzing of electricity goes through it. It makes me shudder.

And it makes me remember the feel of that chair: the straps on my wrists, the cold of the crown on my head.

The fear . . .

How close I came to . . .

And now Isaac . . .

I squint through the darkness. Next to the wooden door, in much smaller lettering, is 'Sponsored by Cyber Secure' and a little motif of a fluffy cloud with a padlock.

I move round to the gate. The path on the other side leads through the grounds, past the tree and around to the entrance where everyone goes for the executions.

The tree, I think, and I'm surprised at the sense of comfort it brings me. I dare to wait just a couple of seconds, and when the bird flies from the branches the relief of it still being alive makes me smile.

The small things matter.

I carry on skirting around the outside, and as I get further away from where the public would ever go, it gradually gets scruffier and scruffier. A few of the streetlights are broken, one flickers constantly, and as I go around a corner the railings are replaced by an old stone wall. I follow it, heading away from the road, and the path turns to grass.

No lights, no cars, nothing.

No sunrise yet.

I can hardly see my hand in front of my face. It's like I'm not in the City any more.

My feet are wet now and the ground feels soft and squelchy.

Of course, all that rain.

As I look up I can make out the top of the wall, but I can't see over it, can't see the other side of the building.

A tree looms up in front of me. Not a massive one, but . . .

I stop and think. I move around it, touching it, working out its branches and opening my eyes as wide as I can to try to see more.

My head's full of ideas that I don't know if I dare do.

What's the worst that could happen? it says to me, and the question hangs like clouds of hot breath in cold air.

I sigh.

What the hell? I think. *What have I got to lose?*

The tree's not difficult to climb, it's got branches sticking out all over, and I get myself to the top of the wall pretty easily. I peer over and I can see the building now. It's not as tall on this side, squat and a bit scruffy-looking. I suppose it doesn't need to look good though, does it? Nobody's looking in, only out.

And I see the windows too.

God, that's weird.

Visions of what's going on inside flash through my head. Is it all still the same? Eve said they change the order round, bring new stuff in. The window on the left is bright white with light, so that one must be Cell 1, still the same. And Jesus it's rained a lot; what number was the cell that leaked? Three? Or is it different now? Some other perverse act of torture under the guise of so-called justice.

Isaac will be in two. They won't have moved him yet. Not till sunrise, and it's, what, maybe about 5.30 a.m. now. What time's sunrise in November? Not for ages yet.

That must be the window for Cell 2, over there.

I scan the row – they *do* get smaller.

I look down at the ground.

If I jump down inside, will I be able to get back up?

I'm not sure.

But . . . that's Isaac's cell. There. Just there. That's where he is.

I jump down before my brain can convince me not to. I land roughly but I'm OK, and without pausing I charge across the grass to underneath his window.

And I stand there, not knowing what the hell to do now.

I stop and think. The window's not very high; I could probably shout and he'd hear me. I could look round, find something to stand on, climb up to the window and actually see him.

Talk to him.

Break the glass, if there is glass – I can't remember – and hold his hand.

Be with him.

Alone.

He's – what? – a couple of metres away from me. Three maybe.

For a second I close my eyes and I imagine him lying on the bed. If only I could stroll into the cell and climb in next to him and we could be in each other's arms and everything around us could just disappear.

If only.

I stand back and suck in a deep breath.

'Isaac!' I hiss up at the window.

I stop and wait. Nothing.

'I love you,' I dare to shout, but the wind blows into my face like a slap and it takes my words.

My eyes sting. I blink the water away, sniff loudly and pull in another deep breath, to shout again, this time as loud as I can.

But, with a lungful of air, I stop.

You can't, I tell myself. *Think what would happen. There's a camera in there watching his every move. They'd be out here in seconds. You wouldn't stand a chance.*

From the darkness below I stare up to the light.

Don't you care about getting caught? I ask.

Of course I do, but I have to do this, I reply in my head.

What? Just to see him one more time?

Yes! And to let him know I'm trying and I haven't forgotten him.

And for him to watch you being carted away again?

I don't have a reply to that.

Give it up, Martha, and get down. It's impossible and it's bloody stupid.

I want to argue with myself for a while longer and try and figure out a way that this *isn't* impossible or stupid, but really I know that I'm kidding myself.

If I wasn't so determined to keep strong, I could just sit here and cry.

Staying tight to the wall, I edge around. It's still dark, but there's a hint of light coming round the corner.

I bend down low, keep close to the wall and shuffle along to the end where I can peer around the corner. I'm looking at the railings now, the front where the road is and where folks queue to come in. I daren't go any further, but that's OK; I can see it now.

There's the tree, close to the window of the old counselling room, stretching its bare branches upwards into moonlight.

What is it about that tree? Why is it so comforting?

Because Eve planted it when she shouldn't have?

117

Because it was a quiet act of defiance?

She was good to me. They all were. I have a lot to pay back.

I turn away. I can't get caught now. But how do I get out?

As I see it, I have three options.

I can go round the back again and try climbing up that wall; I can stroll out bold as brass through the gates, hoping that I look confident enough that no one stops me and that they aren't locked; or I can go over the railings or try to squeeze through them.

None sounds good.

Stupid bloody cow, I tell myself. *Stupid bloody thing to do. Why did you do it, hey?*

I was thinking with my heart, not my head, I reply to myself. So stuff you.

I scan the railings, watch folk lit by streetlights walking past the gates, look back to the wall, wondering if my first option was maybe better, but then I see what I can do.

I suppose that's the thing about these old places with new bits added. Somewhere it's got to join up, and there, where the old wall meets the new railings, it looks as if someone's done a botch job and left a gap.

That'll do me.

Taking it wide, I head for the wall and scurry along it to the railings. I see now why the gap's there – there's a bin concreted to the ground. I suppose it would've been too much time and effort and money to take it out and move it, but I could kiss the workman who made that decision, because I'm up and over and out in seconds.

118

Back to the main road. Bit muddier and a bit smellier. Bit more miserable.

With my head down, hood up and hands in pockets, I walk on.

I don't know what I was hoping for.

Don't know why I came.

There's no way you can get him out, my head thinks. *It's impossible. You know it is. He's going to die. You'll be alone.*

I fiddle with the puzzle ring round my neck, trying to push the pieces together, as if solving it would give me some magic answer.

What do I do?

What *can* I do?

Nothing comes to my head.

Nothing, nothing, *nothing.*

And I feel so damned

bloody

useless.

A car pulls up next to me.

I keep walking, don't look round.

Fuck off, I want to say. *Leave me alone.*

I hear the window wind down – that electric motor sound.

Don't stop, I tell myself.

I look for a left turn, but there isn't one.

Want to cross the road but can't.

I slow a little.

It slows too.

I speed up and now it speeds up.

I turn around, walk back on myself.

Shit, it's stopping, reversing. What now? What do I do?

'Martha?' A female voice comes from the car, a hissed kind of whisper. I look up and down the road, don't know where to go.

'Martha, sweetie, get in the car. Let's talk.'

Sweetie? Sweetie?! What?

I turn around again and go to run across the road, but the car suddenly lurches forward, stopping right at my feet and my hands are on the bonnet and I'm staring through the windscreen.

Patty fucking Paige.

She smiles at me and points inside the car.

Smiles at me.

I don't move.

On the other side of the road a car slows and the driver's window goes down.

'You all right, miss?' the driver asks.

I stare at him.

I'm a rabbit in headlights. I'm drowned in white. Spotlight on me.

I nod at him. 'Fine,' I mumble, and as calmly as I can I walk around to the passenger side of Patty's car and get in.

Right now Patty Paige seems the best option, and that's bloody saying something.

'What do you want?' I say as I slump into the seat.

She pulls away and the doors thud locked; I feel trapped.

I haven't ever been in a car like this; it's shiny and smells funny, there's bright digital numbers saying what speed she's going and other lights for fuel and stuff. And the seat's warm; it feels like I've wet myself.

'That's a fine way to talk to someone who's saving your bacon.'

'Odd way to look at it,' I reply, 'seeing as you nearly ran me over. Someone's already killed a Honeydew woman by car, don't you know? You wouldn't want to be accused of copying.'

She stops at traffic lights; the engine turns itself off automatically.

'Nice car,' I say, 'if you can afford shit like this. Better look after it though – dare say it'd cost a lot to replace.'

'You should watch your mouth; ladies don't swear.'

I laugh at her.

The lights change and she drives on.

'What?' I say. 'You have an issue with ladies swearing, but not with manipulating the whole country into killing innocent people?'

'What are you talking about?'

'Just let me out of here.'

'You don't want to get out.' She taps the indicator and drives onto a dual carriageway. 'I have a proposition for you.'

'I'm not interested.'

'You will be.' She pulls down a well-hidden turning. 'Give me five minutes to explain, then I'll take you back, drop you wherever you want.'

I don't want anything to do with her, but I shut my mouth and watch the headlights lead us down a narrow track that I don't think is any kind of road, bumping us along in darkness to somewhere I don't know and where nobody would be able to find me. I stuff my hands in my pockets, feel Max's phone next to my fingers.

'Where are we going?' I mutter.

'Somewhere quiet,' she replies.

Quiet? I think, and I remember what Isaac's letter said about the money – that he'd leave it to me, not to Patty.

But what if there was no me? If I wasn't here? If I was dead? Where would the money go then?

His next of kin, a voice in my head says.

That's . . . Patty.

Jesus.

She wouldn't, would she?

Of course she would, my head replies.

Why the hell did I get in this car?

We're not going that fast.

What if I jump out?

The door's locked though. Don't know if I can get out.

And what if I did? What would she do? Run me down?

Shit.

Shit, shit, shit.

She stops the car before I do anything, and turns the headlights off.

'Come on,' she says.

She gets out.

I follow, but keep as much distance from her as I can.

My heart's pumping.

My palms are sweaty.

We're by the river; I can hear the water splashing, feel the damp in the air.

'Come closer,' she says. 'The sun's about to rise. It'll look lovely on the water.'

Bugger that, I think. *I know how bloody cold that water is, and Lord knows what's down there – shopping trolleys and old cars probably, enough to break your legs on if you should fall in.*

'I'll stay here,' I say.

'Suit yourself.'

I shrug.

'We share a problem,' she says, strolling towards me. 'Isaac.'

'How is he a problem?'

'His situation is.'

I lean against her car because I think it'll annoy her and I smudge my fingers down it as I listen to her.

'Whatever you may think of me, Miss Honeydew, I do care very deeply for that boy, and I don't wish to see him die. I've lost one man in my life; I have no desire to lose another.'

There's lots I want to say, but I keep my lip buttoned.

'I understand your very deep and real feelings for him, and it's unfortunate the situation's come to this. I think really that the whole . . . *spectacle* . . . could've been avoided. Or dealt with better.'

'*Spectacle?*' I question.

She ignores me.

'Despite everything, he's my son. I've raised him. I have a responsibility to him.'

'And?' I wish she'd get to the point. She's edging closer to me, her hands thrust deep in the pockets of some fake-fur coat. Is she hiding something in there?

'I believe it would be in everyone's interest if we were to get Isaac out.'

My stomach tips. *Get him out? How?*

'He doesn't deserve to die,' she continues. 'Jackson was a pig. I can say that now; before . . . I was under his thumb. He was a nasty, controlling man. I'm sure Isaac's told you?'

She glances at me but I don't give anything away. This sounds like some speech she's rehearsed, and I watch her, the way she moves, what her hands are doing, trying to work out what she's up to.

'Between us we could do it quite easily.' She moves closer.

'How?' I ask, kicking myself for asking but I'm intrigued.

'We blow a hole in.'

I laugh at her. 'You're crazy,' I say. 'Honestly, I think there's something wrong with your head!' I start walking away, relieved. No, disappointed.

'Are you going to sit back and watch him die?' she shouts after me. 'Don't you even want to try? He didn't give up on *you* that easily, did he? You can't love him *that* much.'

That stops me.

In the cold, with the wind blowing over the water and into me, I stand stock-still. I do love him. How dare she say I don't?

Remember what you said last night, Martha? my head asks. *How did you put it?* – 'Every minute, every second I waste not doing anything is a second closer to Isaac dying.'

'But supposing we blow him up by mistake, or kill someone else?' I whisper.

'We don't use that much, you stupid cow.'

Blow a hole in, my head repeats slowly.

'You're talking explosives? A bomb?'

'It's probably wise if we don't think of it in terms of that B-word. People are funny about it and it wouldn't be a *bomb*

124

in the traditional sense you're thinking, more like how you see in films when people use explosives to get into a safe. All we're talking about is a hole that he can climb out of.'

There's all kind of alarm bells going off in my head. As far as any media would be concerned, or the police, or the government, blowing something up sure as shit means a bomb, doesn't it?

But . . . Jesus . . . there's so many buts.

'Why do you need me anyway? So I can take the fall and you can walk away? Clean hands as always?'

'There are some things in life I'm good at and some things I'm not. I admit that. I can arrange the explosives, I know people, but I can't get near the building or into the grounds.'

'What makes you think I can?'

She turns and looks at me with her thin eyebrows raised. 'Don't play dumb with me,' she says. 'Or take me for stupid. You'll regret it.'

'And what about wiring it? You know, making the actual . . . *thing . . .*' I hear these ridiculous words coming out my mouth, but can't think for the life of me why I'm saying them. Why I'm not just walking away and leaving this crazy bitch to her own crazy plan.

Isaac, that's why.

'You wouldn't need to. I have a contact who'll provide the explosives and instruct you on what to do.'

I stare down the river, watching the water flow past us and away.

'And after?' I ask. 'When it's done. What then?'

'Whatever you like,' she replies. 'All I want is for him to be safe and happy –'

'It's nothing to do with money?' I say, interrupting.

She tilts her head to one side. 'Ah. Well, yes. Some financial gain would be expected. I think a fair deal would be for you to instruct Isaac to split his father's wealth with me – fifty-fifty.'

'Why am I not surprised?'

'I would say one hundred percent to me – after all, you can't put a price on someone's life, can you? But I'm not greedy. Plus you'd both be free to go and do whatever you want. I won't stop you.'

'I don't know . . .' I say. 'This is . . . This is serious. If I got caught –'

'You won't.'

'If someone got hurt – killed – and I was caught for it, I'd end up back on death row.'

'Where Isaac is now,' she says, 'for saving *your* life. There isn't time to mess around. If you're not willing to try and save him, I need to know; then I can find someone else.'

Find someone else? I repeat in my head. *Who? What will Isaac think of that? And suppose this* someone else *gets it wrong and ends up killing him?*

'You've got twenty-four hours.' She hands me a card with her mobile number on. 'If I don't hear, I'll presume your feelings for him aren't as strong as you like to make out. I'll find someone who cares more.'

I feel as if I've been kicked in the guts.

I have one more question. 'How can you have enough influence to get these explosives and promise I won't get caught, but you can't get Isaac out?'

She laughs at me now. 'I hate to admit it, especially to you, but some things are out of my reach. Especially since your escapades last week. This way we all get what we want. You get Isaac, I get a fair share of the money and the public's sympathy. Imagine the outcry if he's let off legitimately.

'Jackson was a well-loved man. The public want to see someone brought to justice for it. They need that. It gives them faith in the system, and while they have faith, they won't question.'

However much I dislike this woman, she's not the dumb blonde she pretends to be. She's clever, manipulative, sly. 'But I want them to question,' I say. 'The system's wrong. This is what it's all about!'

'No. You need to let the people *believe* they are listened to and think they have some degree of power. You need to let them *believe* they live in a democracy. But it's a fallacy. Sometimes, though, there's a bone to be thrown. Isaac, at the moment, is their bone.'

'But if we break him out . . . ?'

'Terrorist activity. They'll be behind us even more.'

I stare out across the river, the walls of the Tower of London in the distance, and I think of the people executed there, think of Isaac, moving towards an oh-so-modern equivalent.

How can I do this? I think. *It goes against everything I stand for.* But . . . Isaac.

Four days! How are you going to change folks' minds in four days?

There has to be another way.

I suck in a deep breath.

Martha Honeydew – daughter, friend, girlfriend, lover.

Martha Honeydew – accused of murder, survivor of death row, escapee from the authorities.

Martha Honeydew – bomber?

'Twenty-four hours,' Patty says, and she gets back in her car and drives away, leaving me alone at the riverside to think.

The Stanton house

Eve is sitting up in bed, her hair tied back, her eyes pink and her face blotchy. The curtains are half open and a shaft of dawn light casts its rays onto photographs splayed out on the duvet.

Some of her.

Some of Max.

Some of Max's father Jim.

Some of them all together.

Mixed up with them are old newspaper clippings, yellowing and brittle.

'Justice System Prevails Again', one headline reads.

Another: 'Humanitarian Executed For Inhumane Act'.

And above a photo of his body in the electric chair of Cell 7: 'Jim Stanton: As Dead As His Victim.'

Eve turns them over. Her eyes well up but she blinks the tears away, takes a notepad and pen from the bedside table and, with a shaky breath, begins to write:

Dear Max,

There's never been a right time to tell you this. I would've preferred to tell you in person, but the future is changing so quickly and it scares me this will come out of the woodwork before I've had a chance to explain to you. If you're reading this then they've taken me

away on some charge of helping Martha, and if they've
done that, then I fear it'll only be a matter of time
before someone uncovers a secret I've kept from you,
and if they do they will use it just to sell more papers,
not caring about the effect it would have on you.

I want you to hear the truth before it's
sensationalised by the newspapers.

I want you to hear it from me.

And I want, Max, more than anything, to tell you
I'm sorry.

Next to her, an envelope with his name on waits for her
to finish.

Down the hallway, Cicero, wearing pyjamas and a dressing
gown, shuffles into the kitchen. He sees Max at the table, head
deep in his laptop, an unearthly glow from it on his face, and
a pile of papers and folders next to him.

Max's eyes flick up to him and he frowns.

'I slept on the settee,' Cicero says.

'Press will have a field day with that one,' Max replies,
already back in his laptop. 'They're still camped at the end of
the driveway, you know.'

Cicero shrugs and switches the kettle on.

'Max, there isn't anything –'

'Not my business, Judge,' Max interrupts.

Cicero folds his arms across his chest. 'What are you doing?'

Max doesn't look up, his fingers tapping away at the keys.
'The website was taken down,' he mutters. 'With all the videos.

130

They'd had quite a few views though, and some comments. Some people just shunned it, saying it was all conspiracy-theory crap, but others argued with them. *Some* are listening, but . . .' He shrugs.

'A long process?'

Max nods. 'Yeah, maybe too long, you know, to make a difference soon enough. I'm setting up another site. We'll see what happens.'

'Can they trace it to you?'

'The way I've set it up they shouldn't be able to.'

'What about the *Death is Justice* recording of Martha in Cell 7?' Cicero asks.

Max shakes his head. 'Even if they have kept a copy for themselves, they've increased security around their system. I can't get in.'

He taps at the keys and opens a new page – a login for *Death is Justice*. He taps some more and another link comes up. 'This seems to be the easiest way in. It seems some of the workers, producers or TV crew or whatever, can log into the system. If I could get in that way, I might be able to sidestep through it and find the archives. If they haven't deleted them. But . . . I need more time. And . . .' He shakes his head again.

Cicero moves over to the cupboard and takes out two mugs, listening to Max as he makes the coffee.

'. . . I was wondering how Jackson managed to put everything together by himself. It's pretty complicated . . .'

At the fridge, Cicero pauses and looks at him. 'You're wondering if someone else is involved?'

Max nods.

'Like who?' he asks, pouring the milk.

'Patty Paige?

'Patty Paige?!' Cicero sounds incredulous. 'But she's just some, forgive the phrase, *airhead*.'

Max takes the mug from him and moves back to the laptop, leafing through the folders and papers next to it.

'Look at this list of Jackson's,' he says, spreading it out for Cicero to see. 'Look at the sort of people on it.'

Cicero scans down the names. 'Penny Drayton, DI Hart, Ian Chobury . . . Hang on . . . they were on the panel with me.'

'Read on.'

'Albert DeLonzo . . .' He runs his fingers down the list. 'These are all journalists . . .

Max nods.

'And then . . . politicians . . .' He keeps reading. 'A *lot* of politicians.'

'More politicians than anything else. It's in some kind of order.'

'Hmmm . . . you've got the chancellor, the health secretary, the education minister . . . nearly the whole cabinet . . .'

'All of the most powerful people in the government,' Max says. 'Apart from the PM himself.' He points at the note next to a name. 'If you look at the details, some are pretty serious, like that one next to Jonny West – you know, the TV presenter? That –' he shakes his head – 'that's shocking. But then look at others, like the one next to the home secretary.'

Reading down the list, Cicero stops and smiles. 'The home secretary lost his virginity to a prostitute?'

'I mean, who cares about that?'

'It's all leverage,' Cicero says. 'And the sex stuff, you'd be surprised. When I was a judge, that kind of thing was what embarrassed people the most. When this gets out, if this goes viral . . .' He shakes his head. 'But nothing on the PM?'

'No. And there's nothing about Patty's family either.'

'Her parents had a lot of money and influence,' Cicero says, 'but they lost it all before she married Jackson, and her brother . . . What was it about her brother?' He rubs his fingers down his long moustache. 'Something happened. What was his name? Stuart? Stan? Something like that. I don't remember seeing anything in the papers, but I do remember rumours going around. It could have been some sort of attack? Wasn't he arrested? Oh, I can't remember.'

They both sip at their drinks, thinking.

'It could just be a coincidence,' Max says.

'Perhaps we shouldn't be too quick to allow ourselves to believe in coincidence,' Cicero adds.

As he glances at the list again, the doorbell rings, but before they can react someone bangs and thuds on the door, over and over again, louder and louder.

'What the . . . ?' Cicero says, leaping up.

Max says nothing, eyes grim, but shuffles the papers together, unplugs his laptop and dashes through the house with them.

'If you fail to open the door we will knock it down!' a voice shouts from outside.

Eve runs out of her room, pulling a jumper over her pyjamas. 'What the hell's happening?' she shouts. 'Who's at the door?'

Cicero opens his mouth but Eve's already heading down the hallway towards the front door.

As Max reappears empty-handed, Eve strides into the room followed by three policemen.

'You said I had until noon,' she barks at them.

'Our orders have changed, Mrs Stanton,' one of them says, and his eyes flick from Eve in her nightwear to Cicero in his pyjamas and with bare feet. 'Mr Cicero?' he says, his eyebrows rising up his forehead.

'The settee,' Cicero says. 'I'm a guest. I was sleeping on the settee.'

The policeman's head nods slowly.

'What orders?' Eve says.

'That if you continue to hinder the search by refusing to hand Martha Honeydew over or tell us where she is, then you will be arrested and tried for perverting the course of justice.'

'But . . . I don't have her. And I don't know where she is.'

'We have reason to believe otherwise.'

'I don't know anything. And you can go back and tell your superiors that.'

'I'm afraid that's not an option. We either return with Martha Honeydew or information regarding her whereabouts, or with you.'

'That's ridiculous!' Cicero blusters.

'There is nothing I can tell you,' Eve says quietly.

'Then, Mrs Stanton, we have no choice but to arrest you.'

'She's told you she doesn't know where Martha is!' Max shouts. 'What good is arresting her going to do? So she can *not* tell you in a police station too?'

'We're just following orders,' the policeman replies. 'Mrs Stanton, please come with us.'

134

'And what's the charge?' Cicero demands.

'As we said, sir,' he replies, 'perverting the course of justice.'

'That doesn't make sense,' Cicero insists. 'The definition of perverting the course of justice is in such a case as when a person prevents justice from being served on him or herself or on another party.'

'Perfectly remembered,' the policeman says.

'Explain to me how that is happening here,' Cicero says. 'What justice needs to be served on Martha Honeydew? What crime has she committed?'

'She failed to make it known to the proper authorities that she is underage and living without an adult present. Following the discovery of this, she then failed to hand herself over to these authorities and is thus living in a state of permanent unsupervision.'

'*Unsupervision?* Is that even a word? Do you make everything up as you go along?'

'She has no one who can take full responsibility for her actions, such as a parent or assigned guardian –'

'I said I'd be her legal guardian,' Eve interrupts.

'But you have failed to complete the necessary forms, and until those are received, processed and a decision made, that is not possible.'

'But –'

'As I was saying . . . she has no one who can take full responsibility for her actions, such as a parent or legally assigned guardian, and as she is not housed within a care institution, is not under the control of the authorities.'

'And that's a crime, is it?' Cicero demands.

The policeman ignores him. 'Please, Mrs Stanton, we don't wish to cause a scene. If you could come with us –'

'This is bollocks,' says Max.

Eve throws him a glance. 'Leave it, Max.'

'Mrs Stanton, I'm afraid if you don't come with us peacefully, we will have to take you by force.'

'No!' Max shouts.

Eve lifts a hand. 'Can I at least get dressed?' she asks the police officer.

'I'm afraid not. We have strict instructions to take you in immediately in order for your case to be seen at the earliest possible opportunity.'

'What? I can't even get dressed?'

'Eve, we can fight this –'

'You can't, Mr Cicero, sir. She has committed a crime, and we have a warrant for her arrest signed by the Prime Minister himself.'

'Because she's *that* dangerous?'

'Because Martha Honeydew is a serious threat to our national security and the safety of the public.'

'Don't, Cicero,' Eve says, and she slips her shoes on. 'What's going to happen?' she asks.

'We're not at liberty to say,' he replies.

Eve glances at Cicero and he nods, an understanding passing between them.

'You can find out through the usual channels,' the policeman says, and he hands Cicero a card. 'The information-line number is there, and Mrs Stanton's case number; you can find out how things will proceed through that.'

'At a premium rate?' Cicero asks.

The policeman doesn't reply.

Eve moves forward, takes Max in her arms and hugs him.

'I'll be all right, Mum,' he says.

She pulls away and looks deep into his face. 'Be aware of who you can trust,' she says, and she turns and walks away.

Isaac

I watch the shadow of the railings moving on the wall opposite as the sun lifts, wishing it made a difference to the temperature in here but it doesn't; it's freezing.

I wonder if there's a frost outside. I wonder if it covers the branches of that tree and if the bird's still alive.

The people who designed this are clever. The camera watches me, but the audiences won't realise how cold it is, so I'll not climb under the covers because they'll think I've given up, and I'll not pace back and forth to keep warm in case they think it's nerves, and I'll do my best not to tremble from the cold in case they see it as fear.

Instead I'll sit here, on the edge of the bed, and pretend I'm warm.

For a while I close my eyes and remember being at Bracken Woods with Martha. We've made a fire and it blazes in front of us, crackling and popping as the smoke plumes first one way and then another on the whim of the wind.

She's in my arms and I can feel her warmth too, and her chest moving up and down as she breathes.

She looks up at me and I think about telling her I love her. The words are in my mouth, but it seems too soon to say them in case she doesn't believe me, or in case she doesn't feel the same. The wind played tricks on me last night; I thought I heard, could've sworn I heard, her telling me she loves me. How I wish it had been true, that she had been with me last night, close to me, whispering those words.

If only.

I open my eyes, and the image, the memory and the hopes fade as the cold of the cell floods over me again. I stand, straighten my overalls and take the three steps to the window. There's no glass, and for a moment I lift my face to catch the breeze, but the cold is so sharp it takes my breath away. I gasp but tolerate it; the pain on my skin and in my throat reminds me I'm alive. When I can stand it no longer, I drop my head and stare down at my bare feet.

My bare feet on sand.

Eight-year-old feet that weren't cold on that day; they were burning on the sun-baked beach.

There was another pair next to mine, just as small but with cuts and bruises and chipped nail varnish.

'Put your sandals on.'

I turned and saw a woman wearing oversized sunglasses, a hat and a bright pink bikini, sprawled on a sunlounger. Patty.

She lifted headphones away from her ears to talk to me. 'I didn't spend all that money on them for you not to wear them,' she said.

'*She's* not wearing any,' I replied.

The girl smiled at me and we grabbed hands. 'To the sea!' she shouted.

I wanted to run with her, but Patty's hand clasped around my arm, her fingernails like talons dinting my skin.

'She's not wearing any because she can't afford any,' she hissed. 'She's not our kind of people.'

The girl's skinny face and big eyes pleaded with me to run to the sea and play.

'Why?' I asked Patty.

'Look at her family over there,' she said. 'Cheap clothes and towels that probably came from some *value* store. And look at her *hair*, for Christ's sake.'

I didn't know what was wrong with her hair, or why it was important not to buy towels from whatever a value store was, and nor did I know why you shouldn't have clothes that were cheap. But I did drop the girl's hand and shake my head at her.

The girl ran away, and Patty put the headphones back on and turned over to cook her other side like a chicken on a spit.

As I sat down on the other sunlounger, Jackson came back from the bar with two cocktails.

'Can I go in the sea with someone else?' I asked him.

And I remember so clearly now, and I don't know why I'm *only* remembering now.

'Those trunks –' he asked – 'are those the ones your mum bought the other day?'

I nod.

He glanced at Patty, away in her own world, then back to me. 'No can do then, buddy,' he said. 'She'll kill me if I let you go in the sea in those.' He shook his head. 'They cost too much to be messing around in.'

I watched him balance the cocktails on the wooden table.

'They look good on you though,' he said, glancing back at me.

I slumped back on the sunlounger and picked up my games console.

'Kids nowadays,' he said, still looking at me. 'All this beach to play on and all they want is video games.'

I put it down and stared at my bare feet.

There is so little distraction in here and so much time to think. Memories seep back that I don't want.

I remember that it was always Jackson who came to parents' evenings at school.

Jackson who taught me to ride a bike.

Jackson who built me a tree house.

Jackson who read comics to me at bedtime.

And I shot that man.

Jackson who killed my mum.

Jackson who was a drug dealer.

Jackson who ran down Martha's mum.

Jackson who let others die to save himself.

And I shot *that* man.

I can't reconcile the two; they must've lived alongside each other. Perhaps no one is truly good or truly bad, or perhaps one won out in the end. Or perhaps something happened to push him that way.

2.30 p.m. *Death is Justice*

Heartbeat intro music thuds, the eye logo blinks and shines, and the lights above the studio audience dim as those above the stage grow. In charcoal trousers and waistcoat, and a purple shirt unbuttoned at the neck, Joshua strides out, a wide smile and a welcoming wave.

The audience cheer and clap. He walks centre stage, stops and raises his hands.

JOSHUA: Ladies and gentlemen, thank you and welcome to this mid-week daytime episode of *Death is Justice*!

They applaud louder.

JOSHUA: Later on this evening's show we'll have live updates from all the cells, we'll be looking at the stats and seeing who is likely to die – it'll be a show you will *not* want to miss, but firstly, viewers . . .

He pauses for effect, narrows his eyes and dips his head.

JOSHUA: We, this afternoon, have a very special guest for you.

An 'ooooh' drifts up from the audience.

JOSHUA: But before we find out who that special guest is, let's first catch up with our ongoing drama. Our case that is unlike *any other case* we've ever seen before. Truly a first here on *Death is Justice*. Yes, it's the tragedy of Isaac Paige.

Slower, emotive music begins as Joshua walks to his desk and sits at the high stool on its left. On the screen to the right, the eye logo disappears and is replaced by a live feed of Isaac in Cell 3. The music fades away.

JOSHUA: We all know the story, tragic and shocking as it is. A record 25.5 million viewers tuned in to watch the innocent Martha Honeydew found guilty of the shooting of Jackson Paige, only to have this young man . . .

He raises a hand to the screen.

JOSHUA: . . . admit to his guilt instead. It was a truly heart-breaking and dramatic turn of events . . .

AUDIENCE MEMBER 1: But we still don't know what was said! The signal went down!

AUDIENCE MEMBER 2: You mean a record number of people tuned in to see a blank screen!

143

AUDIENCE MEMBER 3: And it's not on WatchBack. Not on the internet either! Nobody knows what happened!

The audience grow louder. Joshua does nothing to calm them. He grimaces and touches his ear, then he lifts a hand to shield his eyes against the light. Thuds and shuffling come from the audience, the voices quieten. Joshua stands.

JOSHUA: Without more ado, let's welcome our very special guest today . . .

The noise dies down.

JOSHUA: Ladies and gentlemen, viewers at home, please put your hands together for someone who is at the heart of this case, who knows the errant Miss Honeydew as well as a mother could. Someone who I'm certain can offer insight into the alleged relationship between Martha and Isaac Paige. Yes, it's the representative for Isaac Paige, the one and only three times *Death is Justice* guest . . . Mrs Lydia Barkova!

The lights change. The audience applaud. Dressed in her usual dowdy skirt and jumper, Mrs B, horn-rimmed glasses on the end of her nose, shuffles from backstage, across to the desk and perches awkwardly on the high stool.

Joshua stands, shakes her hand and sits back down. The studio falls quiet.

JOSHUA: Mrs B . . . May I call you Mrs B?

MRS B (nodding): You may. You are a gentleman in my book. I respect you.

JOSHUA (frowning, his voice low): Thank you, that's very kind. Now, Mrs B, this has been quite a shocking time for you. I imagine a very distressing and very difficult time.

MRS B: It has, Mr Decker.

Mrs B wrings her hands.

JOSHUA: In fact, if we look over the last year or so for you, you've lost your friend Beth Honeydew – Martha's mother – your son . . .

MRS B (interrupting): Not lost, Mr Decker, that is too nice to put it. They were killed. Murdered.

JOSHUA: Murder is a strong word, Mrs B.

MRS B: What is definition of murder? I check dictionary before. It say: 'premeditated killing of one human by another'. Jackson planned to kill Beth, we know, saw it on that video, that CCTV thing.

Mumbles drift over the audience. A flicker of lights as people take out phones and turn them on.

MRS B: And what is this? Here? This electric-chair thing that took my Ollie, my son, my *innocent* son from me?

JOSHUA: Capital punishment. Justice.

MRS B: Is it not planned killing of one human by another?

Joshua doesn't reply. Mrs B shuffles in her seat and sits up straight. She shakes her head slowly.

MRS B: Mr Decker, you surprise me. I expect that from woman who was here before, what was her name? Skinny woman with plastic face.

JOSHUA: Kristina?

MRS B: Kristina, yes. I expect from her, but you? You are not stupid, and your head not in sand, I see that. You know what is happening. You know truth. But you are clever. A complicated man. You know this is murder. You know it is wrong; I see it in your face. You saw what happened to Martha in Cell 7. You heard the evidence against politicians and important people, didn't you?

JOSHUA: I'm sorry, Mrs B, I don't understand what you're referring to. I believe an inquiry has been launched into what happened with the recording that evening, as well as the state of mind of Martha, but I have no recollection –

MRS B: Is that what the voice in your ear is telling you to say? Make me sound like mad woman? Crazy Russian woman who not understand English? Does it control you, that thing in your ear?

JOSHUA: Mrs B, if we could leave that particular conversation for a moment and move on to Isaac.

Mrs B leans backwards, drops her head and peers over the top of her glasses.

MRS B: Isaac? OK, we do that then, we talk about Isaac. Mr Decker, tell me how these people here and them at home can vote correctly if they not know what happened?

JOSHUA: They know Isaac has pleaded guilty to shooting his adoptive father, Jackson Paige.

MRS B: Do they know why?

JOSHUA: The law states that the reason behind the killing of an individual is irrelevant in the sentencing of an accused. But let's move away from that, Mrs B, and talk about his relationship with Martha.

MRS B: No, let's carry on with law things. I know what law says, Mr Decker, but I want to know what *you* think.

She turns to the audience.

MRS B (shouting): And I want to know what *you* think.

She stands up and moves towards the audience. Joshua watches, dumbfounded.

MRS B: What you think? You want to know why Isaac shot his father? Everyone who was in viewing room know because they saw it on video clip! People who were sitting where you sitting now saw it too! But they say nothing!

She stops at the edge of the stage and jabs the air with a finger.

MRS B: They – authorities and government – they hide truth from people. Stop people speaking out. Stop people knowing truth! People like you do not know Jackson ran down Beth Honeydew with his car, but there is video of it. Jackson, he killed Beth, but my son was executed for it. And Isaac? Isaac shot Jackson to save Martha's life! We saw video

148

of Jackson with belt around her neck, saying he would kill her –

Her microphone breaks up, her voice intermittent.

MRS B (shouting): They stop . . . microphone working. Next . . . stop . . . programme. Or . . . me . . .

Joshua strides from the desk to her side.

JOSHUA (whispering): Lydia . . . come back to the desk.

He flinches and grabs at his ear.

AUDIENCE MEMBER 4: Isaac Paige deserves to die! We deserve justice! Our children deserve safe streets!

AUDIENCE MEMBER 5: An eye for an eye. He shot his dad, I saw it. We *all* saw it!

MRS B: An eye for an eye is crap! It's wrong –

AUDIENCE MEMBER 6: Sympathisers like you should shut the fuck up! Bloody do-gooders. If it was up to you lot we'd let them *all* off! He's a murderer, and we don't want murderers on our streets! We want to know our families are safe!

MRS B (shouting): Abolish the death penalty!

Angry roars from the audience fill the air.

AUDIENCE MEMBER 5: And let child killers off? Let them walk our streets so they can kill again? You're batshit crazy!

MRS B: It isn't justice –

AUDIENCE MEMBER 5: And letting them go is? What justice is that to the victim? But you would say that, wouldn't you? Your son was a murderer.

MRS B (shouting): No!

AUDIENCE MEMBER 4: You sympathisers are as dangerous as the killers. Attitudes like yours should be locked away.

AUDIENCE MEMBER 5: Stick them all in the Rises! They're all scum and sympathisers over there.

MRS B: You are wrong! We have heart. Not motivated by money like you!

AUDIENCE MEMBER5: Put a wall up!

The audience shout and jeer, louder and louder. Some stand and wave fists. Joshua takes hold of Mrs B's arm and tries to pull her away.

JOSHUA: Lydia! Come on!

MRS B: I not back down. I stand for what I believe.

Some of the audience climb over seats, others point their mobile phones around the studio, filming the scene. A bottle of cola flies towards the stage, fizzing and spitting across the stage. A carton of popcorn, a half-eaten burger –

JOSHUA: Come on, Lydia! Now!

Another plastic bottle flies onto the stage, hitting Mrs B square in the chest. Joshua pulls her away with more force. The audience spill from the seats and lurch after them. Lights flicker. Crashes sound.

Above everything, the eye logo comes back onto the screen, flooding it in ice blue as it stares over the scene.

Martha

I need to clear my head. Make my decision. I head deep into the City to hide among the crowds. Hood up and hands in pockets. Anonymous, I hope.

It's heaving.

Christmas shoppers.

Look at all their bags.

Probably full of stuff no one really wants anyway. Someone bumps into me and I turn sideways.

That's when I see it.

There's a newspaper seller, the front page out for everyone to see. And on it, that's . . . that's . . .

Me.

I stop, stare at myself staring back.

It's my mugshot from when I was arrested. I can't move. People are bumping and jostling into me, pushing, tutting, shaking heads.

God, I look awful. My head's shaved and my eyes look wild and frightened. I catch the caption: 'Mental Martha'.

I edge closer, try to lean in without the vendor seeing me, and I scan the article, catching sentences here and there.

'Esteemed psychologist Penny Drayton proclaims Honeydew has severe personality disorder . . . constructed a vast web of lies . . . attention-seeking . . . needs to be locked away for the safety of others.'

My stomach flips over.

They're trashing me. Lies upon lies to cover themselves. Why did I let myself think they wouldn't? Haven't they always?

I can't read any more; I feel sick.

Some woman bumps hard into me.

'You can't just stand in the middle of the pavement!' she shouts. 'Get out the way!'

I'm about to lift my head and answer her back, but something doesn't let me.

'Sorry,' I mutter, and I scurry to the side next to a shop window selling TVs.

And there I am again.

Every screen filled with me!

Oh shit.

It changes. My picture slides to the corner of the screens, and a newsreader is there. She looks serious, but I can't hear what she's saying. I keep watching anyway.

Text runs across the bottom. I blink and blink, trying to focus.

'PUBLIC ENEMY AND THREAT TO NATIONAL SECURITY MARTHA HONEYDEW IS ON THE RUN FROM THE AUTHORITIES. PUBLIC WARNED NOT TO APPROACH. IF SIGHTED, DIAL OUR HOTLINE IMMEDIATELY. REWARD FOR INFORMATION LEADING TO HER RE-ARREST.'

Is everyone staring at me?

Or is that just paranoia?

I'm shaking.

I'm scared.

Jesus Christ.

How can they do this?

What have I done?

Threat to national security?

The screen changes again. Some clip of me running through the gardens behind Eve's house. How did they get that?

A shiver runs through me.

Goose on your grave, Mrs B would say.

I glance past the screens and inside the shop. Some guy's stood there. Looks like a worker. He's frowning at me.

I turn away, step into the crowds and as I do I look up at the massive screen that hangs above the cinema. All pixels and flashing with adverts and stuff usually.

But not today.

That's not an advert.

That's me.

A massive me.

What the . . . ?

I try to look at people from under my hood. So many looking at that screen. Turning to someone next to them and pointing, taking photos of it on their phones.

I haven't done anything! I want to shout, and I'm trembling, tears in my eyes.

Why are they doing this?

I need to get away.

I walk as fast as I can, trying to avoid the people staring up at that screen.

I turn a corner, another newspaper vendor.

More pictures of me.

Shit, shit, shit, shit.

I turn another corner. Down an alleyway. Across a road. Up a side street, without a clue where I am or where I'm heading. Moving and moving. Across a wide road, back down a smaller one and it's quieter. Don't know if that's a good thing.

They're scared of you, that voice in my head says. *They're worried about what you've got.*

But what do I do?

I hear noise ahead. Crowds. Easier to hide. Blend in.

I hurry to the end, out onto a wider road. The Royal Courts of Justice – the TV studios for *Death is Justice* – are in front of me.

All turrets and windows, big doors and railings.

And that eye. That goddamn eye.

But something's going on.

There's a strange feel to the air, like nervousness or anticipation. People are pouring out of the main door and around from the side.

They're shouting, some chanting, sounding angry and loud.

What are they saying?

Some have fists in the air.

I come out of the side street and walk across the zebra crossing, trying to get closer, trying to make sense of all the voices mingling together.

There's more of them now.

Where are they coming from?

I slide into the crowd.

'What's going on?' I shout to one man. His fist is raised and he's glaring at the main doors.

'Bloody sympathisers!' he says.

I don't say anything, keep my head down.

'That Barkova woman!' he continues. 'She called for the abolition of the death penalty. Said we should let murderers off.'

My stomach flips, cold runs through me.

'*Lydia* Barkova?'

He sneers but is too busy punching his fist in the air with the others to look at me.

'Yeah, that woman from the Rises. She was on *Death is Justice*. Been on *three* times now – what does that bloody tell you? Here as Isaac Paige's representative this time. She was ranting, said there isn't any justice, said the death penalty is morally wrong, said we – people who live in the City – don't have a heart, or a conscience. I mean, it's wank.'

'How do you know that's what she said? Were you in there? Were they her actual words?'

'It's all over the internet. Everyone knows what she said.'

He spins around to me, and I pull my head further inside my hood. 'You sound like one of them. Are you from the Rises? Why don't you get back there?' He shakes his head. 'It was bloody right what they said about putting up a wall.'

I move away from him. I've heard enough. This is scary. There's hate in the air and lies being spread. I pass a middle-aged woman peering into her phone; I can see she's on the *National News* website. The headline glares in bold red letters.

'Rises Spokesperson Calls for Freedom for Killers.'

No, I think, *she would not have said that.*

We're being demonised.

They're teaching them to hate us.

Who's the 'they'?

Who's doing this?

And why?

Because you could be powerful, says that voice in my head. *Because they're scared.*

A man next to me pushes into me and catches my eye. I look away but he freezes.

'Martha Honeydew?' I hear him ask.

I try to edge through the crowds and blend in.

'Martha Honeydew?' he shouts.

I push further through the bodies around me, just as the crowd surges and I'm pulled forward.

'There she is!' someone shouts. 'Honeydew!'

Shit.

A jeer and a shout goes up, and folks' heads turn back to the front, attention gone from me, thank God, but what are they looking at?

I turn as well and look with them.

Mrs B.

There she is, coming out of the building.

The crowd roar, pushing hard now. I'm swallowed up, too small to see over heads to make out what's going on. Words they're shouting and chanting are mingling together, names being called. I try to make sense of it but can't.

I try to push through the gaps, but the crowd are strong and people are angry. Another roar goes up, something's happening. I can't see what.

I hear hoofs on tarmac.

The smashing of glass.

A whoosh.

Shouts and screams.

I shove through harder and harder, heading for those black railings and that big door, but I can't get there. I'm forced one way then the other.

Stuff's flying over my head – stones, bottles, rubbish grabbed from bins – folks are screaming.

I'm scared.

'Decker!' I hear someone shout, and I look up between the shoulders around me and there's Joshua Decker pulling Mrs B by the hand.

What's he doing with her?

'Mrs B,' I hiss across the crowds. 'Mrs B.'

She can't possibly hear me, but she turns my way.

I see her face, and we catch each other's eye.

Her smile spreads across her warm face, her eyes crinkling behind her horn-rimmed glasses, her whole body lifting as her arms reach out towards me and she looks the happiest I've seen her in ages.

She is as close to a mum now as I will ever have and I love her.

She is my pillar, my rock, my best friend.

She pulls free of Joshua's hand and strides towards me, her arms ready to welcome me.

And we smile at each other and everything around us melts away.

Mrs B.

My lighthouse.

My rock.

What do I do?

I see Joshua lurch through the crowd after her, shaking his head, looking down.

I hear hoofs again.

Suddenly there are police around me, horses and bodies and I can't make sense of anything.

Some kind of gas spreads across the road and everything is hidden in haze.

'Mrs B,' I splutter. 'Mrs B!' I wade through the haze, arms wide, leaning forward, my eyes stinging. People are running away, some screaming, some crying, coughing as they pull scarves over their mouths and wipe at their faces.

'Mrs B!' I'm screaming myself now.

More things are thrown in the air – stones or bricks or something – but I ignore it all, coughing my way through this cloud, eyes streaming, nose running, knowing she has to be somewhere nearby.

The wind blows down the road, strong and cold, and the cloud is dispersed.

There she is. There she is.

But someone's running towards her.

There's a knife in his hand.

I run.

But he reaches her before I do.

I see her frown at him and shake her head, and I see the knife plunge into her.

'Mrs B!' I shout as loud as I can. 'Lydia!' I scream because now I don't care. And I run to her. With all sorts of crap raining down from the skies, I run to her.

But she's on the ground, and he's stabbing her again.

'No!' I screech.

I see Joshua, heading to her as well, his eyes wide in horror, his mouth open in shock.

The man drops the knife, turns and runs, seconds before I reach them.

I dive to the floor next to her.

'No,' I shout, 'no, no, no . . .'

I touch her face, move her hair, look into her eyes.

Vacant.

'Mrs B,' I shriek. 'Mrs B! No, no. No!'

Her hands flop away from her stomach, blood's pouring from her. I shake my head, pull at her clothes, drenched and red. There's so much blood seeping from her, up her clothes, her body, in a puddle on the ground, on her hands, up her arms.

I'm kneeling in it; my hands are covered in it. I touch her face, move her head, feel for a pulse, a whisper of breath . . .

'Oh shit, oh no, oh no, no . . .'

Joshua's kneeling next to me.

'Did you plan this?' I shout at him.

'I was trying to help,' he mutters low and angry. 'I was trying to get her to safety.'

'Did you know someone was going to stab her? Did you?'

'Of course not!' he hisses at me. His face is pale, his eyes are wet. Do I believe him? 'Martha, you have to go,' he says. 'You have to run. If they get hold of you . . .'

'I can't!' I shout. 'I have to stay with her. I have to fight this. These folks here, they have to know . . .'

He's shaking his head at me. 'Not like this,' he says. 'They're after you. If they see you here, it'll all be pinned on you. They want to make a monster of you.'

'But . . .' I look down at Mrs B. I can't believe it . . . can't . . .

'Martha,' he hisses again, leaning in close. 'Martha! Get up now and run. Look around you!'

Reluctantly I lift my head.

The gas is clearing.

An empty circle is forming around us.

Folks are looming out of the mist like ghosts.

And behind them, clearer, are black helmets moving like ants.

Towards us.

Me.

'Go, Martha!' Joshua pleads with me. 'Go!'

I nod at him and I scurry to my feet. I'm shaking, I feel sick, my head's spinning, but I push through that crowd and get out of there as fast as I can.

The Stanton house

'Riots broke out today in front of the building formerly known as the Royal Courts of Justice, and now home to the *Death is Justice* television studios.' The newsreader on the television shows no trace of emotion as he reads from the autocue.

'Demonstrators became animated over calls from the show's guest – Mrs Lydia Barkova – for the death penalty to be abolished, claiming that "sympathy should be extended to killers and murderers".

'Mrs Barkova was acting as representative to the accused Isaac Paige, having previously campaigned vigorously for her own son's innocence and that of current fugitive Martha Honeydew.

'Spokespeople for *Death is Justice* reiterated that the opinions were solely those of Mrs Barkova and did in no way represent those of the show or An Eye For An Eye Productions.

'Following the show, Mrs Barkova unfortunately met her death in a stabbing incident outside the studios. It is believed the culprit of this crime may be a relative of a murder victim whose perpetrator was found "not guilty" after a borderline vote. If this is the case, it may lead to calls for the parameters of execution to be extended from their current majority ruling, where an accused is released at anything below a fifty percent guilty verdict.

'We will have updates on the crime for you as soon as the police make them available.

'And in other news . . .'

Cicero starts unpacking the Chinese takeaway at the kitchen table and looks at Max.

'Did you know her?'

'No, but I know she meant a lot to Martha,' he says and he takes a couple of forks from the drawer. 'I don't know what to believe nowadays. I mean, that's not exactly what Mrs B said on the programme, is it?'

Cicero shakes his head. 'When do we ever know the whole truth?'

Max stares at the food in front of him. 'It doesn't feel right to be eating, you know. With Mum not here, and Martha, and now Mrs B.'

'You're not responsible.'

Max shrugs. 'It's just so ridiculous. To think that someone would stab a person just because of what she said. Or what they *think* she said. I wonder though . . .' He stops and scratches his head. 'It's pretty convenient, isn't it?'

'What do you mean?'

'That someone who was against the death penalty was killed, someone not scared of being vocal. Who happened to be a friend, and supporter, of Martha's.'

'Are you saying they planned it? To get her on the show to voice her opinion, and shut her up?'

'I'm saying . . . I suppose, I'm asking . . . once someone has lied to you about one thing, how can you trust them to not be lying about something else?' Max puts some food in his mouth and chews, thinking.

'I rang the number to find out about Mum,' he says eventually.

'But I was in a queue for ages and then I was cut off.' He pauses, drops his head a moment and puts his fork down. 'I'm so worried,' he whispers.

Cicero looks up and sees the pain on Max's face that he's struggling to hide.

'I know,' he replies gently. 'I tried earlier and couldn't get through either. I'm sure she'll be fine though, Max,' he continues, but they both avoid eye contact and the words feel hollow.

'I'll try again,' Max says, taking his mobile from his pocket.

'Do it on the house phone, Max. It's cheaper. Your mum had it in her room last.'

Max nods, leaves his food and heads out of the kitchen, down the hallway and to Eve's room. He pauses for a moment, trying to ignore the feeling that he should knock, then goes inside.

Her room is in half-light; the curtains open and the streetlights casting everything in a strange glow. He stares over her room, the photo of their family at her bedside, the teddy he bought her for Mother's Day, a book he chose for her from the library, and her crumpled bed, as if she'd been torn straight from it.

He squints through the gloom. Her mobile phone, sheets of paper, a pen.

'Is it there?' Cicero shouts from the kitchen.

Max glances around the rest of the room and sees the phone on the other side of her bed. As he leans across to grab it, his hand catches on something half hidden under the folds of the duvet. He looks down – it's an envelope with his name written across it.

With the phone in one hand he stands back up.

'Max?' Cicero calls again.

Max stares at the envelope and his name. It's shut and sealed.

'Have you found it? Your food's going cold.'

Max grabs the envelope and shoves it into his pocket. 'Got it!' he shouts, and hurries out the room.

Martha

I'm
numb.
Sick.
Speechless.
Empty.
Crying.
Lost.

I'm
walking.
Walking.
Walking.

There are
no words.
Can't think.
Can't speak.

Sit, Martha.
Sit.
Curl up.
Give up.
Die.

I sit.

Pavement.

Cold.

Wet.

And I curl up.

I hate me.

With a passion, I hate me.

Close my eyes. Let me go. Take me.

Cold wind blows. Through me. Lazy.

I remember you saying that to me once, Mrs B; lazy wind – too lazy to go round – goes through you instead.

You said lots of things.

Keep your hand over your tuppence.

Pears don't fall far from trees.

Your funny ways.

Fall seven times, stand up eight, you said once.

I open my eyes.

How many times have I fallen?

But I have to stand up, don't I?

Give up or get up.

But what do I do?

I remember what I asked myself before: '*What wouldn't you do?*'

As I move, the puzzle ring bounces on the chain around my neck and Isaac's words echo in my head: *It's difficult at first, but persevere.*

Really?

What else did you say?

I hope it inspires you to keep trying.

I take the phone from my pocket. Press buttons with shaking fingers.

Hold it to my ear.

Hear it ring.

'Hello,' a voice says.

Breath judders in and out.

'Martha?' he asks. 'Martha, is that you?'

'Max,' I mutter between sobs. 'I . . . I . . .'

Can't talk.

Just listen.

Nod.

Look round.

'Please,' I whisper.

Mutter the name on the street sign above me and drop the phone.

Lean into the wall and close my eyes again.

I think the smell wakes me.

Coffee and . . . what is that . . . Chinese food?

I open my eyes and there's a blanket round me and there's Max.

'I'm sorry,' he whispers, and he hands me a cardboard cup.

I reach out to take it and pause. My hands are deep red with dried blood. My sleeves too. I look down; so are my knees, my trousers. Jeez.

'Were you with her?' he asks.

I nod.

'They stabbed her,' I mumble.

'I know,' he whispers. 'I'm sorry.'

He passes me the carton of Chinese food. 'You should eat,' he says. 'It's only leftovers. There wasn't much else in the house.'

'Thanks,' I reply.

'What if it was planned?' he says.

I shrug. 'Couldn't prove anything.' I look at him. 'What do we do? Are they ticking us off a list? Getting rid of us or shutting us up. Gus, Mrs B . . . Isaac.'

He sits next to me.

I could cry at the relief of being with a friend.

'My mum's been arrested,' he says.

'Oh God, no. What for?'

He explains and I feel sick. Guilty. Stupid and selfish.

'Do *not* hand yourself in,' he says, guessing what I was about to say.

'But –'

'No. Just no. She wouldn't want that.'

I want to argue with him, but he looks upset enough already, so I leave it, will think on it. I shrug. 'Maybe,' I reply.

'Martha –'

'I have to get Isaac out,' I say through a mouthful of noodles, changing the subject. I swallow and turn to him.

Do I tell him about Patty's offer? Her plan?

Would he talk me into it or out of it?

If I want to see Isaac again, if I want to free an innocent man, if I want him by my side so we can fight the whole lot of this together, then what choice do I have?

Patty and the Prime Minister

'I'm getting fed up with all this sneaking around,' Patty says. 'Cutting through gardens and secret passageways! Why can't I come through the front door like everyone else?'

He leans back on the garden bench. His woollen coat is buttoned to the neck.

'Now that Jackson's gone,' she adds.

He ignores her. 'I presume you've sorted the situation?'

'You know you can always rely on me. I'm luring her into the plan –'

'Luring?'

'Yes, she'll agree. Mark my words.'

'She hasn't yet?'

'Well, no, but –'

'Then you haven't sorted the situation as I asked you to.'

'I'm telling you, she will agree.'

'Patty –'

'I've pushed her into a position where she feels hopeless, so she has nowhere to turn. I paid someone to get rid of that Russian woman friend of hers. I –'

'You paid to have Barkova killed? That mess was you?'

'It's not a mess. It's part of the plan. And it will work. And if it goes wrong, you can arrest her for that murder. She was there.'

'The last thing I want is that girl back on death row and given a voice. She needs muting and she needs to disappear, without any means of coming back.'

'But if she –'

'Stop interrupting me. Remember who it is you're talking to. Do you wonder why I don't share your enthusiasm or your certainty? Could it be because you've promised results before that have never materialised? Assured me that keeping information at your house was a good idea, for example? That it was safe? I don't know why I listen to you, Patty, I really don't.'

'I think you do,' she replies.

'I'd advise against threats to me,' he says. 'I don't think you're quite stupid enough to try to blackmail me.'

He exhales and his breath forms clouds that drift and disperse. 'If we accrue any more loose ends we shall need to go around cutting them off.' He stands and straightens his coat. 'I'll allow you the benefit of the doubt this one last time, Patty, but I want to be informed immediately of any developments in this *plan* of yours.'

'What? Why? I said you can trust me.'

'You are to ring Sofia with updates. As I told you to before.'

'But I've got it sorted.'

'Courtesy, Patty, and respect. That's what I've always asked from you. Don't fail me now.'

Briefly he rests a hand on her shoulder and then melts away into the shadows.

Martha

Max gets me a room in a B&B. Pretends it's for him. He sits with me for a while. The company's nice, but I tell him to go. Don't know if Cicero knows about him meeting me – didn't ask. Eve's on *Buzz for Justice* tomorrow.

The room's pretty shit.

The wallpaper's coming off in places, the window rattles and a gale of a draught blows through. There's a weird stain on the carpet, and the bed sheet's so thin you can almost see through it.

Can hear folks walking up the stairs too. Laughing or talking. Can hear folks walking around above me, and whoever's in the next room has got the bed banging on the wall good and proper.

But . . . what the hell. Beggars and choosers and all that.

I'm dry. I have food. I've had a shower even if it was accompanied by spiders and woodlice. And I can sit here in these clothes he's brought me and watch you on TV, Isaac.

The TV looks like the newest thing in the room, but it's padlocked to a bracket on the wall. Would folks really steal it?

I stare at it, watching you.

He's waiting for you, my head says.

Looks like you've lost weight, Isaac. You look ill. Sitting on the edge of the bed like that, staring around, moving all jagged.

What's going on with you?

What are they doing to you?

I touch the screen, wish things were different . . . wish . . .

What a day.

What a week.

Year.

Fucking lifetime.

What are you going to do, Honeydew? I ask myself.

What choice do I have?

With a sigh, I take the phone out of my pocket and I dial the number on her card.

'Patty,' I say into the phone as it's answered. 'I'm in.'

I hate that bitch of a woman, but I love her son.

DAY 4

The Stanton house

'Ready?' Cicero pulls a long, waterproof coat around himself and a woolly hat on his head.

Max walks down the hallway. 'Judge, you don't have to do this.'

'As far as I see it, Max, we do this or we do nothing.'

'But it's your money.'

'What else am I going to do with it?'

Max shrugs. 'Honestly, Judge, I can think of a million things.'

'Probably not the kind of thing I'd want to spend it on.' His smile stretches underneath his long moustache, and behind his thick glasses his eyes give a rare sparkle.

Max grabs his hat from the coat rack. 'Come on then,' he says. As he reaches into his pocket for his keys, the envelope he found on his mum's bed rustles against his fingers. He pauses.

'Are you all right?' Cicero asks.

Max closes his eyes and breathes deep.

'Max? Are you all right?'

'It's . . .' His hand grips the envelope.

'Your mum's a strong lady. We're going to sort this and have her home tonight.'

Max lets go of the envelope.

'Yeah,' he sighs, 'you're right.'

* * *

Out of the house and down the drive, battling through journalists shoving microphones in their faces and paparazzi flashing cameras.

'What will you do when your mother's sent down?' one shouts.

'Are you upset about losing another parent?' asks another.

'Is it true Cicero and your mother were having an affair?'

'What's it like to be the child of a criminal?'

'Ignore them,' Cicero mutters close to his ear. 'They want reaction, that's all. Don't feed it.'

'Do you think it runs in the family?'

'Are you angry she's put your future in jeopardy?'

'How do you feel?'

Question after question bombards them like a hail of bullets.

'Come on,' Cicero says.

He opens the car door and Max climbs inside.

Still the faces leer at the window and the lights flash in his eyes.

Cicero starts the engine.

Another of the journalists bangs on the glass. 'Give us something for the front page,' he shouts. 'Unless you want us to go delving into her past.'

Again Max touches the envelope.

The car drives away.

Cicero pulls into a parking space on a side street and he and Max climb out. The noise of the doors banging shut echoes off the walls of the buildings towering above them, and for a second Cicero lifts his head nervously to all the dark, anonymous windows looming down. With his hands stuffed deep into his pockets and his hood pulled up, Max walks away, and trailing behind, glancing down every alleyway they pass, Cicero follows, with his woolly hat on and his collar turned up high.

Their footsteps are heavy and lonely.

The City bears down on them, its buildings full of history guiding them under a dark and heavy sky; a storm is brewing.

They turn one way, then another, and noise from traffic nearby growls through the silence. They turn again and voices can be heard, gradually drowning out the sound of their shoes on the pavement.

'Here we go,' Max says, and he takes a deep breath.

Next to him Cicero nods.

They step around a corner and looming above them is the Old Bailey, Lady Justice high in the air with her arms stretched wide, her scales in one hand, sword in the other.

Cicero and Max stop and stare around.

The roads are closed. Yellow police tape stretches across bollards keeping traffic out of the area. Horns blare from cars hemmed in, drivers shout out of windows, police cars stationed at road blocks flash their lights intermittently. Ticket touts shout their wares, newspaper vendors wave the latest edition and fast-food sellers announce their prices.

'That's a lot of people,' Cicero says.

'It's as if the fair's in town,' Max says. 'Is it always like this?'

Cicero shakes his head. 'It's *never* like this.'

Staying close to each other they ease their way through the crowds. Gangs of well-dressed teenagers film each other on phones, a gaggle of suited men talk business and a crowd of pristine mothers with expensive prams form a circle, passing around flasks of coffee and elaborate home-made snacks.

'Why are this many people interested in my mum?' Max asks.

'I don't think they necessarily are,' Cicero replies. 'This seems somewhat organised.' He veers left, slows down and edges towards a security guard. A barely discernible nod passes between them. He and Max stop.

'Judge Cicero.' The guard's voice is quiet. 'Good to see you.'

'You too,' Cicero replies. 'It's been a long time. I'm sorry you lost your job at the court.'

'Hey, we all did, didn't we?'

'Well . . .' Cicero shrugs. 'By the way, this is Max, Eve Stanton's son.'

'Pleasure,' he says, extending a hand to Max. 'Shall we move on to business, Judge? We shouldn't risk being seen.'

'Ah, yes,' Cicero replies and he pulls a bulky envelope from his coat. 'As we agreed.'

With a nod, the man slides it into an inside pocket.

'Tell me,' says Cicero, 'who are they?'

'OK,' he whispers. 'You've got three men. Women tend to be more sympathetic so maybe that's why there aren't any, don't know. One of the blokes, guy called Lucas, is sort of well-dressed; he's wearing a suit and tie but his coat is scruffy. Like he's wearing Sunday best that he's had for years

180

but his coat he wears to work, you know? Grey hair, forehead the size of an ironing board but with loads of wrinkles. You'll spot him a mile off. But . . .' He pauses to think, wiping a hand over his face and sighing.

'Tricky because I reckon he's had dealings with you, Cicero. His daughter was murdered back when we had courts. You were the judge on the case.'

'Don't tell me, I can guess – the guy they had it pinned on didn't go down?'

'Exactly. Perhaps best if the boy does that one. Anyhow, another of the blokes is massive, shaved head, rough-looking, you know the kind. His name's Jase. Probably actually owns a chihuahua or something, you know?'

Cicero nods, scanning ahead in the queue and seeing the man he must mean.

'But he's got debts his wife doesn't know about, and I can't see him as the sort who really wants to be here. I'd put money on him applying for the ticket thinking he could sell it on at an even higher price and make some cash. The other bloke, Raif, is uptight-looking, suited, the carry-an-umbrella-all-the-time kind, belt and braces. You know what I mean?'

'I get you.'

'I think he could be tricky too, and I couldn't find out much about him neither. No internet stuff. Seems he keeps things close to his chest. Sorry I couldn't find out more. It was pretty short notice. With a bit more time –'

'It's fine,' Cicero assures him. 'I can run with that.'

'People will do anything for money, Judge.'

'*Most* people,' Cicero says with a smile.

181

The man nods. 'You were always the exception to every rule.'

Cicero stuffs his hands in his pockets. 'Say hello to your wife from me. Tell her I miss her chocolate cake.'

'Will do, Judge. Take care. You too, Max. Good luck.'

Martha

I drifted in and out of sleep all night.

Kept seeing Mrs B lying there. That image of her over and over.

Who would do that? Was Max right? Was it really planned?

Jesus, say it out loud and it makes you sound like one of them conspiracy-theory folk who hole themselves up in tiny rooms, walls plastered with papers, bits of string attached to photos, until they get carted away as some sort of loon.

I'm not one of them, am I?

I snuck out the B&B while the reception guy was on the phone in the back. There was a newspaper on the desk with my photo on it, and on the TV the newsreader was talking about Mrs B. I couldn't bear it. I froze for a moment and I'm sure I heard my name, sure I heard the word 'reward'.

I dropped the key onto the desk and scuttled away without grabbing any breakfast, didn't dare risk it, and I headed out into weather as frosty as this government's attitude to us folk with no money.

I don't know why they pretend to offer us concessions. It's all lies. Give with one hand, take more with the other.

They may as well just ignore us.

It's obvious we're hated.

* * *

The crowds get thicker the closer I get to the Old Bailey.

There's a funny buzz in the air.

I don't like it. It makes me nervous.

I turn the corner and . . .

Jesus . . .

There's crazy and there's crazy.

But this right in front of me now is some really crazy shit.

How many people?

And they all seem so posh!

It's like they've packed up all the folk from the City and the Avenues and brought them on some day trip here to the Old Bailey and told them all to wear their best bib and tucker.

Why are they all here?

Why are they so interested in Eve's case?

Jesus, if I'm spotted I'll be lynched.

But I can't leave. No, I will *not* leave.

There's TV cameras and reporters and they're interviewing these folk. Not going to get much of a balanced opinion, are they? I don't see anyone who looks like they've come from the Rises.

Jeez, there's even folks selling balloons! And flags! And popcorn to take in like it's some spectacle or show.

Rome.

Gladiators fighting to the death.

Who says we're more civilised now?

Un-be-fucking-lievable.

What does that banner say over there?

'No Sympathy for the Sympathisers.'

And what's on the sticker that guy's wearing?

'Cruel Justice for Some is Kind Justice for All.'

What the . . . ?

And another –

'Kill the Killers.'

I've heard that one before.

There's a cameraman halfway up a lamp post filming around the area. Yeah, that's right, show the one opinion and make it out to be everyone's. This is planned; this is manipulating, discrediting.

Propaganda.

Some woman's being interviewed. I move closer, keep my back to them, but listen.

'Well, I for one am extremely worried about the situation and I fear for the safety of our children. Martha Honeydew is very obviously a cold-hearted, self-absorbed individual and I agree wholeheartedly with the authorities' claim that she is mentally unstable. Personally I would go so far as to say she exhibits psychopathic or sociopathic tendencies. Clearly she influenced the unfortunate Isaac Paige, and now we, as law-abiding citizens, have no option: if we wish to abide by the laws our government has set, which of course we do, we must sentence the poor boy to be executed. He killed a man.'

'You believe the law is right?'

'It is *law*, it is there to be upheld, not questioned, and Mrs Stanton, especially given her previous position of authority, ought to remember that. She has clearly abused her power to affect the situation.'

'And if you had a ticket on the panel today, what would you be doing?'

'There is no question. She is guilty. In my mind, she does not even need to *speak*. What she has done is unforgivable and she should be made an example of, given the strictest and longest prison sentence available for the crime. By aiding and abetting Martha Honeydew, she has perverted the course of justice and set this country along a very unstable path with the safety and security of the public endangered. It has been stated frequently, even by the Prime Minister himself, that Honeydew is a threat to national security, and I follow his lead on this.'

I keep my head down, but I feel her turn to the crowd.

'Do we want our children to be able to walk to school in safety?'

'YES!' they shout back.

'Do we want to travel on buses and trains without fearing Martha Honeydew has been there before us?'

'YES!'

'Do we want our country to be run in a fair and democratic manner?'

'YES!'

'Do we believe Eve Stanton has abused her position of authority?'

'YES!'

'Then she should go down!'

'DOWN! DOWN!' the crowd cheer, and it's deafening.

Shit, I think. *Holy shit.*

Max and Cicero

Max adjusts his hood to obscure more of his face and sidles up to a lone man in the queue – razor-sharp seams ironed into his trousers but a jacket covered in dog hair.

'Excuse me,' he says. 'Lucas?'

The man's eyes narrow as he looks towards Max. 'Yes,' he replies. 'Can I help you?'

'I think I can help *you*,' Max says. 'I have an offer for you –'

'I'm not interested. I suggest you go away.' His voice is low and controlled. He pulls his hands from his pockets and tries to square his scrawny shoulders.

'I think you would be, if you –'

Lucas flies forward, grabs Max under his chin and lifts him up.

'I can assure you that I will *not* be interested,' he hisses, his face contorting and sweat beading on his high forehead. 'I've waited a long time for this, and no little shit like you is going to spoil it for me. Now –' he eases him back down – 'do one.'

Max opens his mouth to argue, but Lucas lifts a finger in warning.

'OK, OK,' Max replies, and walks away.

Cicero moves through the crowd, quickly changing his glasses, pulling his hat down and his scarf up to obscure his face. He

187

focuses on the big man, edges close to him, and stops right next to him.

The man – Jase – glances at him.

Cicero flicks him a smile. 'It's cold today,' he says, rubbing his hands together.

Jase nods.

Cicero takes a hip flask from his pocket, has a slug and offers it to the man.

'Brandy,' he says. 'Keep you warm on a day like this.'

'Cheers,' Jase replies, and takes a swig. 'Have you got a ticket?' he asks.

Cicero shakes his head and returns the flask to his pocket.

'Are you looking to buy one?'

'Maybe.' Cicero shrugs. 'Why, are you selling?'

Jase glances around, sighs and turns to Cicero, his head angled down to him. 'Tell you the truth, I bought the ticket for my wife. We've been having a tricky time and I wanted to surprise her.'

Cicero nods. 'I understand.'

'She threw it back at me when she found out it cost so much. So I thought, well, screw you, I'll go on myself.' He laughs.

From under his bushy moustache, Cicero gives a wide grin.

'But I'm regretting it a bit now.'

'Women, hey?'

'Tell me about it. Are you married?'

'No,' Cicero replies.

'Never met the right woman?'

'Something like that. I tell you what though – we could help each other out here.' He pauses and leans in, trying not to flinch from the man's smell. 'There *is* a woman, you see. Well, hopefully. She went to school with Eve Stanton and remembers her when she was a lawyer. They were friends, and *she*, this woman . . .'

Jase nods as he listens.

'. . . she reckons Stanton's just gone off the rails with the stress of losing her job and needs some time. She tries to see the best in people, especially people like us, people from the City and the Avenues. She's quite upset, and I wondered if . . . perhaps . . .'

Jase laughs and nudges Cicero with his elbow. 'You want to impress her!'

'You could say that.'

'You want to stop this Eve Stanton going down? You want to buy this ticket off me so you can make a statement for this woman of yours?'

Cicero scratches his head. 'I'd like to, but I don't think I could do television. Perhaps we could come to a different arrangement.'

He lets the words hang for a moment.

'You don't want me to press the buzzer.' Jase's eyes narrow as he thinks. 'I do have my own thoughts and morals on this, you know.'

'Obviously,' Cicero replies. 'And I respect that. But if you were willing . . . I'm sure we could negotiate something. Make it worth your while . . .' He takes a wad of notes from the inside pocket of his jacket. 'So much now, so much later. As long as you don't buzz.'

Jase smiles.

'I don't care what you're offering me,' the last man, Raif, says to Cicero, his thin lips stretching across his teeth and his nostrils flaring, 'an example needs to be made of her. She flouted our laws and endangered our country by harbouring a known criminal. And if you persist in badgering me, I shall be forced to call security, who will be very interested to hear of your attempts to bribe me, I'm sure.'

Cicero nods, retreats inside his oversized coat and steps back into the crowd. Raif's high-pitched voice has attracted too much attention and people are looking their way. He moves first in one direction then the other, covering and recovering his tracks.

Only one, he thinks to himself. *I hope Max got to the other.*

Music starts, loud and dramatic, drums thudding like a heartbeat, and people stop walking, pause in their conversations and look around them. So does Cicero. To one side a large screen whirrs down from a huge metal stand, and as it flickers into life Kristina Albright's smiling face appears.

'Ladies and gentlemen, viewers, audience, guests,' her voice sings over the crowds as the music fades, 'we are delighted at your attendance. We will shortly be opening the doors to our esteemed panel and the studio audience, but in response to the numbers surrounding the building today, we will be providing a live feed on this, our innovative outside screen, so enabling you to watch along with us.'

The crowd applaud and whoop.

'All for free!' Her painted lips part in a wide smile.

The crowd cheer again.

'This has been made possible with donations from our sponsors – Cyber Secure – and the generosity of you, the viewing public. We hope the weather stays fine and we hope you enjoy your afternoon's entertainment with us.'

Applause sounds over the streets.

The music begins again, and as her face fades away and is replaced with the eye logo, the queue slowly eases forward.

Max watches them, his mum's fate in the hands of three, and he glances at the others, watching the queue disappear, spotting Cicero with his straight back and his hands in his pockets. He moves his gaze further around and stops.

A little distance away, someone is staring straight at him.

Eyes peering from inside a hood, just as his peer out.

They lock, each knowing who the other is, and give the smallest nods of recognition. Then, unseen to anyone else, Max indicates his head to one side, turns and moves slowly through the waiting crowds.

The other follows, eyes fixed on Max, stepping around people, across to the side, this way and that, but finally back into the shadows of the side street.

'Well?' Martha says to him. 'How'd it go?'

'You shouldn't've come here,' Max replies.

Cicero comes around the corner.

'Martha?' he breathes.

'I know what you're going to say, both of you, but I had to.'

Cicero moves forward and rests a hand on her shoulder. 'It's good to see you,' he says, 'but it's not safe.'

'Nowhere is,' she whispers. 'But I had to be here for Eve.'

10.30 a.m. Credits roll for
Buzz for Justice

The jaunty intro music thuds across the studio. The lights ping on and dance around and the audience sit up, an excited murmur drifting over them.

MALE VOICEOVER (loud): Ladies and gentlemen, viewers at home, our audience outside, welcome to today's episode of . . . *Buzz for Justice*!

The audience applaud and cheer.

MALE VOICEOVER: With your host . . . Kristina Albright!

From behind the stage bounds Kristina, wearing a tight duck-egg blue dress, ruched at one side and with a plunging neckline; high heels to match. Her blonde hair bounces as she waves to her audience, and her teeth dazzle as she smiles.

KRISTINA (shouting over applause): Thank you! Thank you, ladies and gentlemen!

The applause dies down.

KRISTINA: And welcome to the show you've all been waiting for! What excitement this is for a daytime show. More thrilling than our sister show, *Death is Justice*, has been in some time, that's for sure. And that's because we bring you *all* the cases; from acid attacks to abduction, battery to brothels, counterfeiting to car crashes, we truly are the ABC of justice. And aren't they exciting cases too?

She nods and glances around the audience.

KRISTINA: I said, aren't they exciting cases?

AUDIENCE (together): Yes!

KRISTINA: Yes, that's right, they sure are! And today's case is no exception, because today we have the culmination of the long running drama and scandal of Eve Stanton.

There's an audible intake of breath across the seats.

KRISTINA: Of course, we know that you loyal viewers have been following the ups and downs, the trials and tribulations of the Paige saga. The tragedy that began with the shocking gunning-down of our hero Jackson, followed by the scandal when we discovered that the beastly Miss Honeydew had manipulated Jackson's son into his murder! And the . . .

She pauses, sighs and shakes her head.

KRISTINA (quietly): The utter *shock* when we realised that the action he was talked into ultimately means his death if we are to uphold the principles by which we live.

She strolls across the stage, spotlight following her.

KRISTINA: All of which makes today's case so much more pertinent. It is imperative to our national safety and security that Martha Honeydew is found, taken into custody and assessed properly and thoroughly. Without this, who knows what she will do next or who could be tricked by her cunning ways.

She stops in front of the audience. They hang on her every word.

KRISTINA: Yet it seems our safety and security is not of interest to today's accused, who has consistently withheld information regarding Honeydew's whereabouts and in doing so has endangered the lives of ourselves and our loved ones: our husbands and wives, children and parents, our elderly and frail, our young and our vulnerable.

A selfish act, an act of defiance and disrespect of our laws and our leadership. Ladies and gentlemen, esteemed panellists, if I were sitting in those chairs, with those buzzers in front of me, I wouldn't hesitate to send her down. After all, what is the alternative? Stand by and wait for others to be killed or manipulated into committing the most heinous acts?

She pauses, looks around the audience and at each member of the panel.

KRISTINA: Let's bring her out!

Music jangles, lights dance from the ceiling, the audience applaud. Escorted by a security guard, Eve, with unkempt hair, no make-up and still dressed in pyjamas and her old jumper, walks from backstage.

The audience boo and jeer. With her head down, Eve takes her place in the witness box. Kristina stands tall and confident. The music stops and the lights dim over the audience while those over the panel, and Kristina and Eve, still shine.

KRISTINA: Mrs Stanton, you've been brought here today to face some very serious allegations. Allegations which could affect the lives of thousands, if not millions, and could see you imprisoned for a very long time. Your son's future, already greatly

195

under threat from having been raised by a single parent, is in serious jeopardy. After all, who is going to employ the son of a convicted felon?

Eve doesn't react.

KRISTINA: Mrs Stanton, for the audience's benefit, to make sure our panel here have the relevant information and to ensure we follow the democratic rule allowing you time to speak, let's start by running through a few facts. Firstly, is it true that you were the designated counsellor for Martha Honeydew?

Eve leans towards the microphone.

EVE: That is true.

KRISTINA: Answer yes or no, please.

EVE: Yes.

KRISTINA: And is it true you developed an attachment for this girl, that you believed her innocent and tried to persuade her to change her plea?

EVE: She *was* innocent. To execute her would've been –

KRISTINA: Yes or no, Mrs Stanton?

EVE (quietly): Yes.

KRISTINA: And could you comment yes or no on this question, please? Did you take Martha Honeydew to your home to live and did you keep her from the authorities when they came to take her into care?

EVE (sighing): Yes, but –

KRISTINA: A final question. Since the introduction of Votes for All, and the current death row system, our justice system has seen a fall in violent crimes of 87% and has been proven to take violent and dangerous criminals off our streets and thus make them safer. Despite this, is it true that you continue to be a staunch opponent of our systems and of the death penalty and campaign for its change, which may in turn put more lives in danger?

EVE: Your words are misleading.

KRISTINA: Yes or no? Failure to answer will result in your immediate incarceration.

EVE: People said the courts were unfair and manipulating, yet now we have *this*? How is this better?

KRISTINA: Final warning, Mrs Stanton. Please answer: do you wish to see the overthrow of our current judicial system?

EVE: Yes.

KRISTINA: Thank you. So, to recap – Mrs Eve Stanton has stated that she believed Martha Honeydew innocent during her time on death row and encouraged her to change her plea; she is a fierce and outspoken opponent of the current system – a system that saves innocent lives every single day – and she purposely kept Martha Honeydew, a threat to our safety, from the hands of the relevant authorities and so endangered the lives of every single member of society.

Kristina lets silence fall over the studio and her words sink in. She shakes her head slowly. Eve says nothing, but stands tall.

KRISTINA: Let's turn to our screen and find out exactly what crimes she's accused of.

To the left of the large screen the word 'CRIME' is illuminated in large blue lettering. Underneath it, rows of LEDs flash.

KRISTINA: Tell us the crimes!

The tension builds. The lights stop with a bang. One line reads, 'AIDING AND ABETTING A KNOWN CRIMINAL'. Then the next: 'PERVERTING THE COURSE OF JUSTICE', and finally: 'ENDANGERING THE LIVES OF OTHERS'. The audience murmur.

KRISTINA: We have three crimes committed! And serious crimes they are too. Let's move quickly on, and find out what Mrs Stanton's prison term will be if – *when* – she's found guilty.

The audience cheer and nod their approval. Kristina turns back to the screen. Underneath the crimes, next to the word 'TOTAL', LEDs flash before stopping with a bang. The audience fall silent.

KRISTINA: Oh my. I believe that is the highest prison term we have ever seen here on *Buzz for Justice*. Completely warranted of course, but nevertheless I'm certain that will come as a shock to you, Mrs Stanton, and to your family.

In the witness box, Eve's face pales as she stares at the screen's decision – 30 YEARS.

KRISTINA: Indeed, Mrs Stanton, by the time you are released, your son will have finished school, been to university and found himself a job and a partner in life. Most probably at the age he will be by then, he will have had children. Grandchildren you will not have met. I wonder how old they will be by the time of your release. And how old you will be upon release, Mrs Stanton. In fact, will you even survive that long?

She steps across the stage as she looks into camera.

KRISTINA: A life-changing moment for Mrs Stanton and her family here, but of course, something she should've thought about before committing her crimes. Let's move over now and meet our panellists.

EVE (shouting): What about my thirty seconds? I'm allowed to make my case for thirty seconds!

Kristina turns towards her with a wry smile.

KRISTINA (laughing): Eve, did you not hear what I said before? The questions I asked were your opportunity to speak. They allowed you well over the allotted thirty seconds.

EVE: No! That's not fair. I want to speak to my family. Max, listen, Max, don't believe –

The microphone is turned off. Her words stop abruptly but her lips still move, her face contorted in anger as she thumps her fists on the glass of the witness box.

KRISTINA: Now, now, Eve. Temper never solves anything, does it now? You know that.

She smiles to camera. The thudding continues in the background.

KRISTINA (louder): Eve Stanton may have seen her son in freedom for the last time. She may have experienced her last ever breath of free air, she may have already eaten her last meal as a free woman. It may seem harsh justice, but Eve Stanton, of all people, was aware of the risks when she committed the crimes. Panel, the decision is yours. The responsibility for the safety of our nation lies at the tips of your fingers. But before we find out, let's hear from our sponsor. Join us again after the break.

She smiles and the Cyber Secure cloud and padlock icon pops up in the corner of the screen.

Outside the Old Bailey

'What if I hand myself in now?' Martha says as they watch the live feed from under the shadows of the awning of an empty shop.

'It won't make any difference,' Max says. 'They'll have the two of you then.'

'But they wanted me; that's why they took her.'

'Max is right,' Cicero adds. 'They won't back down now. They'll say they're making an example, but really they just want her out of the way.'

'I'm starting to think they want us all out of the way,' Martha says. 'We're trouble, aren't we? These folks here, the ones with money, they're not questioning or even really listening because they don't want to, they don't need to. They just think, Isn't me, doesn't matter. Till it is them of course.'

'Present company excepted,' Max says.

'She's right,' Cicero mutters as he stares into the distance. Martha looks to see what's holding his attention. Up on the screen is a mugshot of herself with the word 'WANTED' stamped across it and a number to call with information.

'I think I got the first man,' Cicero whispers to himself. 'But the others?' He shrugs. 'Who knows?'

Martha's image fades.

Buzz for Justice

The theme music dims to a heartbeat thud. Eve stands in the dock, her expression fixed, the toughened glass still surrounding her. Kristina's face is solemn as she strides to the panellists.

KRISTINA: Welcome back, viewers. It's decision time.

She stops walking, and the lights angle down.

KRISTINA: Panellist number one: Raif, thirty-nine, married with three children. Children, no doubt, you would do anything to keep safe. Raif, you've heard Eve's replies to our questions and seen what she stands accused of. You now have thirty seconds to decide whether you trust Mrs Stanton to have seen the error of her ways, or whether the risk to the safety of others is just too great. Your time starts . . . now.

On the screen a digital timer counts down from :30, while next to it images are shown of crying children on dusty streets.

RAIF: No-brainer.

He slams the buzzer, the eye flashes open and the glare of blue light shines down. The audience fall into silence.

KRISTINA: One down, two to go, but will they make their decision as quickly as Raif? Clearly he is a man who takes his duty to society seriously, but is it a *no-brainer* for each of our panellists? It certainly would be for me. Let's move on. Panellist number two: Jase, a motor technician, married to his teenage sweetheart, who he claims is still his sweetheart. How cute. Jase, you have thirty seconds to decide your vote.

The timer counts down :29, :28, :27. Eve's head drops. Calmly Jase looks over the audience at the sea of faces.

KRISTINA: Fifteen seconds left now, Jase. If you wish to make a difference to the security of our nation, now is *your* moment. Twelve seconds.

The timer reaches :10 and ticking sounds over the studio, the lights throbbing with each beat. Jase reaches out his chubby hands.

KRISTINA (along with the timer): Three . . . two . . . one . . . zero.

The lights around Jase turn off and plunge him into darkness.

KRISTINA: What a surprise this is turning into. Ladies and gentlemen, I don't mind telling you, I'm shocked. I thought this was a cut and dried case, yet clearly not. But it is a sad state of affairs when an individual is judged more highly than the collective. Clearly Jase is disillusioned and struggling with his priorities. Perhaps our final panellist is of a higher moral standing. Hello, panellist number three: Lucas. Lucas, this case is important to you, is it not?

LUCAS: Yes, Kristina, and thanks for letting me talk. My daughter, Anita, was murdered fifteen years ago. The man *accused* of killing her was tried under the old system. He was set free. Judge Cicero claimed there was insufficient evidence.

KRISTINA: Lucas, I'm so sorry for your loss. You truly have our greatest sympathies. This must be an emotionally charged case for you, especially as Eve Stanton is a close friend of the man who released your daughter's murderer. I doubt you need reminding, but you are voting on one of the most, if not *the* most, important cases we have ever seen on *Buzz for Justice*. I'm sure you're ready, but I will just remind everyone that we currently stand at one guilty, one not guilty. Lucas, the balance lies with you. The responsibility is heavy. Remember as you consider your vote what exactly is at stake here. Lucas, your thirty seconds starts now.

The timer ticks down. Lucas stares at the buzzer for a moment and then looks up. The timer reads :20, :19, :18 . . .

KRISTINA (whispering to camera): This last vote is needed to ensure Mrs Stanton receives the justice she is due.

The timer reaches :10, the ticking gets louder, the lights throbbing with the beat. In the witness box Eve stands tall, eyes and face fixed. Lucas lifts his head and stares at Eve. The timer reads :05.

KRISTINA: Lucas, your decision, please.

:04

KRISTINA (shakily): Seconds left, Lucas . . .

Lucas lifts his hands.

:03

KRISTINA: Three seconds.

He moves them towards the buzzer.

:02

KRISTINA: Lucas.

And lifts them in the air.

:01

LUCAS: The man they accused of murdering my daughter
was innocent. The real killer is still at large. Bring
back the old system, I say!

:00

Lucas disappears into darkness. Kristina stands in shock. One
person in the studio audience claps slowly. Kristina touches
her ear, gives a plastic smile and looks to camera.

KRISTINA: Well . . . viewers, audience, you can't say we
never bring you drama! What a surprise. I
for one will be very interested to understand
Lucas's reasoning. But for now, what does the
future hold for Mrs Stanton? Will she be able to
walk safely through our streets? Will suspicion
hang over her at every turn? Will every other
member of society accept this judgement? Only
time will tell.

She turns to Eve as the camera moves to take in the full
studio. Jeers sound from the audience, and there's a noise of
people moving around.

KRISTINA: Eve . . .

AUDIENCE MEMBER (shouting): You selfish bitch!

Something thuds against the toughened glass. Eve jumps and lurches backwards. Broken egg runs down. Another thud, another egg. Another, then another. Eve crouches down. Security guards stride forward. The audience shout and jeer more, pushing and charging onto the stage, feet like thundering horses.

KRISTINA (loudly): Well, I think we are seeing just how high feelings are running right now. Join us again . . .

The picture draws tightly on her; bodies run in front of the camera. She's jostled back and forth.

KRISTINA (shouting): . . . when we'll bring you the case of a couple accusing *each other* of physical abuse. What a show that will be!

Outside the Old Bailey

'Thank God,' Max sighs, and he turns to Cicero and Martha. 'But we need to get her to safety.'

'You'll need a car,' Martha says.

Max peers around the corner to the outdoor screen; the image shows his mum cowering against a security guard as eggs and flour bombs are pelted at her. The picture changes, feeding live from the CCTV cameras around the outside of the Old Bailey. Zooming in randomly on people's faces twisted in anger as they gesture or chant their disagreement.

'Cicero's is parked too far away,' he says. 'But there's one of the show's support vehicles at the front. Judge, get her home in one of those. I'll meet you there later.'

'Where are you going?' Cicero asks.

'To get Martha out of here,' he replies.

'I don't need you to look after me,' Martha says. 'Your mum will want to see you.'

Max shakes his head and stuffs his hands in his pockets, the edge of the envelope touching his fingers. 'She'll understand,' he mumbles.

Watching him, Cicero nods slowly. 'OK,' he says. 'We'll meet you back at the house.'

As he disappears into the crowd, Martha turns to Max.

'What's up with you?' she asks.

'What do you mean?'

'That. You lying to him. What's going on? What's in your pocket?'

He shrugs. 'I don't know what you're talking about. Come on. Let's get out of here.'

'This way,' she says, turning her back on the Old Bailey. 'I know you're lying though.'

6.30 p.m. *Death is Justice*

A dark blue screen with flecks of white buzzing and crackling. 'An Eye For An Eye For' spinning in the blue of the eye logo.

The caption – 'Sofa on Saturday' – drifts across, and the theme tune begins, sweeter and calmer than on weekdays. The caption disappears and lights come up on a smaller studio. Joshua, subtle check trousers, sky-blue shirt and a navy tie, sits cross-legged on a slouchy leather sofa, the day's newspapers splayed across the coffee table in front of him.

JOSHUA: Good evening, viewers, and welcome to today's episode of *Death is Justice!*

There's muted applause.

JOSHUA: And joining us today in our 'Sofa on Saturday' studio are two special guests. Firstly, we have one already familiar to you all: Detective Inspector Hart.

The camera moves sideways to show DI Hart leaning backwards on the other leather sofa, his chubby legs wide and his belly straining at his uniform. He gives a thin, reluctant smile.

JOSHUA: And secondly, a new face. One that usually stays at the sidelines of media, but a very important and well-informed one nevertheless. Ladies and gentlemen, please welcome none other than personal aide to the PM Sofia Nachant.

Sofia, dressed in grey trousers and a smart sweater, walks into the studio. Joshua stands and extends a hand, smiling widely as he welcomes her. DI Hart doesn't move, only giving the smallest nod of acknowledgement.

JOSHUA: Thank you both for taking the time out of your hectic schedules to join us today. It is an absolute pleasure to have you here.

SOFIA: It's a pleasure to be here, Joshua, and to finally meet you in person, DI Hart.

DI HART: Quite.

JOSHUA: Sofia, this must be an incredibly busy time for the PM. I'm surprised he can spare you.

SOFIA: Well, ideally he would've liked to have made another appearance himself, but was unable. He does send his regards, and I can speak on his behalf.

JOSHUA: Excellent. So, Ms Nachant, we've had some truly scandalous developments recently that have rocked our nation to the core. Perhaps you can share his thoughts on that with us?

SOFIA: Forgive me, Joshua, but I think you underestimate the resilience of the people. Yes, we've had some *disturbing* events: a high-profile murder, the near execution of an innocent teen, the revelation of a young man shooting his father, an elderly lady knifed in broad daylight, insinuation of corruption at the highest level –

JOSHUA: If I can just stop you there for a moment, Sofia. You say, *insinuation of corruption at the highest level.* Wasn't that investigated by the police and shown to have been invented by Martha in an attempt to slur the government? I'm surprised you should bring it up.

DI HART: It was a load of old tosh. And disrespectful to the hard work my officers do. For them to put their lives on the line every day and then have some head-in-the-clouds girl come up with claims like that? It's an insult.

The audience cheer and clap. Sofia gives a vague smile and nods.

SOFIA: I hear you and understand your frustration, but the last thing the Prime Minister wishes is for society to think we have in any way brushed it under the carpet. After all, she did claim that you yourself, Inspector, were guilty of crimes of a *sexual* nature . . .

DI Hart splutters and turns to Sofia. The audience look around, confused. Joshua freezes, his mouth agog.

DI HART: Now, see here, young lady . . . I could have you done for slander . . .

SOFIA: I'm purely stating facts.

DI HART: And Steve's authorised you to say this on his behalf, has he?

SOFIA: Steve?

DI HART: The Prime Minister. Steve. He's allowing you –

SOFIA: That's a very familiar way to speak of the Prime Minister.

JOSHUA (laughing): First-name terms there, ladies and gentlemen. But I suppose those are the perks –

DI HART (jabbing at the air): And furthermore, Mrs Nachant –

SOFIA: It's Ms not Mrs, if you don't mind. My marital status is of no relevance.

DI Hart shakes his head and tuts.

DI HART(louder): – *Ms* Nachant, where exactly would we see these claims you say she's made? When exactly is she supposed to have said this?

SOFIA: I think you know when.

DI HART: This is not a discussion for primetime viewing, *Ms* Nachant. This is –

SOFIA: To be discussed in private? Away from the public eye? Surely not. And I'm certain in another situation you'd be advising caution, Inspector Hart, otherwise such quotes as *thou doth protest too much* may spring to the public's mind, don't you think?

DI HART: You fucking –

JOSHUA: Er . . . if you could please refrain –

DI HART: I don't know what game Steve thinks he's playing here –

The camera zooms in on Joshua. He touches his ear and smiles nervously. DI Hart's loud voice can still be heard, but Joshua talks over him.

JOSHUA: My sincere apologies for the language, ladies and gentlemen, children at home. I do hope no offence was caused. Time for a break, I think. Join us again . . .

DI HART (shouting): Lies, fucking –

Loud theme music covers their voices and the title screen replaces the shot from the studio.

The Stanton house

Curled up in the corner of the settee, a blanket wrapped around her and a wine glass poised at her lips, Eve stares agog at the television. On the floor next to her, poker in his hand aimed at the crackling fire, so does Cicero.

'Sofia Nachant?' Eve questions, still not moving.

'Mmm,' replies Cicero. 'She's . . . erm . . .' He searches for the right word.

'Got some balls?' Eve asks, finally taking a mouthful of wine. He nods and jabs at the fire. 'Quite,' he replies.

Isaac

Cell 4; they all look much the same, but each one's smaller.

And some are hotter, some colder.

Solitary is hard.

I remember at school we studied Nelson Mandela and how he was incarcerated on Robben Island for eighteen years. One visitor a year, and only for half an hour, two letters a year, a small cell, a bucket for a toilet and a bed on the floor.

I'm here for seven days; I've done three and a half of them.

There is no comparison.

I wonder how many of those days he believed he would die in there?

There is so much time in here to think, and those lessons about him have been going over and over in my head. This stays with me –

I learned that courage was not the absence of fear, but the triumph over it. The brave man is not he who does not feel afraid, but he who conquers that fear.

I feel afraid, and I am scared of dying.

I don't think I'm scared of being dead, more the physical act of dying.

I don't know how to triumph over that.

I spend my days wanting to cry and trying not to.

I'm not brave.

But I'll pretend to be, and I'll try to remember what I've had and be grateful that it has been more than many others have had.

But remembering is hard.

Someone once told me that memory is subjective, but what I'm remembering is not, and slowly it's showing me how I was really living.

I remember the time when Patty dragged me into a shop with deep-pile carpets, walnut shelving stacked with shirts of all different sizes and colours, brass rails with jackets hanging, waistcoats, hats, cummerbunds, ties. Even top hats and bowlers.

The kind of place where opening the door triggers a little bell and the staff look you up and down as you enter, judging you on the clothes you wear and how much they must've cost. Or not cost.

Patty made me try on trousers and shirts, different jackets and blazers, and an old man with creaking knees took my inside leg and pinned the cloth with such enthusiasm I was sure I was going to bleed all over it.

'One presumes there must be a special occasion, madam?' he asked, a creamy voice with rounded vowels; certainly no time spent in the Rises.

Perched on the edge of a velvet chair, Patty folded her legs and smiled at him.

'I suppose it would be for *some*,' she said, her fake posh accent stressing the last word so much I thought she said *Sam*, 'but it is becoming somewhat of a regular occurrence for myself and my husband. We're lunching with the PM.'

'How pleasant,' the man replied. 'I trust the boy here is joining you?'

'Steven – the Prime Minister, that is – is especially keen to meet him.'

I'd heard mumbles and whispers before about her and Jackson and the PM, but never as blatant as this, and it was most definitely the first I'd heard about me meeting him.

I watched the interchange between Patty and the tailor. It was like a dance, Patty continuously trying to impress, not realising he was looking down his long nose at her as if she were mud on his shoes, and deaf to the thick sarcasm in his tone.

There was a hierarchy of posh and clearly she was at the bottom.

There isn't a great deal I remember about meeting the PM for the first time though.

I caught snippets of their conversations –

'. . . must work their way out of poverty . . .'

'. . . the monetary value of information . . .'

'. . . mutually beneficial . . .'

Flashes of replies from Patty –

'. . . whatever we can do . . .'

'. . . public persona . . .'

'. . . arrangement between us . . .'

Anything else is hazy, but I do remember that his handshake was firm but cold.

That his smile was wide but felt fake.

And that his voice did fade to listen, but his replies were always loud, commanding the room and the conversation.

And I do remember, very clearly, wondering why Jackson was so quiet, and how Patty knew the PM anyway.

And why the tailor in the shop, who was *just* a man who sewed clothes, had been so condescending of her, yet the PM, the leader of our country, was inviting her for lunch and laughing at her jokes?

To that eleven-year-old me, it made no sense, but it did make me question.

It put me on edge and frightened me, but I couldn't figure out why.

For years I've been aware of the eyes of the PM and those who work for him peering into heads to read every thought and into hearts to look for weakness, and for years I've been watching his whole being ooze, not just with power, but with the thirst to keep it.

And for years I've remembered those snippets of conversations even though they didn't seem to make any sense without context. But yet . . .

. . . shivers run down my spine.

I close my eyes and imagine myself back in the tailor's shop.

The clothes folded between tissue paper and boxed or bagged for us to take. The smell of the shop like fresh laundry and beeswax, the smooth wooden counter beneath my fingers, the sound of the till as he rang up the bill. The total figures stretching across the display.

Patty opening her purse, her painted fingers resting on the gold credit card.

The tailor smiling at her moments later, the card in his hand. 'My apologies, madam, but it's been declined . . . Most likely a technical issue . . . Surely not insufficient funds.'

'Go wait outside,' she told me, and I did. For ages.

'He's going to deliver them tomorrow,' she said as she came out of the shop. 'Save us carrying them.'

I nodded and believed her.

'. . . monetary value of information . . .' the PM had said.

'Insufficient funds,' the tailor had said.

Coincidence? I ask myself now. But they weren't short of money, were they?

Were they?

Or was this a way to make themselves even richer?

Greed over principles.

Too many questions in my head that I will never know the answers to now.

I wish I could discuss them with someone, or write them down for someone to find after I've died.

Or write you a letter, Martha.

Yes, that I'd like to do.

I close my eyes, imagine writing it. *Dear Martha* . . .

No, I'll imagine you reading it. You're walking through Bracken Woods, the low winter sun is lilting through the branches of the trees, twinkling on the frost carpeting the ground. You come to our clearing and you sit down on the log near to where we made the shelter and take the letter from the pocket of the jeans you're wearing. Your fingers unfold it and your eyes dance slowly across it, taking in every word.

I hope I managed to write something that makes you smile and makes you understand how much you mean to me.

Martha, I love you?

Martha, I miss you?

They're just words, and words that aren't good enough.

If only I could do away with words and pull the feelings from inside me instead and put those on the paper for you.

I cringe at myself; how ridiculous I sound.

Letters, sunlight, feelings . . .

I open my eyes.

I need to forget letters, Bracken Woods and seeing the girl I love, because all the future holds for me is four walls.

And a painful death.

Martha

'Why are we here?' Max asks, and I watch him strolling up to the end of the dock and staring into the water below.

'It's quiet,' I tell him. 'There's no people. No posters of my ugly face. Nobody watching.'

'You're not ugly . . .'

I shrug at him. Nice, but yeah, he would say that.

We sit down and dangle our legs over the edge and watch the sun beginning to dip below the horizon and the orange stretching down the river and dappling its surface.

I wish I could follow it to where it shines next.

'I never said thank you,' I whisper. 'For what you did with the computers and that. And the glass in the cell to get me out. And everything. I should've said it before.'

'You don't need to thank me,' he replies.

'I do. And thank you for yesterday too. I thought I was going to have to sleep rough again.'

'Do you want to go back there tonight?'

'No, I think they clocked me.'

'Somewhere else then? A different B&B.'

I shake my head. 'Thanks, but I daren't risk it.'

We're both quiet for a moment, but he's fiddling with his fingers and I can tell he wants to say something.

'Would it be that bad?' he finally asks. 'A care institution. I mean, I don't see what the alternative is. On the run till you're eighteen? That's two years.'

Something I'd been trying not to think about.

'They're horrible places,' I whisper. 'I had to spend a month in one once when my mum was in hospital. The doctors had sent them to get me. You're treated like an animal. Fodder. Do this job, that job, save them money. Like prison. I don't mind work, I'm not scared of getting my hands dirty, but it wasn't like that. It was like . . .'

'Like the Victorian workhouses?'

'I suppose. I mean, you are educated and fed and that, but all individuality and character and personality's knocked out of you. But . . .' I stop, sigh and look back to the setting sun, as the last tiny sliver drops away, plunging us into gloom. *Take me with you*, I want to say to it. 'I don't think I'd ever get out,' I whisper. 'I think they'd find excuses to move me from that institution to another. I think . . . I think . . . that would be the end of me. A free me anyway.'

He nods. 'I get you.'

'I'm sorry it's all come down on your family,' I mutter. 'Your mum, she –'

'Have you managed to watch Isaac at all?' he interrupts.

'A bit last night,' I reply. I want to ask him what the stats are, but daren't.

'He's been really strong.'

Kind of him to say.

'What about the websites?' I ask. 'Is anyone paying any attention?'

He shakes his head in despair.

'I can't believe the public turn their backs on it. These folks – pop stars, TV presenters, actors, whatever – are supposed to be role models, and we're showing what they've really been up to, but nobody wants to know.'

'The websites keep getting taken down. Every time. Some people saw them. Some messaged me, told me how shocked they were,' he says. 'But more people told me I'm a liar and should stop rocking the boat.'

'Those that are all "I'm all right, Jack", hey?'

'Exactly. Some think we're conspiracy theorists. But others, I think they're scared. The people with money, people in the City, in the Avenues, or even families like mine who live just outside, they're scared that if they kick up a stink or do anything against anyone, then they could lose their jobs and end up in the Rises.'

'It's not *that* bad. We're not all drug addicts and prostitutes and murderers and that.'

'I know,' he says. 'Drug addicts in the City wear suits, that's all.'

'And the prostitutes have designer knickers,' I reply, trying to make light of it all.

He smirks. 'Same but different.'

'Mrs B used to say, "Same meat, different gravy",' I add. I want to smile at the memory, but I can't.

We're both silent for a while.

'I don't know what to say about Isaac,' he whispers. 'They've upgraded their system; I can't get into it to change the vote like I did before.'

His words hang in the air while I think about Patty, what I've agreed to do, what it'll mean.

'Don't worry,' I reply eventually.

'But, he'll . . .'

I turn to him. The words are in my mouth, but I can't tell him.

His eyes flick around. I hear crinkling, his fingers fiddling with something.

'What is that in your pocket?' I say.

His faces changes before he looks away. 'Nothing.'

I've touched a nerve. 'Like hell.'

He takes his hands out of his pockets. 'Nothing important. A letter, that's all.'

'From who?'

He picks some loose stones from the ground and throws them one by one into the water.

'My mum.'

My brain does somersaults. I listen to the *plop* as he throws more stones.

I bet Eve thought she'd be sent down. I bet she was thinking about what the press might dig up on her. I know something Max doesn't. I bet she decided it was best if Max heard it from her first.

'What does it say?' I ask.

'I haven't –'

'What did she tell you? To read it if she was sent down?'

'After they took her . . . I went in her room . . . it was on the bed, under some papers and things . . .'

'She doesn't know you've got it?'

He shakes his head.

Oh hell. What would Eve want? What should I do? *Think, think.*

'Give it to me,' I say.

'What?'

'Give it to me. I'll open it, read it, then I'll tell you what it says. That way she can't be cross with you for taking it, can she? You can't get the blame. Give it to me.'

He pulls it from his pocket, the wind flapping at it.

'Give it to me,' I whisper.

Slowly he stretches out.

'Sometimes,' I say, taking it off him, tearing it open and pulling out three loose sheets of paper, 'you think you want to know stuff, and then when you do know, you wish you didn't. Temptation and all that, you know?'

I unfold the papers, stare at them, leaf through them slowly.

One . . .

Two . . .

Three . . .

In the struggling light from buildings above us, Eve's secret in handwritten guilt.

A secret that killed her husband, his dad, changed lives.

He nods at me.

'You know nothing good can come of it, don't you?'

'I suppose.'

'Good.'

I rip the papers in half and in half again.

A secret that could only cause pain.

'What are you doing?' He reaches out to grab them from me, but I lean back, ripping them again and again and again. Into smaller and smaller pieces.

'Stop!' He lunges for them, but I tip them, like confetti at a wedding, over the edge and into the water. 'What the hell did you do that for?' he shouts at me.

'If she wanted you to know, she would've given you it herself!'

'It was addressed to me!'

'But you *took* it!' I shout.

'That doesn't give you the right –'

'No, but it doesn't give you the right to read it either!'

'Why do you get to decide that? Why is everything about you?'

'It's not –'

'So your mum was murdered and everything else, but shit happens!'

'Don't I know it!'

'And now my family, my mum, is dragged into it, and me, and she's put on trial and my life's torn apart and we can't even go outside, and it's all because of *you*!'

I open my mouth to argue, but he's right. He was dragged into this. Wasn't his doing, his responsibility or anything.

'You've read it, so you know what it says, and I don't. How is that fair?'

It's not, I think. *But what is?*

I stand up and retreat from the dockside, the wind howling now, heavy drops of rain splattering onto my stubbled head. I pull my hood back up.

'I was protecting you!' I shout over my shoulder, but the second the words are out I know they're wrong.

'Protecting me? I don't *need* protecting. I don't *want* protecting. You of all people should understand that. You blunder into our lives and all of a sudden you know my mum better than I do?'

I bite my tongue. Don't tell him you knew before you met her. Don't tell him about all the other people who probably know too. I could, and I could really hurt him. But I'll stand here and I'll take it instead.

'I'm sorry,' I mutter. 'I get that you're stressed, but please don't shout at me.'

'*Stressed?*' he spits back at me.

Damn it, I think. Wrong word again.

'Too right I'm stressed, because some girl dragged me and everyone else into her screwed-up life and then ran away, leaving everyone else to deal with the mess because she can't handle it!'

Oh, now I can take some crap, but that is too much. I turn around again and walk back to Max, angry now, my finger jabbing at him, the rain faster and heavier, the wind stronger.

'Can't handle it?' I scream at him. '*Can't handle it? I am* handling it!'

'How? I don't see you doing anything that's remotely *handling* it.'

'I . . . can't tell you.' Bloody hell, Martha.

'Something else you can't tell me? Why's that?'

'Because you don't want to know. You're better off not knowing.'

'Something else I'd be better off not knowing!' he spits, furious now. 'Tell me, or tell me what was in my mum's letter.'

Oh, I'm so crap at arguing.

'No,' I say. 'It's not my place to tell you about your mum. That's her business, not mine, and not yours either. And the other? Because . . . because . . .'

I turn back to the river. Don't cry, Martha. Come on, be strong. Like Isaac.

'What?'

I'm looking at him and my eyes are full of tears, but I will not cry. 'I can't tell you, I can't say the words . . . I'm . . .' I swallow hard. 'Oh Jesus, I'm scared, OK? I'm scared.'

He steps towards me, his face softening. 'What is it?' he whispers.

I shake my head, tears on my face now, rain mixing with them, and I don't want to be there. 'Somebody,' I mumble, 'someone . . . *approached* me with an idea. A way to get Isaac out.'

His eyebrows lift. His voice drops. '*How?* There are cameras in the cells, the computer system's impregnable – believe me, I've tried. That place is harder to get in than . . . than . . . I don't know, Alcatraz, Fort Knox or something.'

'You can get into the grounds.'

'Maybe, but that's all. And it's no use anyway, and there are still cameras here and there. The only way you'd get in, or out, of the actual building is by . . . by . . . I don't know . . . blowing your way in, I suppose.'

I glance to him.

'No,' he replies. 'That is *not* a good idea.'

'Tell me a better one,' I say.

We drift away from the dockside; it's cold, wet and the wind is battering us, so we head back towards life, looking for cover or warmth, and we find a bus shelter and stand in it, shivering while rain hammers on the tin roof.

I watch cars and lorries zipping down the road, their headlights blurring and distorting and their tyres splashing torrents of water onto the pavements.

231

Rain's dripping from the front of my hood.

'Go home,' I say to Max.

'Not unless you come with me,' he replies.

'You know I can't.'

'A B&B then, or a hotel. Something.'

A bus pulls in. I glance at the steamed-up windows, the lights inside glaring through the dark, and I flinch. There's that mugshot of me again, pasted to the side of the bus like some film publicity poster.

Max sees it too.

'You know I daren't,' I reply.

A man gets off the bus, throws a look our way and walks off. The bus revs back into life and falls in with the rest of the traffic.

'You need to get off the streets,' Max says.

I don't answer. Don't know where I'll be best. Out here or holed up somewhere. Hiding in plain sight, people passing but probably not paying attention, or risk one receptionist, cleaner or guest recognising me.

Swings and roundabouts?

No.

'It's too risky,' I say. 'I'll find somewhere out here.' I walk out of the shelter and down the road. He follows me.

'In the rain? No –'

'Go home, Max, I'll be fine. Go on. Your mum will be worried.'

'I'm not leaving you.'

'You can't stay out here with me.'

'Go back to the Rises then. Someone will put you up there, surely. They'll protect you.'

I stop walking and stare at him. 'At what risk to themselves? I'm not asking anybody to do that for me. Can't. Can't ask you either.'

I carry on walking, don't know where I'm heading.

He follows me, down a path, near some railings and we stop. Rain still pours, sheets of it captured in the dull streetlight above us.

'Go home,' I tell him again. I want to be alone.

He shakes his head.

'You've already done too much. Go home.'

'But –'

'Please.'

We stare at each other for a moment.

'Do you want me to,' he whispers, 'or just think I should?'

'I want you to,' I say.

'What will you do?' he asks.

I give him a weak smile. 'Survive.'

'Make sure you do.'

He hugs me. It's warm and comforting. But that's no good. Can't be doing with letting my guard down, can't feel weak now.

I watch him walk away.

Be strong, I tell myself, don't run back to him, don't plead with him to take you to his house. You don't want a hot bath, or something to eat, you don't want to see Eve and Cicero and actually feel like you belong somewhere.

As if you really are wanted.

And liked.

As if you really could be someone else's friend.

You're in this alone – keep thinking that because you need to believe it.

It's your responsibility, no one else's, and you can't risk endangering them. They've done enough. Let them go.

He's disappeared now, swallowed by bodies and darkness.

I shouldn't've told him about blowing into death row, I think as I turn and walk away. Should've kept my mouth shut. Shouldn't've ripped up the letter. Shouldn't've got involved.

Shouldn't've started this whole damn crazy thing.

Should've just kept to what I know – nothing – and dreamt of being nothing more than I am – an orphan girl from the Rises – because when that was all I was, everything was safer, simpler and easier.

Really? my head argues with me. *Easier? Your mum dead, cleaning toilets to live hand to mouth, no future, no prospects, no hope.*

But I still have nothing, I reply to myself.

In fact I have less: no home, no friends, no family, no job, no money, no education . . .

You have the chance of more –

What, the money from Isaac's will? I won't see any of that. I'd have to hand myself in, and then what? Don't want it anyway.

You have hope and possibility and determination, and those are worth more than money.

At this moment, right now, I have nothing.

Friends. Eve –

No. I don't want that, them feeling obliged. And I've caused too much pain, too much . . . Jeez, and now all I'm doing is moaning. I don't want sympathy. Just honesty.

I feel bad about everybody. Can't stop seeing Mrs B. She did so much for me, and all I did was –

234

I don't know what to do. Feel empty. Selfish. Stupid. Alone.

Want to go somewhere, but don't know where. Want to be with Isaac. Don't want him to die.

Can only see one option, but I don't like it.

I pass a corner shop – the door beeps as someone comes out – then an off-licence, where some suit bungles out shouting into his phone, a bottle in his hand wrapped in a paper bag, and walk past a restaurant that smells so good it feels as if my stomach is turning inside out.

I head down a couple of side streets, don't know where I am, don't care. There's a subway entrance further up and I head for it. It'll be dry if nothing else.

I edge into it, away from the rain and the wind, but from the light too, and the shadows start to play tricks on me.

I think I hear scurrying, like massive rats or scratty dogs.

It's hellish black inside.

Hellish scary too.

Scarier than in the Rises.

My legs ache, and my feet. I don't want to think about what's on the ground but I slump down and sit against the wall anyway, pull my knees to my chest.

I could die here and nobody would know. Few would care. Some might celebrate.

How can folk hate so much and so easily?

How can folk decide about me and judge me just on what they read in the papers and what the TV tells them?

That's not me.

I'm Martha Elizabeth Honeydew. My birthday is May 31st. I like dogs, but cats make me sneeze. I once had a pet goldfish called Swampy. My favourite chocolate bar is a Twix. I don't like beetroot. I prefer to wash the pots than dry them. I drink builder's tea – two sugars and milk – and I love biscuits.

That's me.

I like trees and I like watching birds in them.

That's me.

I cried on my first day of school. I didn't have a best friend but all the other girls did.

That's me.

The song I chose for Mum's funeral was the one she used to sing to me when I was little. I've felt hollow ever since she's been gone. For the first month after she died I slept in her bed, in the same sheets so I could smell her.

That's me.

My eyes sting. I blink. Sniff. Shake my head.

Come on, girl. Don't cry, I tell myself. *You're stronger than that.*

I have no qualifications. No education. No family. No real friends. Except Isaac and he'll likely be dead in a few days.

That's me.

I wipe the back of my hand across my nose and rub my eyes.

Don't do this.

I have no future. No hope. Nothing.

That's me.

A sob bursts out of my chest.

Don't give up.

I have nothing and nobody.

That's me.

I blink and tears fall.

Don't. Give. Up.

But I can't go on.

There is nothing more I can do.

I slide to the ground, rest my head in the dirt and cry like some useless, ridiculous, helpless *waster*.

Don't be weak, my head says.

But I am, I tell it.

I am weak.

And I'm done.

The Prime Minister

With his tie securely in place and his jacket buttoned, the Prime Minister stands in the centre of the room, watching the ten o'clock news as it plays footage of Eve being dragged from the Old Bailey towards a waiting car. Her hair is matted with raw egg and pieces of shell, her pyjamas and jumper are spattered too, and dusted with flour.

His eyes narrow.

The rest of the room is lit only by the dull glow of a table lamp and the flicker of the open fire.

'Did you catch "Sofa on Saturday" this morning?' Sofia asks from the shadows.

'Did I need to?' he replies coolly. 'That was your responsibility. I presume it went well.' He twists the buttons of his jacket, slips it off and hangs it over the back of the upright chair.

'Are you going to watch it back?' She takes one step forward but still the light doesn't reach her.

'Again, do I need to?' he asks.

She pauses. The fire pops, shadows play across the floor and the light flickers up the walls and heavy curtains.

'No,' she replies. She takes another step forward and the firelight dapples her face as she pours him a drink from a lead-crystal decanter.

'They've been studying all the camera footage from the area,' she says.

'They?'

'Your employees in the blue room.' She passes him the drink.

'Did they find anything?' he asks.

'Yes,' her voice is quiet. 'They saw –'

'Let me guess,' he interrupts. 'Cicero et al?'

She nods.

He lifts the glass to his mouth and sips at the alcohol. 'Seems they're turning into quiet revolutionaries.'

'They're also reasonably certain that –'

His phone rings from his jacket pocket and he raises a hand to silence her.

'Patty,' he says into the phone. 'I told you to update Sofia, not to bother me.'

His face is stern as he listens. 'I see. With the Stanton boy?'

He pauses for a moment.

'I'm certain we can get that fed back to you and then you can sort it.'

He takes another sip of his drink, and a sly smile comes to his face.

'The *National News*? Yes, excellent. In fact, pull out all the stops on this one. You are the master of this, and I take my hat off to you for your wonderful idea. You've truly excelled yourself.'

He ends the call and holds the phone to his face as he thinks.

'One stone,' he murmurs with a smile. 'Many birds.'

DAY 5

Martha

My eyes are closed.

I think it's still dark.

Things feel weird.

I'm thinking, thinking . . . trying to remember . . .

I was with Max. Cold, wet . . . it was raining . . . there was the bus, then we walked . . . I told him to go . . . stopped at a subway. Then what?

Then I got miserable. Lay on the floor like some kind of loser. It was cold. Wet. I was really wet.

But . . . now I'm not . . .

I'm on something soft and there's something else on top of me. Warm and dry. Blankets? A duvet?

Things smell nice.

It's quiet.

I wiggle my feet – they're dry.

I shuffle my body. What am I wearing?

Where am I?

What the . . . ?

What happened?

I sit bolt upright. Open my eyes. Blink. It's dark but there's a dull light, like a lamp, coming from somewhere. I blink a bit more, open my eyes wider. I'm on a bed, a great big soft duvet over me, and I'm wearing fluffy pink pyjamas that come right over my hands. I peer around the room as best I can; can't see anyone. I try to make sense of where I am.

Curtains over a window, bookshelves, posters on walls, a desk . . .

The door opens and light streams in. I blanch, raise a hand and peer through my fingers.

'Good morning, sleepyhead!' A shrill, high-pitched voice.

'Patty?' I croak. What? 'What the hell?'

'Fine way to greet your host and to thank someone for saving your life.'

I stare at her. 'What?'

'I found you slumped at the side of a road unconscious, and I risked my own safety by putting you in my car and bringing you back here.'

'What?' I repeat. 'Why didn't I wake up?'

'Well,' she mutters, 'I didn't want you to get all stroppy on me, so there was a little chloroform involved.'

'What?!'

'No lasting damage, don't you worry.'

'And where am I now?'

'I told you. My house.'

'Your –'

'Well, if you're going to get shitty about it, then technically Isaac's house, but as he's currently unavailable, then . . .' She shrugs. 'You're actually in his room. Clean sheets though, don't fret. I would've put you in one of the spare rooms, but one is filled with clothes, another has suitcases ready for packing to go away and the big one of course I'm using as a gym while the regular gym is refurbished.'

I look around. His posters on his walls, his schoolwork on his desk, his clothes in his wardrobe, his photographs propped on his shelf. I squint at them. Photos of me and him, one of us at Bracken Woods, one of me sitting on the swing, smiling.

'I can't believe you chloroformed me.'

'I was worried about you. I thought it a sensible way to get you here.'

I stare at her. 'Yeah, right. And now tell me why you really brought me here.'

She sighs, folds her arms across her chest and leans back against the wall. 'Thought you might die if I left you there –'

'And you care?'

She shakes her head and tuts.

'Oh, I get it,' I say. 'You don't, but you need me.'

'You did agree that you're in,' she says, waggling her mobile phone in the air.

'In reality you couldn't give a shit if I die or not, but you need me to break Isaac out of death row. Is that about right?'

She doesn't reply.

I swing my legs out of the bed. 'I don't get how you found me though. Were you following me?'

'Kind of.'

The clothes I was wearing are in a heap on the floor. Next to them is the phone Max gave me.

'Well, cheers for that, but I'll be on my way now.'

'No, you won't.'

'Er, yes, I will.'

She strides across the room and turns the TV on. 'No, young lady, you really won't. Not unless you want to be caught, and that won't suit either of us, or Isaac. How would we get him out then?'

She flicks on to some news channel and there I am, that mugshot of me again.

'Thought you would've noticed all the wanted posters of you out in the streets.'

'I don't need you. I can fight my own battles.'

'Yet here you are.'

'I didn't choose to come here. You kidnapped me. Drugged me!'

She laughs at me. I want to punch her.

'If I hadn't picked you up and brought you here, you'd be dead by now. Or handcuffed to some hospital bed.'

'They want to send me to a care institution, not prison.'

'I think you realise it's gone past care institutions.'

'I haven't done anything.'

'Surely you know by now that nobody gives two hoots whether or not you've actually *done* anything. Fact is, you're here, you're not going anywhere, so put up and shut up. Get showered – you *reek* – put some clothes on and come downstairs. We have plans to sort – you need to learn how to set off an explosive.'

She turns and flounces from the room.

'Bitch,' I whisper under my breath.

Isaac

Everything in here is memory; everything the past because I have no future.

I sit on the edge of this mattress, remembering that seven days ago you, Martha, were in here.

How did you stay so strong?

What did they do to you in each of these cells?

From the outside, watching you through the cameras, the cells seemed bigger, more comfortable and *easier* somehow. But like I said before, the people who run this place are clever and sly; what the people at home see is not what's really happening.

In today's cell, the walls and the bed and the floor are all white as usual, the window is even smaller and there are no bars again, just gap. There's not enough space to drag the bed over to it, and even if I could it's too small to see out of. But I can see the sky, and I can imagine the streets and the buildings, and remember the tree and the bird.

There are four cameras, one at the top of each wall. I know which one is filming at any time, because a small red light comes on, much like the red light in *Terminator* that follows you around.

As I turn, a different camera will film so they're always getting a good view of me.

It's a strange game I play with them, turning to one, then another, then the next, as fast as I can, trying to catch them out.

I settle on one and stare into the red and memories flicker through, like being at the opticians, or brake lights in the dark, the standby button on Jackson's huge television, or the switch on Patty's laser weight-loss machine.

Memory is a strange thing, and it's strange what comes into your head and when.

I close my eyes, thinking of all the *things* they had, like the state-of-the-art burglar device, the latest entertainment system linked around the house, the underfloor heating, the remote-control curtains, the –

I stop, open my eyes. There's a whirring noise . . .

What is that?

The wall in front of me is changing. There are different colours on it, mingling, images appearing, photos.

Where's it coming from?

I look behind; the whirring's coming from the camera opposite.

It's a projector as well.

I look back. A picture of Martha is coming into focus.

Her hair is still long; it must be from before she was arrested. She's smiling, laughing. She looks so happy.

I smile back at her, but it changes. The colours mix then disperse, and there she is again.

Her hair's long but there's a different look to her. Her eyes are staring towards me like they're pleading. I reach out a hand even though I know she's not real.

Where did this come from? Who took this photo?

It changes again.

A close-up of her face. Jackson's belt going round her neck.

Changes again.

Freeze-frame on her flinching as the bullet hits Jackson. Flecks of blood paused mid-air.

And again.

Zooms in on both of us, that same night, staring at each other, looking so scared and confused. And audio now. Her voice – 'I can be the martyr, Isaac, I can do that, but the fighter has to be you.'

'Be you' echoes.

The image changes again.

Just her.

Blue lights flash on her skin, her hands are in the air.

Changes again.

A razor passing over her head. Hair falling. She's crying.

Again.

Lying on the floor of this cell. White overalls, blood on her fingers.

Again.

In Cell 7, the crown lowering.

Again.

Again.

Again.

I turn away. Can't handle it.

The whirring stops.

But in seconds it starts again, from one of the other cameras this time, and in front of me the images start again too.

Her hair is long. She's smiling, laughing; looks happy.

Dread fills me; it's on a loop. I know what it's going to show me next.

Belt.

Bullet.

Blood.

Martyr.

Fighter.

Be you . . . you . . . you.

Blue flashes.

Hands in the air.

Razor on her head.

Hair falling.

Tears . . .

I close my eyes.

Can't bear it.

I turn again, to my side this time, and I open my eyes.

A red light flicks on that camera too now. And the projector opposite it whirrs.

Here come the images.

The torture.

Always directly under the camera filming me, so never seen by the viewers at home. All so clever and calculating.

I turn away again, and so it starts on *that* wall in front of me.

Turn again. Now on that one instead.

What must I look like to the people watching? Turning this way and that, shaking my head?

A lunatic.

Not the sort of person who's safe to be released into society.

I'm playing into their hands.

I'm doing what they want.

I close my eyes, but part of me can't resist looking at her and so I open them.

Jackson's face is added to the loop now; that leer of his, and Patty's too, laughing that awful high-pitched laugh of hers, piercing into my head and making it pound and bang.

The lights of the images flash bright and I have to close my eyes, but I'm certain when I do that they make the noise and the voices louder and more shrill.

I put my hands over my ears too.

I'm angry now at being manipulated and tortured.

I close my eyes, hum to try to block out the sound, rock backwards and forwards trying to calm myself.

Try to breathe . . . in . . . out . . . in . . . out . . . calm . . .

I bury my head in the mattress but I can still make out the flashing, and even with my hands over my ears I can still hear Patty's laugh, Jackson's voice, Martha's crying.

I try to put myself somewhere else, imagine myself away from this, but I can't hold a train of thought in my head, and instead questions and thoughts that I don't want fire into my brain.

Patty's laugh.

Should've acted before.

Jackson's voice.

Should've listened, questioned, acted.

Martha's crying.

Her mum would still be alive.

Feel guilty. Am guilty.

Mrs B's heartbreak over Ollie.

I deserve to die. Should die.

'Arghh!' I stand up and shout and scream at the images. 'Arghh!' And I thump the wall, driving all that anger through my arm and fist and into the stone and hell does that hurt.

I fall to the ground.

My head pounds and now my fist does too. The images carry on above me, and the sound all around me. I lift my injured fist into the rays of the projector and Patty's face is cast onto my skin instead of the wall.

I move it so her mouth is on my bleeding knuckles. 'Kiss it better,' I whisper. 'No, you never would. What was I ever to you? A commodity to be rolled out at functions, or for magazine articles? The poor orphan boy you saved from poverty?'

I rest my hand on my chest and close my eyes.

'What a joke.'

Patty – *Proper Parenting*'s Mother of the Year two years running, who was always talking and smiling at everyone, but never at me.

Mother of the Year who was forever hissing down the phone, plotting and conniving. Conversations I couldn't help overhearing while I tried to watch TV, or while I boiled the kettle to make her another cup of tea or opened a tin of beans to make my own dinner.

'. . . and if I do that, you can guarantee me how much?' I heard her mutter.

'Well, *I* have the purse strings now.'

'And that amount is in exchange for photos of them together? Yes, I understand, as long as it's something you can use . . . And we could have the same arrangement again sometime? Yes, of course with someone else, someone high profile.'

Blah, blah, blah, I used to mimic her as I buttered my toast and poured on the beans.

Mother of the Year?

Yeah, right.

I stop.

My head clears.

Suddenly I'm awake and I sit up.

How many of those phone calls did I overhear? All along the same lines.

In front of me the images still flash on and off, but I'm ignoring them now.

Thinking.

'A good agreement for us both,' I heard her say.

Remembering.

'Yes, I agree – secrets *are* ammunition against others, and sharing them with you is funds in the bank for me.'

Everything – *everything* – was, or still is, money and manipulation.

But how much of that was Patty?

Max

In the quiet of his room Max switches on his computer and sits down in front of the screen. As it hums into life, he clicks onto the internet and types in the address for his website. At the top of the page the circle turns and turns as he waits.

He leans back in his seat and takes a swig of lukewarm coffee.

Eventually the screen changes. 'THIS WEBSITE DOES NOT EXIST' it tells him.

He frowns, leans forward and again types in the address, this time slower and more carefully. Again the circle turns as he waits, but again the same message comes up.

With a sigh, he takes out his mobile phone and tries on that instead, but still there is nothing.

He turns back to the computer, his fingers hovering over the keyboard, but before he can think what to try next an email pings.

He clicks on the screen to retrieve the message.

'The website you created has been reported to be in violation of government guidelines with reference to national safety and security. Following an investigation under the updates to the Anti-terrorism laws, it has been taken down and history of all content has been destroyed. You are forbidden to republish any of said data and violation of this may result in your arrest and subsequent incarceration.'

He puffs out his cheeks and exhales noisily. '*Anti-terrorism?*' he whispers, shaking his head.

Tapping sounds on his door and he turns from the computer.

'Can I come in?' Eve asks.

'OK.'

She shuts the door behind her and sits on the edge of the bed. 'Are you all right?'

'Yeah,' Max replies. 'I'm glad you're home.'

'Me too,' she breathes. 'I think Cicero had something to do with it, but he won't say.'

Max shrugs.

'And I imagine you were involved too?'

He doesn't reply.

'Just be careful,' she says. She stands to leave but pauses at the doorway. 'Max . . . I left an envelope in my room before they took me, but I can't find it now. You don't happen to know where it is, do you?'

He shakes his head. 'What was it?'

'Something that would be better spoken, not read.' She waits for his reaction but his phone sounds with a message and he turns away from her.

'I don't know, Mum,' he replies.

'Never mind,' she says, and with a nod she steps out of his room and closes the door.

Max stares into his phone.

He blinks at the text, shakes his head, looks away, then back to it.

'The websites won't work. Stop them. There is another way. You are not alone.'

He looks at the number, not one he recognises.

'Who is this?' he taps to reply.

A moment later the answer comes back. 'A friend. A sympathiser.'

He pauses for a second, then his thumbs dart over the keypad. 'What's the other way?' he types.

He stares at the screen, waiting for more.

Another ping sounds. 'Not yet. Be careful. You're being watched,' it reads.

'Watched?'

The reply comes quickly. 'No more right now. Wait. I'll be in touch.'

Absent-mindedly he looks out of his window. Something at the top of the telegraph poles the other side of his garden catches his eye.

He steps closer, staring at the trees they're half hidden by, sure he saw movement. A shiver runs through him, and even though it's daylight, he pulls the curtains across.

The message tone on his phone goes off again and he glances down.

'You can close your curtains, but they still know where you are,' it reads.

His legs buckle. He staggers backwards into his seat and the phone falls from his hand.

In the gloom, the brightness of the screen and its warning stare up at him from the floor.

Martha

I sit here on his bed, surrounded by his things – a photo of him as a boy on a beach, a T-shirt he's taken off and dumped on the floor, his school bag with books spilling out – while I watch him on his own TV.

I've been watching it all day. Went to the bathroom, wandered downstairs, came back again.

It's real quiet. So different to the Rises. There's no shouting and fighting outside, no fireworks going off to let folks know that drugs have arrived and are on sale. The radiators work and the hot water doesn't run out, the windows shut properly and the door lock can't be undone with a butter knife.

It's the simple things, I suppose.

So far I've not seen anyone else but Patty. She was chatting into a phone, mouthed something about talking to me later and disappeared.

You know what I miss in all this batshit crazy stuff? Someone smiling at me when I walk in a room, someone asking if I want a cup of tea, someone putting a hand on my shoulder. Company.

Mum did all that.

Then Mrs B.

Isaac.

Eve.

This bloody machine that is *Death is Justice* and *Buzz for Justice* and the rest of the crap that goes with it has swallowed us whole and it feels like we're fighting from the inside to survive.

I can feel it rotting me away like the digestive juices in some massive evil whale.

Maybe the whole country's the whale. No, the system, the government. Yeah, the government and the authorities that allow this, they're the whale, and us, the little folk, we're the . . . what is it now? Krill?

I have been pushed to a point where it seems inevitable I'm going to become the criminal they say I am.

Either I watch the man I love executed for saving my life and fighting for justice for my mum and Ollie and everyone else, or I agree to blowing a hole into death row and helping him escape.

Either I stay here and become that criminal, or I climb out the window and run away.

My conscience says I have no choice.

Max

Max staggers down the hallway to the kitchen, shaken and still in his pyjamas. His laptop's under an arm and a microphone in his hand, cables dragging behind him. Eve and Cicero watch as he blunders in, their hands around mugs of coffee, plates with uneaten sandwiches on the table in front of them.

'I've got an idea,' he says. 'It's phone-ins on *Death is Justice* today, isn't it?'

'Yes, it is,' Eve replies.

Max places his laptop on the table. 'Good. Remember what we did before, Judge? With the phone?'

Cicero nods.

'And Martha has a phone too,' Max says.

6.30 p.m. *Death is Justice*

The theme music pounds with a rhythmic heartbeat thud. Flecks of white buzz and crackle around the eye logo. The music fades, the logo moves to the edge of the dark blue screen and Joshua strides out onto the stage. In a tailored blue suit, white shirt and burgundy tie, he smiles broadly, and whoops sound from the audience. He stops, spins and strikes a pose. Wolf whistles soar across the studio and he winks.

JOSHUA: Ladies and gentlemen, good evening to you all and welcome to the show! Have we got an evening's entertainment lined up for you today! Yes, indeed. Just sit back, grab a drink and that chocolate you so deserve, put your feet up and let us transport you away from your daily worries.

He pauses as the audience cheer and applaud.

JOSHUA: As I'm sure you're aware, Sundays usually see us with guests on our 'Judge Sunday' show, but we thought this week, for your viewing pleasure, we'd mix things up a little. Yes, on today's show not only do we have . . .

He turns to the screen. The display splits into seven rectangles, four occupied, the faces of the accused leering out. The first rectangle flashes brighter and moves to the centre of the screen. The man in it is visibly shaking and his eyes dart from one side to the other.

JOSHUA: A brand new inmate in Cell 1 . . .

The first rectangle moves back into place again and the fourth takes centre – a man lying on the floor, his hands over his face.

JOSHUA: All the juicy details of the murder allegedly carried out by Cell 4 occupant, Bill Dandy . . .

Bill's cell recedes. Cell 7 now takes centre, its occupant prowling the floor, his face gaunt.

JOSHUA: Final-decision time for our man in Cell 7 – is he that trigger-happy bank robber or not? It's for you to decide . . .

Cell 7 moves back into line with the others. Joshua turns to camera.

JOSHUA: But, ladies and gentlemen, of course we have *that* case to discuss. Yes, the one you've all been waiting for, the icing on the cake, the cherry on the top, the one you're all talking about. Our *water-cooler* moment. The name on everyone's lips, in all the newspapers, and the hashtag you're all following. None other than son of murdered celebrity millionaire, orphan boy from the Rises and, ironically, named teen ambassador for justice in last year's *Celebrity Now!* magazine, yes, in Cell 5 it's Isaac Paige!

Again the audience applaud, and as the lights dim over them, Isaac's cell takes centre and the others fade away. The camera focuses in on his swollen face and red eyes as he lies on the mattress, staring at the ceiling.

JOSHUA: He's looking pretty broken there. I wonder how many of you have sympathy for him, or how many will be helping to rack those guilty numbers higher and higher. Well, this is your chance to tell us, because today we are taking your calls on this one, viewers. Yes, we want to hear your thoughts and opinions. Lines are open. Get your fingers dialling! And while our lovely ladies are taking your calls, let's have a look at the stats in this case. How do you, our loyal followers, judge Isaac Paige? Guilty or not guilty of killing his father, Jackson Paige, charity worker and self-made millionaire, who rescued him from a life in the Rises and shared his wealth, experience and opportunities with him?

Joshua's smile never falters and his voice rings with charm, but his eyes are dull. He wanders to the screen as the feed from

Isaac's cell moves to the right-hand side and two columns appear on the left. Above one is the word 'Guilty', the other says 'Not guilty'.

JOSHUA: Show us the stats!

The levels on the columns move up and down, adjusting dramatically alongside a loud ticking. Suddenly it stops. The 'Guilty' column is high, the 'Not guilty' one low.

JOSHUA: Well, would you look at that? Seems pretty clear-cut to me – doesn't it to you, audience? Yes, that reads 99% guilty, 1% not guilty. Tell me, caller number one, what are your thoughts on that?

Crackling sounds over the studio as Joshua strolls back to the desk and takes his seat. The camera zooms in on him.

JOSHUA: Hello? Do we have anyone on the line? Caller one, are you there?

CALLER 1: Hello. Hello?

JOSHUA: We can hear you, caller one. What is your name and what would you like to say about this case?

LUTHER: My name's Luther. I wanted to say . . . well, I wanted to ask something. I missed last week's programme with Martha in Cell 7, so I was going to see it on WatchBack, but when I go to play it, there's nothing there. It's just blank, like it's been taken down. And it's –

JOSHUA (laughing): Luther, I think you've dialled the wrong number! You need technical, darling!

The audience laugh with him.

LUTHER: No, because my neighbour said the same, and the shopkeeper, and the blokes at football whose wives tried WatchBack. They all said the same thing happened to them. It's nowhere on the internet either.

JOSHUA: Luther, if I could stop you –

LUTHER: And friends of mine said Martha was talking about this corruption scandal and what people had done but had been covered up, and they said there were some pretty serious crimes there, and –

JOSHUA: Luther, my sweet, it sounds as if you haven't been keeping abreast of the situation. If you had, then you'd know that these allegations have been fully investigated –

LUTHER: No, I did hear that, but I don't see how something that serious can be *fully* investigated in such a short time. Especially when it usually takes so long for the government –

The line goes dead.

JOSHUA: Oh dear, it seems we've lost Luther there. What a shame.

He winks to the screen and touches his ear.

JOSHUA: Let's move on. Do we have someone else on the line? Caller number two is . . . Malcolm. Are you there?

MALCOLM: Hello, yes, I'm here.

JOSHUA: Thank you for joining us. Tell us what you have to say about this case, Malcolm. Do you have any opinions on Isaac Paige? It is yet another teenager on death row after all. Does this illustrate a decline in society in general or specifically within the teenage community? Do you think we should fear our own teens? Media have suggested there's a need for underage curfews. Do you have any strong feelings on that?

MALCOM: I have strong feelings on lots of things, but I'll tell you something you'll find interesting, Joshua. Something that I think everyone will find interesting. This Isaac Paige case isn't as simple as you think it is. I work for a major national newspaper, and I was in the viewing area last week at Martha's Cell 7. What a sham that was! I can tell you that what Luther was talking about, those documents –

Joshua frowns, touches his ear subconsciously and shifts in his seat.

JOSHUA: Malcolm, I'm afraid I have to interrupt you there. Discussion into police investigations is not allowed.

MALCOLM: You said *fully investigated*. Finished. Done. So . . . as I was saying, the documents . . . I was there to record the event and I taped Isaac's victim speech, where he showed the documents. I purposefully zoomed in on them and I'm telling you they weren't fake –

JOSHUA: Malcolm, I have to warn you that making allegations against people publicly –

MALCOLM: Is slanderous, yes, I know. But not when it's true. And I know what I saw is true. I know for a fact that Albert DeLonzo – editor in chief of the *National News* – was previously arrested for supplying class-A drugs, but was later released without charge. I know that Penny Drayton's charge of child abuse was swept under the carpet. I know countless claims of a sexual nature against TV host Jamie Howdinger were ignored by investigating officers because someone higher up told them to. I know DI Hart only holds that position because of the people he bribed, not because of aptitude, and I know that all this was documented by Jackson Paige so he could use it to get off whatever crimes he committed and carry on his privileged life. Not only that, but also shown that evening – though interestingly also unavailable since – was clear video footage of Jackson purposely killing –

Again the line goes dead. Static fills the air. Joshua leans back in his seat and steeples his fingers. The audience are silent.

JOSHUA: I can only apologise that we must have a technical glitch this evening, viewers. We do seem to be struggling to get into any sort of debate today. But let's move swiftly on. Do we have caller three on the line? Caller three? What's your name, please, and what do you have to say?

CALLER 3 (female): Hello, Joshua. Thanks for having me on.

JOSHUA: You're welcome. I'm sorry, caller three, I didn't catch your name.

CALLER 3: If I tell you my real name you might cut me off, or that voice in your ear might. I think you're all right really, but that voice in your ear doesn't like stuff being said that actually makes folk think and question.

JOSHUA: You're baffling me, caller three. Yet I'm intrigued.

CALLER 3: That's good. How many folks are watching, Josh? What are your *viewing stats*?

JOSHUA: I'm afraid I don't have access to those right now –

CALLER 3: What does the man in your ear say?

Joshua sighs heavily, raises his eyebrows and touches his ear.

JOSHUA: He says that it's usually around twelve to thirteen million, but the current public interest has upped it, so probably well over the fifteen mark.

CALLER 3: That's a lot of people.

JOSHUA: All waiting to hear what you have to say.

CALLER 3: OK. I want to try something, but I'll need folk to play along. Like a party game. Promise you it's nothing illegal or rude, right? And it's relevant to Isaac. OK?

JOSHUA: I'll humour you. For now, at least.

CALLER 3: OK, everyone, viewers at home too, close your eyes and think of the person you love the most in the world. Who is it? Your mum, your dad, your brother or sister. Best friend maybe. Or your husband or wife, partner, whatever. Imagine you're with them right now, they're sitting opposite you. You're smiling at each other. You're happy. You love them, they love you, you can't imagine ever being without them. Yeah, Josh, you got it?

JOSHUA: Yes, I'm with my partner.

The camera pans over the audience, whose eyes are closed, some holding hands with the person next to them, others clutching their mobile phone as if it's their link to a loved one.

CALLER 3: Everyone feeling warm and cosy? Well, now imagine someone comes up behind you and whispers they're going to kill you. They put a rope, or a belt, around your neck. My God, you are scared. I mean, you are so scared. You're thinking, This is it, I'm going to die. And you are *terrified*, and you're still looking at the person you love and they're still staring at you, and you know that in a few minutes' time, or seconds even, it's all going to be over because some nutter

269

is going to squeeze the breath out of you, and
you are frightened!

She pauses. The studio is silent.

CALLER 3: You with me?

JOSHUA (quietly): Yes.

The audience mumble.

CALLER 3: That person you love and who loves you back
can stop it all. He, she, whoever, can save your
life because they have a gun. They raise it and
they shoot the person who's about to kill you.

There's a collective sigh of relief.

CALLER 3: But now that person you love is going to be taken
away and he – or she – is going to be executed
for saving your life. He took a life, so, as our law
demands, his should be taken. But he didn't act
out of violence or hatred; he acted out of love.
Our justice system has no room for love, and I say
that's wrong. That's what happened to me, that's
what happened to Isaac. He killed Jackson because
Jackson was about to kill me. Nobody knew – well,
hardly anyone – because they took the evidence,
they destroyed or hid everything. It's wrong.

JOSHUA: Martha, is that you?

There's a mutter over the audience.

MARTHA: Our system sees only black and white. We need grey and we need love, or at least compassion. We need to stand up for this and stand up for each other. The only way we can do it is to buck the system. Isaac *is* guilty – yes, he killed a man – but I plead with you to see the bigger picture, see the grey, and vote him not guilty and make it a vote against the system too. Prove that together we have power and toge—

For the third time the line goes dead. Again the studio is silent.

JOSHUA: My, my! Well, it does seem like we're experiencing some technical issues here, and I do apologise for that. We had a queue of callers lined up to discuss this fascinating case, but it seems it will be necessary to –

AUDIENCE MEMBER (shouting): Turn the debate to the floor!

JOSHUA: – resume the calls after –

AUDIENCE MEMBER (shouting): We want to speak!

JOSHUA: – this message from our sponsor. But what
fascinating calls we've had, including an exclusive
from the delightful Martha Honeydew. Join us
again . . .

He stops talking and stares over the studio. He takes his
earpiece out.

JOSHUA: In fact, yes, why not? We'll go to that message
later. Right now, let's turn the debate to the floor.
Ladies and gentlemen, please remain seated. I shall
come to you.

He stands and strides towards the audience.

JOSHUA: Please raise your hands if you wish –

The studio is plunged into darkness. The audience shout
and jeer.

JOSHUA: Remain calm, please, ev—

His voice is silenced.

On screens in homes, shops, offices and on mobile devices, the
link to the studio is cut and an automatic video plays. A blue
sky with white fluffy clouds. Text, photos and information
drift into one of the clouds, and a padlock forms and clicks
onto its corner.

FEMALE VOICEOVER: Here at Cyber Secure, sponsor of *Death is Justice, Buzz for Justice* and key shareholder of Eye For An Eye Productions, we take your virtual safety and security seriously and guarantee to hold all your information in line with the strictest safety policies and procedures in the world . . .

Martha

'Nice party trick,' Patty says, barging into the room. She grabs the phone from me, throws it to the ground and stomps her heel through it. 'I take it your cosy little Stanton friend did that? The one who thinks he's so clever with technology?'

'Cleverer than you,' I reply.

'Is he your backup in case Isaac dies?' A revolting smile spreads across her stupid face.

'You're a bitch,' I tell her.

'Yeah, and proud.'

I could quite happily punch her ridiculous face in.

But I won't.

'Why did you even bother? People aren't going to vote him innocent. He did it.'

'It'd be a statement. A "fuck you" to the authorities.'

'Mind your dirty mouth.'

I lift a middle finger to her.

'I suppose you're not to blame for your filthy mouth and habits. It's your upbringing after all, your mother's fault.'

'Circumstance taught me to swear,' I tell her calmly. 'Can blame your husband for that one. Who gives a toss anyway? Certainly doesn't sound like you care much about Isaac or you'd be thanking me. I really don't get you. Tell me you want to save him, then –'

Patty sighs, shoulders slumping and eyes rolling like she's some stereotypical teenager. 'I *told* you it doesn't work like that. People need a scapegoat and to see justice done or the whole balance will shift. People need to know who's in charge and what will happen if they disobey. Fact.'

'You do talk a load of crap.'

'You are my case in point.'

'You are a disillusioned cow-bag of a stupid woman. That's my polite version.'

'Do you want me to ring the authorities and tell them you're here?'

'Do what you want. Why did you bring me here anyway?'

'We have an arrangement. You have things to learn.'

'Oh yeah, right. You want to turn me into a terrorist. There's a good adult influence for me.'

'Hardly a terrorist. Don't go filling yourself with delusions of grandeur!'

'I'll go along with your plan, but not if the stats go down. If it's looking like he'll be voted free, then I'm not doing it.'

'Clearly you *are* deluded. Do you know what the stats are? They've never been recorded this high or this consistent. He's ninety-nine percent guilty, and I'm guessing the one percent is something to do with you and all those phones the PM gave out. Good move on his part – let people think they're making a difference.'

'I'm not going to argue with you,' I tell her, managing, God knows how, to keep calm. 'Teach me what to do, but like I said, if it's looking like he'll be released –'

'Which it won't.'

'– then I won't do it,' I repeat.

She pouts and folds her arms across her chest and stares at me. 'You're naive and stupid,' she says.

'Do you always need the last word, Patty? How old are you really?' I say.

She turns around, walks to the door, makes a show of opening it and pauses in the hallway. 'No,' she says, closing the door before I can reply.

Immature cow, I think to myself.

Joshua

Joshua sits on a chair in the middle of a room. It's so dark all he can see are the vague shadows made from the lights filtering in from the street far below him.

'Where am I?' he says into the darkness.

'Top floor,' a male voice replies.

'Why?'

'You need reminding of the job you do and the responsibility you hold. You've been letting personal feelings enter into your delivery. That cannot be tolerated.'

'But –'

'There are many people who think you're sympathising with the accused.'

'It wasn't my fault with the phone calls today.'

'The callers were allowed to speak for far too long. You could've interrupted.'

'I didn't have the power to cut them off – you did.'

The shadow of the man's body looms over Joshua.

'Hang on – you're not from *Death is Justice* or An Eye For An Eye Productions, are you?'

The man doesn't reply.

'Where are you from? The government?'

The man moves across the room, his shoes clicking on the floor. He stops, and suddenly the light of a TV screen blares into the darkness. Joshua flinches and turns from it.

'So the government now controls what's allowed on television? What people say?' he mutters.

'Both are concerned with the safety and well-being of the nation and its people,' the man replies as he strides back across the floor. 'Watch,' he says, his voice coming from behind Joshua.

The screen flickers slightly and then a recording begins.

Joshua is sitting at the desk of *Death is Justice* with Kristina and Eve. He looks to Eve, rests a hand on hers, and says, 'I'm so sorry.' The recording changes, shows him passing her a box of tissues, changes again and he says, 'We're all your friends here, Eve. We all support you.'

A different recording comes up: the feed is grainier, a street view in evening time, a few cars rumbling along, people walking one way or another. A solitary man moves into the picture from the right and the camera follows him down the road. It watches him stride up the steps of a large Edwardian house and holds steady as he first scrabbles in his pockets, then gives up and presses the doorbell.

The camera zooms closer as he waits for the door to be answered, and slowly a face appears out of the pixels.

In the room, Joshua barely moves as he watches the door being opened by another man and himself entering his own home. But as the door begins to close and the picture freezes, and captured on the screen is an image of the two men kissing their hellos, Joshua's eyes turn skyward and his head shakes.

'So?' he says, staring at himself and Pete on the screen.

'I don't care,' the man says from behind him, 'but plenty will.'

'I don't know what century you think we're living in –'

'The public like you, but –'

'Don't underestimate our public. They're supportive, thoughtful, open-minded –'

'*But* there are many bigoted people out there. High-powered influential bigots.'

'Are you threatening me?'

He doesn't reply.

The image on the screen changes again. A different view from a camera looking down at the front of the Old Bailey. A huge crowd are chanting and jeering and pushing. The camera flicks from one face to another, pausing briefly on each as if taking a photograph.

Suddenly the noise gets louder and the camera pans away. Coming out of the Old Bailey is Joshua, gently guiding Mrs B. The camera rests on them each individually for a moment, then follows them into the crowd. Their faces are lost as it focuses on others close to them, those holding banners or shouting, or those raising fists into the air.

Seen from above, the crowd moves like a flock of starlings, first one way then the other, then without warning it parts, an empty circle forming but for one figure in the middle. Mrs B, lying on the ground, blood leaking from her stomach and forming puddles and rivulets on the path.

Someone rushes forward and the camera zooms and pauses on her – Martha. As it pans away Joshua can be seen running towards them.

In the room, Joshua doesn't move, only listens as the sound crackles and the recording of his voice cuts through the air – 'Martha! Get up now and run.'

The image freeze-frames on the two of them and Mrs B's lifeless body.

'A strange allegiance forming there,' the man says. 'Why would you tell her to run?'

Joshua doesn't reply.

'You know she's wanted by the authorities.'

'Yes.'

'And it's your duty as a citizen, your responsibility for the safety of your fellows, to report her whereabouts.'

'Explain to me why she's wanted by the authorities,' Joshua says.

'She's a danger to the safety and security of our country.'

'What if I disagree?'

'That's irrelevant. Did you help her in any other way?'

Joshua shakes his head. 'No.'

In front of them the screen changes to a satellite picture of London. Behind him Joshua hears the man tapping at some sort of device and two red dots appear on the screen. It zooms, focuses, zooms again, until it's tight on one address – Joshua's. As the feed moves to street level, names appear next to the red dots –

Martha Honeydew.

Joshua Decker.

'How . . . ? What . . . ? I didn't –'

'Did you invite her to your home?'

'No!'

Martha's dot moves across the road while Joshua's goes into the house. A few seconds later Martha's shifts again, going up the steps of the house before pausing and moving down towards the windows of the basement kitchen.

'I didn't know she was there!' Joshua says.

'Do you like your job, Mr Decker? Do you like *having* a job?'

'Yes,' he says. 'And I didn't know –'

'Do you like your home? Your cosy life with your partner?'

'Of course I do.'

'Then I suggest you choose your actions wisely.'

Joshua stares at the screen.

'Because you won't be told again.'

The man's shoes click away across the room. The door creaks open but no light comes in, and as it shuts again Joshua sighs heavily, leans back in his chair and shakes his head.

Martha

'It's really very simple,' Patty says.

'So simple that if I get it wrong I'll kill myself.'

'Do you have to be so awkward?'

I look at her. I want to say something like, *Do you have to be so corrupt or so hateful, or so mean?*

'*You* could do this,' I say to her instead.

She tuts and doesn't reply.

'I just want to make sure I get it right,' I say. 'I don't want to end up killing us both. Or anyone.'

Patty just walks away. The woman does my head in. If there was another way to get Isaac out I sure as hell wouldn't even be entertaining this nonsense, but . . . well, there you go.

I look back at the man sitting with me in Patty's garage. A skinny guy with big curly hair and glasses. Would look like some mad professor if he was older.

'You would literally have to be sitting on top of this for it to kill you,' he says.

'How do I know I can trust you?' I ask him.

'Trust me?' He pushes his fingers through his hair; I imagine mice getting caught up in there. 'Do you have any choice?' He smiles but it's weird; perhaps I'm his science experiment.

'It's very easy,' he says. 'And as long as you follow the instructions, nothing can go wrong.'

'What if I blow myself up?'

'What did I say a minute ago?' His eyes swim behind his glasses.

'Err . . .'

'You would literally have to be –'

'Yeah, sorry, got you.'

He talks for ages about what's in the bag, where to put it and all this other stuff, and my brain loses it after a while and I'm just nodding and agreeing.

'Questions?' he asks.

I stare at him blankly.

'What if he's right on the other side of the wall to where I put it?'

He folds his arms across his chest and his eyebrows lift as he stares at me. I get the feeling that he's already covered this at some point when I wasn't quite paying attention.

'According to the plans I've been given, the point of the explosion – the drain next to the wall – is a position within the cell where he is highly unlikely to be, either seated or standing.'

I close my eyes, rub my fingertips across the itchy stubble on my head, trying to remember . . . think . . .

It'd be Cell 7. It's bigger than the others. From what I can remember, it'd be across the other side, away from the door.

Did I ever sit near there?

Walk near there?

Can't remember.

Can't think.

'What about the folk in the viewing area? What if . . . ?'

'Remember what I told you – it'll only be a relatively small explosion; there is near zero chance of anyone being injured. You would literally have to be –'

I nod again.

'OK,' he says. 'Go through what you'll do.'

I shift nervously. 'This is like being at school,' I mutter.

'Did you blow things up at school?'

'Errr . . .'

'Get on with it.'

I close my eyes, picturing the route. 'I climb over the wall around the corner where I did before, and I stick close to the building and move around till I get to where Cell 7 is – I can work that out. Right up against the wall is a bush, and next to the bush is a drainage grille. I pull the grille off and push the backpack into the gap. Then I go back over the railings –'

'No. If you go back over the railings, then you won't be able to help him.'

'Yeah, yeah, sorry. I go back as far as I can, staying in the shadows, and then I press the detonator, which is the mobile phone . . .'

As I say that, I lift it in the air.

'And then?'

'And then as soon as the explosion goes off, I run back over, drag him through the hole it will have caused and we both climb over the railings where I did before, near the bin.'

'And then?'

I sigh. 'And then you will be waiting around the corner, you'll pick us up and drive us away to somewhere safe, wherever you decide that is.'

He gives me a double thumbs up, and his eyes narrow as he does his weird smile thing.

I imitate it back. 'What could possibly go wrong?' I say with sarcasm.

Patty comes back into the garage. 'Nothing will go wrong,' she says.

With those words I'm suddenly very, very scared.

Isaac

The images have stopped.

And the guards have left.

I counted them out: three sets of boots marching one at a time down the corridor. Three times the main door opened and three times it shut.

Now there aren't any feet, or keys, or even any whistling.

In silence the sun went down, and nobody turned the lights on.

But at home, on TVs or computers, people will still be watching, and they'll see this cell better than I can. In a green hue of night vision.

Are you watching me, Martha?

Can you see me?

What are you doing right now?

How has your day been?

I wish you could tell me.

I want to hear that the public are listening now, that they finally know about the injustice and corruption.

I want you to tell me of their shock and horror at discovering what those in power, and with power over us, have done to keep it.

I want to know that the papers printed these stories because they had a duty to, and that the television news ran it as headlines so every household was reached.

I want to see your smile, Martha, as you tell me that what we fought for is beginning to happen. Slowly, perhaps, but as the crimes committed by DI Hart, Albert DeLonzo and their like become public knowledge, then all those who've abused their positions will fall like dominoes, and only the people who've distanced themselves from the corruption will remain standing.

In this darkness I can imagine you standing tall and explaining to the public who are listening now; the sense of pride I have for you lifts me from the drudgery of this place and reminds me there is hope.

I accept it will be too late for me, but, Martha, stretching out in front of you now is a good life with possibilities for your future.

I wonder what you will do.

Go back to school, then perhaps to university?

Train to be what, I wonder?

After all this, perhaps a lawyer, fighting for the rights of others. Yes, I can see you doing that.

You'd be good at it.

In the darkness I see you still; older, wiser, standing in front of a courtroom filled with people. Yes, the court system is back, because you, and others alongside you, have fought for it and won.

You argue well. You're passionate, but calm. You're respected; people know your past and how hard you have fought to succeed.

I imagine you standing there, cross-examining a witness, or questioning the accused, your hands come together and your fingers touch. In my imagination I see a ring glint on your finger; five small bands entwined together. My mother's puzzle ring.

Because you solved it.

'It's difficult at first,' I wrote in that letter to you, 'but persevere' and I wrote that you'd lit my life and it was time for you to light others' too.

You did persevere.

And I know, even from the depths of this cell, that you will light other people's lives.

And I know you will think back to this time and remember I loved you.

Even though it will be after I have died.

DAY 6

Martha

I couldn't sleep last night.

It's too warm in Patty's house. I'm not used to it. I opened the window, let the wind and rain howl in; it made me feel alive.

Then I got some of Isaac's clothes out his wardrobe – some joggers, a T-shirt and a hoodie – and I wrapped myself up in them, hung out the window with the lights off and watched the City.

Crazy, fucked-up place full of crazy, fucked-up folk.

You know what it feels like? You know when you're in school and you see a bunch of students having a go at one kid who's by themselves, and you sidle in and tell them to stop being a bully, expecting them to just back off, but they don't, they just let that person go and then start on you instead, so you try telling them it's not your fight, but they don't listen, or they're not interested, and the next thing you know is that they're *always* at you, *all* the time and you just can't escape?

That.

Except I've dragged everyone else in too.

I'd just like to go home.

Walk through the door, throw my school bag down, and sit at the kitchen table. Mum would make me a hot chocolate and ask me about my day. I'd tell her I hate maths and she would pass me a biscuit. Then I'd tell her that old Mrs Seaton farted when she was writing on the board and we'd snigger together.

She wouldn't've had time to cook because she'd've been at work all day, so I'd run down to the chip shop while she'd fry some sausages and eggs, and I'd see Ollie down there. I'd moan at him about maths and he'd say I won't need that kind of maths when I've left school anyway and not to worry. He'd hug me like I was his little sister or something, and as we came back up the stairs to his flat, Mrs B would pop her head out and give me some of her honey cake to take home for tea.

We didn't have much then, but we had each other.

Life's like a house of cards sometimes, isn't it?

Knock one by accident and the whole lot comes tumbling down on you. Right now, what's left of it is balanced above my head, and wobbling.

There's a tap at the door.

I turn around and Patty, dressed in some ridiculous pink garb, wanders in.

'Why's the window open? It's November! I'm paying for that heat going out there, you know.'

I can't be bothered to argue with her, so I sit on the bed while she pulls the windows closed and ramps up the radiator. When she turns back she looks me up and down, and I feel like I should say something about wearing Isaac's clothes, but in the end my 'screw you' attitude beats my 'I'm sorry' feelings.

'It's Lydia Barkova's funeral today,' she says, all matter-of-fact.

'Where is it?' I ask.

'You can't go,' she says.

'I asked where it is, not whether I could go,' I reply, trying not to rise to her.

'How should I know?' she says all indignant. 'Some awful place on the north edge of the Rises. Some crematorium.'

'No,' I say. 'She didn't want to be cremated. She wanted to be buried. She told me so. There's a plot next to her husband and Ollie. That's where she wanted to be.'

She shrugs. 'Don't shoot the messenger. She's dead anyway; she won't know.'

Stupid insensitive cow.

I blink my eyes. I will not cry.

'I'll be sure to have them lob you on the city dump when you die,' I mutter. 'You can be seagull fodder for a few days.' I look her up and down. Slowly, on purpose. 'Or a few weeks,' I say, 'or months,' and I can't help but smile.

I pull open Isaac's wardrobe and take out a dark jacket with a hood.

'Where do you think you're going?'

'Out,' I tell her.

'You can't; what if you're seen? Our plan . . .'

I walk out the room.

'You'll get caught!' she shouts after me.

I'll take that risk.

The High Rises

Eve clicks the indicator, pulls to the side of the road at the underpass and turns off the engine.

In the passenger seat next to her, Cicero sighs and stares out of the windscreen at the tributes for Jackson. Once in brilliant full bloom and covering the grey of the pavements, now their colours are gone, and dead or dying petals have flaked off and been swept into gutters by the biting wind or the rain or left on the path to turn to stinking rot.

Max leans forward from the rear seats. 'What happens to them?' he asks.

'I'm not sure,' Eve replies. 'I think usually people would take them to his grave, or at least take the dead ones away.'

'The true marker of a man,' Max says, repeating words from *Death is Justice*, 'is what people think of him upon death.'

Cicero continues to stare at the flowers. 'Rotten,' he replies.

Eve climbs out of the car and the others follow. The wind blasts them, and from her bag she takes a woolly hat, pulls it over her head and shoves her hands deep into her pockets. Max loops his arm through hers.

As they pass the corner, the shopkeeper comes out and Eve turns to watch him locking the door and pulling down the shutters.

A little further along they pull across the park. There's nobody on the bench, nor the swings, and nobody standing against the bin; just a couple of figures in the distance, heading towards the street far off to the right.

Memories fly through Eve's head of being here before, seeing Gus, remembering him, going to see Mrs B. The photos on her wall, the knick-knacks of her life, all to be wheeled off to a charity shop or thrown away.

'You OK?' Max asks.

She nods, but he knows she's not.

Finally they step into the street near the crematorium. Crowds of people mill around, dressed in suits and ties, or with smart overcoats or rain macs pulled in tight around them. Men shaved and their hair perfect, women made up and manicured. Some chat away on phones, others scribble notes on pads. Few just wait.

'There are a lot of people,' Eve says to Max and Cicero.

Cicero glances around, carefully and slowly taking in the whole situation.

'These aren't Rises people,' Max whispers.

The rear doors of a van nearby open and a man with a video camera tumbles out.

'No,' Cicero says. 'They're press.'

'Lots of press,' Max observes.

Cicero nods. 'I hope Martha doesn't turn up.'

The crowds around them turn and the cameras follow, focusing off into the distance as silence falls and the air prickles.

Max, Eve and Cicero glance at each other, faces frozen, then they look to what the cameras see.

Herds of people are walking towards them, silently and slowly moving across the stubby grass, faces lifted but solemn.

'*They're* Rises people,' Cicero whispers.

They move with peace and calm. Some in groups, some singly, some with chins raised and chests out, others with tissues to noses and red eyes.

Dignified.

A cloud of dark clothes drifting as one. Formed in pain, united in grief, bound by respect.

The press, the journalists, the cameras and the grief-tourists part like the Red Sea for them, and as Mrs B's coffin, flanked by friends and neighbours, comes into view, heads are bowed and hands are placed over hearts.

Cicero takes Eve's hand and squeezes it.

And with Max at their side and ignoring the cameras pointing at them, they watch and wait as the coffin moves slowly towards them.

Martha

Feels good to be back. Somewhere I belong, where folks know me, recognise me. Understand.

I keep my head down though. Can't trust everyone. There's still them who'd be thinking they could get a reward for dialling that number and having someone come and arrest me. I get that though; that's life-changing money. Could pay your rent or mortgage, pay off debts, you could go on an actual holiday or, hell, you could even send your kid to university, give them a fighting chance of some kind of future.

Takes a lot to turn away from that when it's in outstretched hands for you to take just for pointing in a certain direction.

Think of the food you could have.

Think of telling that boss who's been a shit to you for years that he can go jump.

A bank statement that's not written in red.

Or having the heating on all winter.

Powerful thing money.

Don't we just know it?

Yeah, good to be back, but wish it was for better reasons. Wish I could stay too.

I'm walking with a group of them next to the coffin. I wanted to be one of the bearers, but folk look too much at the bearers, so I stay between them instead, my right hand brushing against the wood and my head down.

Oh, Mrs B . . .

The shoes in front of me belong to Sam. The toes are scuffed but it looks like he's gone over them with black marker pen. Black marker pen like he drew all over Ollie's hands with when they were in primary school, and Mrs B went ballistic, because one of his scribbles looked like a penis and it wouldn't come off. And then she apologised because she'd made him cry.

Behind me is Asa. Can hear him sniffing and his breath rattling in and out. No brothers or sisters, no real friends. Real enthusiastic football player even though he was crap. Can hear him now. 'Gis a game, mate,' he'd shout to Ollie even when it was pissing down. Ollie was too kind to say no, but Jesus would he get a going-over from Mrs B when he got back wet through. He never told her why. Just shrugged like it wasn't anyone's fault but God's for raining.

Opposite him, the old guy, that's Mrs B's *gentleman friend*, as she used to call him. Mr Stanley. I never found out if Stanley was his first name or last. Teased her about him once. 'He is friend, that is all,' she said, and I saw her look at the photo of her long-dead husband and I didn't say any more.

I glance sideways to see his face. His head's up, his chest out, and there's tears pouring down his cheeks. He doesn't hide it; he shows his grief and pain to everyone.

I'm sorry, I think, but wish I could say. *I'm sorry. I'm sorry. I'm sorry.*

The wood knocks against my hand again and I think of Mrs B being inside this box, but it doesn't seem real. Can't imagine her body in there. Can't imagine her not being *here* any more. Not answering her door in some terrible pinny she'd bought from the market, not hearing her 'secret' knock on my door telling me tea was ready, not that smell of her honey cake, not the only thing wrong with her cooking: that God-awful gravy that clegged your mouth up and formed like jelly if you left it on the plate.

Not . . . being . . . *anywhere*.

Not . . .

Just not.

Just being dead.

Too much death and too many funerals and too much pain.

Everything blurs in front of my eyes and I suck a deep breath in, trying not to cry, and I blink and look to the bearer at the front but I can't tell who it is from behind. Somebody in the crowd to his left catches my eye though and I flick a look.

Eve.

She's staring straight at me.

My stomach flips and I want to run over and throw my arms around her. Want her to hold me and take care of me, like she did last week.

I'm so tired of having to be strong, tired of being alone.

She nods at me, and I nod back, more with my eyes than my head, and I keep watching her as we draw closer, coming up level to her near the doors of the crem. We pause, someone at the front clearing the way or opening the doors or whatever.

Something touches my hand and I jump. It's Eve.

'Don't turn,' she whispers in my ear. 'The authorities and the press are everywhere.'

I put my head down; the people around me are so much taller I can hide among them.

'I'm sorry about Mrs B,' she says.

I can't reply.

Pull yourself together, I think.

But I'm shaking now, my whole body trembling and tears are pouring.

'Oh, my poor girl,' she says, and she squeezes my hand tight, 'I wish I could fix it all for you . . .'

The crowd moves forward again and I'm carried along with them. She stumbles next to me, forcing her way through.

'Meet me afterwards,' she whispers.

Quickly I wipe my face and I frown at her. 'Where?'

But the crowds drag me on and swallow me up and she's lost.

I put my head back down and shuffle forward.

The concrete steps of the crem come up and I see my own feet step up them and remember the time before.

Mum.

And now Mrs B.

Who next?

Isaac.

I touch the ring that I still haven't fixed, dangling on the chain around my neck.

The chapel is full. Every single seat taken. Folks standing down the aisle. More at the back where I am, hidden between bodies who care for me, though to them I'm almost a stranger, a name they know, who watched me nearly die, who saw me at my weakest. I feel naked to them, like they know everything about me without knowing me.

You're their hope, that voice in my head says.

They know the truth, they voted your innocence. Spent their money on you, someone they didn't know but trusted to do the right thing.

You owe them.

I owe Mum, I think to myself, and Ollie and Mrs B. And I owe Eve for caring, Cicero for speaking out, Max for helping. Isaac. Isaac for . . . for . . . everything.

How did I end up owing so many?

I stare at the coffin and can't help but imagine Mrs B inside it, and like a punch in the chest, the air goes from me.

I want to run away, leave everything, forget it all.

Too much pain. Too many memories.

I can't see for tears.

'Hey,' a voice hisses in my ear.

Slowly I turn towards the voice; some girl is right next to me.

'You have to come outside with me,' she whispers.

I catch her eye. 'What?'

'The authorities are about to come in here and check everyone. You need to get out of here now. Come on!'

She tugs at my arm.

'Who are you?'

'I was in your French class last year. Come on,' she pleads. 'Quickly!'

'But –'

'It's for your own good. You have to go!'

I glance back to the coffin. 'I can't –'

'You have to. Mrs Barkova wouldn't want you to be caught, would she? Come on. I'll help you. Come on. Before they turn this whole thing into a circus.'

She pulls at me.

She's right, I think, can't let Mrs B's funeral turn into some witch hunt all about me. This is her time. Swallow it, Martha, and get out.

I follow, pushing through the crowds with my head down, standing on toes and bumping into folk.

Jeez, this feels disrespectful.

She pulls the door open quietly and I have to shade my eyes because the sun's so bright after being in there. It clicks shut behind me, and she drags me a few steps away from the building.

Then she lets me go.

I blink against the light again.

'She's here!' The girl's voice pierces through the air.

I flinch against it, my stomach tipping.

What did she say?

'I claim the reward for catching Martha Honeydew!' she shouts. 'She's here.'

Shit.

'What?' I hiss at her. 'Who are you? Why would you . . . ?' I squint through the sunlight at her; her designer jacket, her hair extensions, her false nails. 'You're not –'

She smiles, teeth so white I reckon they could blind me.

She said French class; I haven't done French since Year 7. She said Mrs Barkova; no one calls her that. This girl, she's no Rises girl. She's come here from the City or the Avenues on the gamble I'd be here and she could find me.

'You bitch!' I say. 'How dare you pull me out of my friend's funeral? How *dare* you be so selfish?'

I'm mad; fucking, spitting, bastard mad. I want to smash her ignorant face in.

How dare she?

'I claim the reward!' she shouts again, and tries to grab me round my arm.

'At a *funeral*!' I scream at her, squirming from her grip. 'You utter scum!'

I hear the crem door open and slam shut again.

'Martha.' Eve this time. 'You have to go,' she says.

I glance to where she's pointing, blink the tears from my eyes and can see the authorities jostling towards me, journalists following them with cameras balanced on their shoulders.

I'm sorry, Mrs B. I've brought this to you. I've caused you so much pain when all you ever did was support me and Mum, and now I can't even stay at your funeral. I'm sorry.

'Martha!' Eve's running down the steps towards me.

'I know,' I mutter. 'I know.'

But I can't go without doing something.

I charge up to that smug cow with her smirk and her white teeth and her manicured nails, and her hands rubbing at the thought of the reward money, and I stand in front of her and I spit in her stupid face.

'They won't catch me,' I hiss at her. 'You won't get the money,' and I turn and I run.

6.30 p.m. *Death is Justice*

The theme tune pounds over the studio and the lights dip and dazzle. The camera soars around the applauding audience before settling on a subdued Joshua. In brown checked trousers, double-breasted waistcoat, dark blue shirt and tie, he's already seated to the left side of the desk. On the large screen to the right, the eye logo blinks and shifts as if taking in the view of the studio.

The music fades.

JOSHUA: Hello, ladies and gentlemen, and welcome once again to the flagship show of Eye For An Eye Productions. We have a splendid evening's entertainment lined up, with some extraordinary news that will have you gasping with astonishment!

The audience make pretend shocked noises; Joshua laughs gently.

JOSHUA: We'll have up-to-date figures on all of our death row prisoners, and we'll be giving you the juicy details of our brand-new inmate in Cell 1 – quite a

case that one is. Yes, ladies and gentlemen, in Cell
1 we have Mrs Georgina Parsons, an *87-year-old
woman* accused of suffocating her husband.

He pauses as a sudden intake of breath is heard over the
studio. The camera zooms closer to him.

JOSHUA (quietly): Her terminally ill husband. A moral
conundrum? Or a clear case of guilt? And does it
matter? We'll be discussing that later, but first . . .

The camera draws out.

JOSHUA: Ladies and gentlemen, tell me, what would you
most like to see today?

The camera roves over the audience as the lights above
them brighten.

AUDIENCE MEMBER 1: Execution!

AUDIENCE MEMBER 2: Martha back again!

AUDIENCE MEMBER 3: Isaac Paige suffering.

JOSHUA: Close, ladies and gentlemen, but no cigar.

He pauses, stands up from the desk and moves over to
the screen.

JOSHUA: This evening, for your entertainment, not only are we going over live to Cell 6 to our resident father-killer, Rises-sympathiser, lover of Martha Honeydew – Isaac Paige – but we're also going to be speaking to him. Live. On. Air!

He points into the camera.

JOSHUA: And you too, yes, you, viewers at home, have an exclusive opportunity to apply to speak directly with our inmate. For only £59.99 you can enter our competition to be one of only three people who will be able to speak to, and question, our death-facing criminal. How do you win this privilege? I hear you ask. Well, it's easy. Simply dial the number 0909 87 97 76 and leave the question you'd like to ask on the answerphone. Alternatively log onto www.aneyeforaneyeproductions.com, pay your fee and enter online.

He pauses and moves to the side. On the right of the stage, the screen changes: the eye logo moves into the corner as the live feed of Isaac in Cell 6, sitting on the mattress on the floor, fills the middle. The voting information runs along the bottom.

JOSHUA: From the entries we will be picking the most original, the most inquisitive and the most challenging, so get your thinking caps on!

306

The camera focuses in on Isaac, his fingers tapping at each other as he mouths something into the air. His eyes stare off into the distance.

JOSHUA: You could learn what makes this young man tick, ask about his feelings for Martha Honeydew, his relationship with his father, or why he felt the need to pull that trigger and end a life. This is a once-in-a-lifetime opportunity for an amazing low fee of £59.99. Increase your chances of winning this incredible prize by entering as many times, with as many questions, as you want. This is a not-to-be-missed chance to understand the inner workings of a murderer's mind.

Joshua comes back into shot, standing next to the screen.

JOSHUA: A troubled young man there. What *is* going through that head? Well, this is your opportunity to find out.

He winks at the audience and a rumble of appreciation goes round.

JOSHUA: Get those fingers dialling, get your entries in and join us after this message from our sponsor to find out what questions will be posed.

The camera pauses on him, catching his fake smile slipping.

Martha

I run.

Feet on path.

On grass, up steps, through alleys, past buildings.

I run.

Further, faster, harder.

Round Daffodil House, between bins, across Tulip Place.

I run.

Lungs burn, chest screams, heart thuds.

I'm tiring.

Come on, Martha. Keep moving!

I glance behind.

Can't see.

Run, girl, run!

I am.

I do.

Away to where the lights don't reach and the streetlights stop.

Thankful for a dull day, a short day, a winter's day.

Getting darker. Can't see my feet. Can't see the path.

Could be anyone there. Or anything. Or nothing.

I slow down, move sideways. I know where the bushes are, the hedgerows, and I edge back like when I'd play hide-and-seek with Ollie.

Quiet now. Quiet.

Shhh, Martha, shhh.

It's only dusk, but the shadows are long and they trick you.

My breathing's screeching in the silence.

Like I'm squeezing a guinea pig.

Or an accordion.

I pull my shoulders back and open my lungs, taking big, deep mouthfuls of air.

My legs are like jelly.

Slow down, I think.

Swallow.

Calm.

I peer out from behind the bushes and I can see them in the distance. Just shapes, dark and blurry, but I can tell who's leading the way.

That damn girl from the City. All she's interested in is money. But why should that surprise me?

All that money, all that opportunity, but zero morals.

Mind you, she believes the press, thinks I'm what they say, so why wouldn't she report me?

She's pointing over here. She knows where I went. She's probably got some bloody night-vision camera, some crap Daddy bought her, and can see me crouched here.

But . . .

I'm guessing the others are from the authorities. They're standing there, hands on hips or just in pockets. There's crowds round them – folk from the Rises, I reckon – and they're in the way, but peaceful, not shoving or shouting or anything. And the authorities folk aren't doing anything to get past them.

309

The girl? She's shouting now, I can just hear her. And she's pointing over here and jabbing into the air, but they don't do anything. They just watch her, almost like . . . almost like they're not bothered.

I stretch up a little so I can see better.

She's screaming at them now, but still they're not moving, not even trying to get past the Rises folk.

Why is that?

Why would they let me go?

I don't know, but I'm not going stick around here to find out either.

Death is Justice

On the screen is an oversized image of a white, fluffy cloud on a blue sky. A sparkling gold padlock is clipped to the left of the cloud, while random streams of text and fake personal details float through the sky and into the cloud.

The words 'Cyber Secure' form. A lightning bolt hits the cloud, but the text remains in place.

FEMALE VOICEOVER: Cyber Secure. Securing your details from every eventuality.

The cloud drifts away and the screen fades to black as the eye logo appears in the middle. An unseen audience applauds as a heartbeat gently thuds.

MALE VOICEOVER: An Eye For An Eye Productions welcomes you back to . . .

The eye is replaced by Joshua seated at his desk, smiling.

MALE VOICEOVER: *Death is Justice!*

The heartbeat fades, and Joshua raises his hands to quieten the audience.

JOSHUA: Welcome back, ladies and gentlemen, viewers at home, people watching on their mobiles, computers, indeed so many ways to keep up to date with all that is happening here on *Death is Justice*. And keep up to date you must, as we are constantly bringing you new innovations and developments. Before the break we gave you the ultimate opportunity to pose a question to death row inmate Isaac Paige.

He stands and wanders to the screen.

JOSHUA: Have your dialling fingers been busy over the break? Have your brains been working overtime, thinking of all those questions you're just *dying* to ask? Have your conversations been filled with queries and curiosity? Well, I hope so, because lines are now closed.

He turns to the screen. The eye blinks away in the top right corner, while in the middle a digital display reads a series of zeros.

JOSHUA: Let's see how many entries our once-in-a-lifetime competition has received.

The zeros flicker and numbers scroll, then stop with a bang. Joshua gives a low whistle.

JOSHUA: Proving once and for all the incredible reach of our show. Look at that, ladies and gentlemen, a total of 12.15 *million* entries! Wow!

The audience whoop and applaud.

JOSHUA: But which lucky contestants' questions have been chosen? Before we find out, let's head over to Cell 6 and see how our inmate is doing.

Still with the eye logo in the corner, the rest of the screen changes and fills instead with a live feed from Cell 6. Isaac sits on the edge of the mattress on the floor, looking up towards the high window. His white prison uniform is dull and dirty and he taps his fingers in some sort of rhythm.

Isaac

I'm going to die tomorrow.

Tomorrow.

I think the words. I whisper them too, but my brain can't process them.

Tomorrow morning I'll be moved to that cell. I'll be fastened to that chair, my arms and legs strapped down. The helmet will lower, and with all those people watching, the electricity will tear through me and I will die.

Last week, when Martha was in there, I searched on the internet to see what happens to your body.

I read over it a few times because I couldn't believe it. Why would that be legal? How could any government allow something so horrific to be done to someone?

I decided it must be for the spectacle. The same reason people peep through their fingers at a horror film, rubber-neck at a car crash, leer at an operation on the television while saying how frightening, or terrible, or disgusting it is.

Sensationalist, thrilling, the buzz of adrenaline running through your body and the relief that it isn't happening to you.

Thousands watched gladiators fight to the death in Rome, flocked to the guillotine in France, threw rotten food at those led from the Old Bailey to be hanged. It seems human nature hasn't altered much.

Here and now it's the same, except with a little show business. Some pizzazz and style and a hint of glamour, with tickets and a running commentary. And the ongoing assertion that we are all *doing the right thing*. By ridding the country of these people we are *making the world a better place*.

I don't swear much, not even in my head, but what bollocks that is.

We, the ones voting, are the criminals and the murderers.

We, from our safe homes, with our well-stocked fridges, our warm beds, our massive TV screens and our plump sofas, pick up our telephones while grabbing a beer or a coffee or putting a pizza in the oven and make a call on someone's *life*.

We scan newspapers that talk of the crime committed and utter our abhorrence, glance at the accused's face, pixelated and blurred, and send a text while we wait to be served in a supermarket or a takeaway, and we cast aspersions and make assumptions based on the way someone looks. Eyes too close together, hair too thin, forehead too big, bum too fat, neck too thick.

'He looks like a murderer,' I've heard people say.

'She looks shifty.'

And I've seen them coming out of the viewing area with smiles on their faces, shaking hands or giving a high five. Coming out into a world they view as a little safer now that evil has been eradicated. Yet the evil lives on in them.

After I've died tomorrow this world will be no safer, and no more dangerous, than it is now or it was last week. I only hope that my death makes at least one person question, or one person act.

The rest of them with their high fives and their smiles and their congratulatory messages to each other? Bollocks to them.

'Isaac Paige, good evening. This is Joshua Decker live from *Death is Justice*.'

Where's that coming from? My head?

'Don't be worried, Isaac.'

There's a speaker in the wall.

Or am I going mad?

'The nation is watching you, Isaac. Would you like to say hello?'

The nation? Everyone? Martha?

'Whh . . .' My voice feels strange. I cough. Try again. 'Whhhich cam . . . mera?'

'The one on the wall in front of you. Do you want to wave? Isaac, you've become quite the cause of fascination here. We have lots of people who are just dying to speak to you.'

'M . . . Martha?'

'No, not Martha. Do you need some water? There's some to your right.'

That wasn't there before. I lift the plastic cup. That feels good.

'Isaac, while you're drinking, let me put you in the picture. Here on *Death is Justice* we have been running a competition to give members of the public the opportunity to ask you a question, and believe me, young man, you are quite the hot property. I'm sure you can appreciate just how excited people are feeling to be able to chat with not only a death row inmate, but someone who has murdered his own father.'

I try to stand up . . . my legs wobble . . . feel light-headed. I want to get closer to the camera but it's too high up.

316

'We are about to announce the winning entries and put them through to you so they can ask their questions directly.'

Is Martha watching?

'Our first competition winner is Shamra from Norwich. Shamra, pose your question, please.'

Norwich. We went there once. Cathedral. River.

'Hiya, this is Shamra. I'm so excited! I can't believe I'm talking to an actual murderer!'

'Ask your question, please,' I hear Joshua say.

'Ha ha! Yeah, course, I'm just so . . . like, thrilled! Hi, Isaac, it's amazing to be able to speak to you, my friends are going to be so jealous and –'

'Your question, Shamra?' he says again.

'Oh yeah, my question is – Isaac, if you could spend your last day with someone famous who would it be and what would you say to them?'

'An excellent question from Shamra there. Isaac, what would your answer be?'

'Martha.' My throat still hurts. 'I'd spend my last day with Martha. I'd tell her I'm sorry. And that I love her.'

'No, I meant someone famous, like a pop star or something, y'know?'

'Martha, just Martha.' I sit back down on the edge of the mattress and stare up to the camera.

'Thank you for your call, Shamra, and congratulations on being the first member of the public *ever* to speak to a death row inmate! Moving on to our second caller.'

Am I imagining this?

'Martha, are you watching?' I mouth. 'Are you there?'

317

'Our second winner is Elspeth from Whitby. Congratulations, Elspeth.'

Whitby. Let's go to Whitby, Martha. Walk in the sea, read *Dracula* to each other in the wind at the abbey, eat fish and chips.

'Thank you! I can barely believe I've won. I've never won anything. I'm . . . I'm . . . completely gobsmacked!'

'Your first ever competition win and the second person in history to speak to a death row inmate and celebrity murderer live on national television. What a coup, hey?'

'I know, Joshua. And speaking to you is such an honour as well. You are such a lovely man.'

'Now, now, Elspeth. It'll go to my head. Please, Isaac is here, waiting for your question.'

'Errr . . . wow . . . OK. Hi, Isaac.'

Why does this woman want to speak to me?

'Isaac, are you there?'

'He's there, Elspeth, please go ahead.'

'OK, well, my question to you is – if you could change one thing in your past, what would it be and why?'

'What an excellent and well-thought-out question there from Elspeth. Isaac, would you like to answer?'

'Nothing,' I say.

'Nothing? What, *nothing*?' she says.

'No,' I repeat. 'Nothing.'

'I spent £59.99 and you give me a one-word answer? That's not fair. I demand more than that. Or I want my money back.'

'The Ts and Cs of the competition clearly state no refunds, I'm afraid. Isaac, perhaps you could expand on your answer for Elspeth here . . .'

'Yeah, Isaac, expand,' she says. 'You really wouldn't change *anything*? Not even shooting your father?'

Why can't she understand? 'If I hadn't shot him, he would've killed Martha,' I tell her. 'I didn't want to but –'

'Oh, come on! We all know that's crock.'

'What? The video with Martha –'

'What video?'

I stand up and step to the camera, leering up to where it's attached at the very top of the wall. 'You must've seen the video. I showed it when I made my victim speech. The video of Jackson threatening Martha. The feed from the CCTV camera. And the documents, the evidence. You must've seen it.'

'Nope. I've seen the one where you shot Jackson. Martha wasn't on it though.'

'What?' I say. I rub my head. I'm confused. 'But that doesn't make any sense. He had a belt around her neck. He was going to strangle her.'

She laughs, actually laughs, and it echoes round the cell like a horror film clown. 'No, he didn't. I think you've gone a bit stir crazy. I mean, why would Jackson Paige do that? You *really* are losing it. You shot your dad. There was just you and him. It was on the video.'

Are they trying to trick me? 'No, that's wrong,' I say. Stick to what you know, I remind myself. Keep calm and focus. 'That's not what happened. You're talking crap.'

'*Me*? *I'm* talking crap? *You're* the one making stuff up.' She laughs again and I cringe against the sound of it around me. 'I tell you what, I hope the authorities catch that Martha and she pays for her part in all this too.'

'Catch her? *Catch her?* What?'

'Y'know, I came on here because I wanted to believe the best of you. Everyone deserves a second chance, I thought, and perhaps if you were sorry about what you'd done then I'd vote you innocent, because you are, like, *famous*, but you're not sorry. You really are a cold-hearted murderer who deserves to die.'

'I don't understand!' I shout into the camera. 'What the hell is happening out there? What do you mean, *catch Martha?* What the . . . ? And the video? Joshua, you know the truth. Tell her. Tell them all. I . . .' My head's all over the place. I don't know what's going on. *Catch* Martha? Catch her? *What?*

Are they doing this on purpose to wind me up? For reaction? For *good television?*

'Jackson killed Martha's mother, he killed my mother,' I shout up to the camera, 'and he was going to kill Martha. That's why I shot him.'

'You are truly a disillusioned young man, and for that I feel sorry for you, but I honestly believe the world will be a better and safer place without you in it. And for everyone else listening, I hope you do too.' Her voice is quieter now, and serious. 'Y'know, I heard the PM speaking the other day. He said, "Secrets are ammunition against others," and he's right; if you know a secret about someone who's up to no good, then you can use it to stop them, but *your* secret – that you were seeing Honeydew – that blew up in your hand!'

What?

What?

I'm so angry I'm shaking and burning, my fingers twitching.

I drag the bed to underneath the camera and stand on it. I can reach now, and I pull at the mount but the camera won't come loose. I feel around it for wires but can't find any.

The woman, whatever her name was, is still jabbering on, but I'm not listening.

Calm, I tell myself. *Don't do anything in anger.*

I glance around the cell. I know what I want to do, but can't see anything to use. So I stare into the camera, lift my right hand and slam my fist into the lens.

Bits of glass stick in my knuckles. It hurt before, from yesterday, but hell, that hurts even more now. I steady myself though and move the bed to the next camera and I slam my fist through that one too. And the next. Until there is only one left.

I won't be your creature in a zoo any longer, I think. This is now on my terms.

Standing on the edge of the bed I peer right into it.

'If you can bear to hear the truth you've spoken
Twisted by knaves to make a trap for fools,' I quote,
'Or watch the things you gave your life to, broken,
And stop and build 'em up with worn-out tools:'

Keep it together, I tell myself. *Be strong. Keep going. Remember Kipling, come on. You learnt it once.*

'If you can talk with crowds and keep your virtue,
Or walk with Kings – nor lose the common touch,
If neither foes nor loving friends can hurt you,
If all men count with you, but none too much;
If you can fill the unforgiving minute
With sixty seconds' worth of distance run,

Yours is the Earth and everything that's in it,
And – which is more – you'll be a Man, my son!'

My hand throbs. I have only one thing left to say now. I've been their clown and their stooge, but now I'm resigning.

'Martha, I love you.'

Those will be my last words.

The brain is a strange and clever thing; it's shown me many memories while I've been in here, things I'd seen, heard or knew about but hadn't been able to put together.

I think today I finally have.

That phrase the caller quoted from the PM – *secrets are ammunition against others* – I've heard it before, and now I remember when.

I punch out the last camera.

Death is Justice continued

The studio is silent. Joshua stands in front of the static-filled screen. His shoulders drop as he exhales, and he closes his eyes and shakes his head before looking up into the camera.

JOSHUA: I don't know about you, ladies and gentlemen, viewers at home, studio audience, but after seeing that, and hearing that poem, I don't feel much of a man.

Walking across the stage towards his desk, he loosens his tie and undoes the top button. After a judder of unexpectedness, the camera follows.

JOSHUA: I feel a cheat and a liar instead, and I think it's time for me to stand up, take inspiration from these brave young people, and be truthful and honest to myself. For a long time I've been treading a very thin line between my public persona and my personal life, and perhaps the time has come for one to take precedence.

He sits at the desk; the camera hovers on his face.

JOSHUA: There are many people who know the truth, but few who speak it.

He lowers his head, sighs long and heavy and looks back to camera again.

JOSHUA: The CCTV video that both Martha and Isaac have talked about on this programme was edited so you couldn't see Martha, but she was there, and Jackson really did threaten to kill her. He really did place a belt around her neck, and that is why Isaac killed him: because he loves Martha and would forfeit his own life because of that love. Jackson also killed Martha's mother and let Oliver Barkova take the blame. He killed Isaac's mother and adopted the boy in order to make himself look good to the public. If you'd been present at Martha's Cell 7 last week you'd know all this, but all recordings of what happened were destroyed and everyone who knows has been silenced in some way.

He pauses, swallows hard.

JOSHUA: I can no longer sit by and watch the injustice mount up. I don't know how much time I have before your screen goes blank and I'm cut off, but I'm certain there won't be time to explain everything, so instead I beg you to go out and question, seek the truth about your country and your leaders.

Start by tracking down the few remaining copies of that feed from the other day, last seen on websites purposely set up to show you the truth, but which the government has had taken down. You think you have freedom of speech? Question that.

He pulls off his tie, stands up and strolls towards the audience.

JOSHUA: One final thing – ever since An Eye For An Eye Productions found out I'm gay they have used it to manipulate and control me, threatening to destroy my career here or anywhere else, as well as that of my partner. They told me this country is run by manipulative bigots. They're right, of course. Manipulative bigots who will do anything to keep hold of their power. But I believe the people of this country are better than our leaders. I believe they are kind and compassionate, understanding and tolerant. And I believe they have love in their hearts. I pray they do. And I pray for a better future for us all. I doubt I will be on this stage again, so I beg of you all, live with your eyes and your hearts open, question what you are told and form your own opinions, whatever they may be –

Martha

The static on the TV screen fizzes on my fingers. There are trails where I've dragged my fingers through the dust as I touched Isaac's face.

He knows the truth now, that I'm on the run. I wish he didn't.

I've failed him. Am still failing him.

Need to change that.

I'll get you out, Isaac, I promise. I can do that. I owe you that.

He looked awful. So tired, his head shaved to his scalp, little nicks from the razor, scratch marks from his fingers. His skin looked greasy, his lips cracked, his eyes bloodshot.

I want to take him, hold him, bathe his face and his head, clean his hands, bandage his knuckles.

He looked broken.

I'll fix you, Isaac.

They put the eye logo back on the screen. I watch the words spin around the iris – An Eye For An Eye For An Eye For An . . .

Around and around and around.

A continual loop.

We kill the killers; we become the killers.

Show me Isaac again. Please.

There'll be uproar. They said three questions. They only managed two. Folks won't get their money back though. There's always a clause.

Show me clips of him then, recordings.

Look to your memories, my head tells me. *Better there.*

I don't want memories. I want now. I want him here with me. I don't want this crazy fucked-up mess of a world. I want peace, justice, truth. I want Isaac. Please. I'll pray for it, I'll go to church, I'll believe, I'll have faith. Please, God, please, help me.

I rub my eyes, blink the blur away.

The stats come across the bottom of the screen. What was it yesterday? Ninety-nine percent guilty.

I stare at the screen, stretching my eyes wide.

That can't be right. That says sixty-seven percent guilty.

Really?

Really?

I head out the bedroom and down the stairs. The carpet's so thick my feet sink into it, and the house is so big it feels like I could walk around it for half an hour and still find new rooms.

I hear Patty though, talking into her phone. That laugh of hers shrill.

Why is she laughing?

Her son's on death row. Her husband's dead. She's lost all her money. All but some living allowance anyway, whatever that is.

She sees me standing in the doorway.

'I have to go,' she says down the phone. 'Chat later. Bye.' She actually waves down the phone.

'Stats are sixty-seven percent,' I tell her.

Her drawn-on eyebrows rise up her forehead and she shrugs. 'And your point is? That's still a majority.'

Heartless bitch. I ignore her comment. 'Did you just watch *Death is Justice?*'

'I did. Stupid man. He's thrown his career away. Everyone pretends to be all open-minded and that, but they're not. People are as prejudiced now as they ever were.'

'No, they're not. I don't give a hoot whether he's gay or not.'

'Maybe you don't, my dear, but believe me, those in power, those who make decisions, they do.'

'I like him.'

'You like him because he's a sympathiser and now people know that, people from the City and the Avenues, people who *matter*. He'll get no job around here. People employ their own kind.'

'You're full of shit.'

'I'm full of truth.' She laughs at me, flicking her hair to one side. 'The key thing you're missing here is the divide between the two. Now that –'

'Would be less important if people knew the truth.'

'Oh, shut your face.' She throws her hands in the air. 'I cannot be dealing with you and all your morals right now. I have no interest in you.'

'I only came down to remind you that if the stats *are* low, I won't be going ahead with breaking Isaac out.'

'You said that already.'

I shrug. God, I hate this woman.

'If you want to leave his life in the hands of these people you seem to despise so much, that's up to you. Personally I thought you had more about you. A little more . . . *guts*.'

'It's not about guts,' I reply. 'It's about trust. And you're missing the point – why would we break in and risk everything, if they're going to release him?'

'You are a misguided fool, Martha Honeydew, but if that's your decision . . .' Her voice trails off without answering my question. 'We'll see what the stats are tomorrow. Now, if you'll excuse me.' She picks up her mobile phone again and starts jabbing at the buttons.

Isaac

I see my mother in dreams, but only snapshots. Her blonde hair in a ponytail, creases around her eyes, the blue jeans she always wore, her hand holding mine, my fingers exploring that puzzle ring of hers.

I can never hear her voice, or see her whole.

Now I wonder if I'll see her again. Will I recognise her if I do? And will she recognise me?

I'm sorry, Mum.

You gave so much for me.

Do you think I'm throwing that away, or do you see it as I do? I have no idea now.

Catch Martha, she said. *Catch her.*

Is she on the run?

And why?

Why?

What the hell is going on? She was found not guilty. She should be fine.

The Prime Minister

Stretched back in a reclining leather chair, the PM watches over the banks of screens in front of him. Nobody else is with him in the blue room, and he absent-mindedly flicks through the various feeds with the controller, bringing each up in turn and scanning it briefly. With his other hand he toys with a tumbler of whisky.

Next to him his phone goes off, and as he glances at the screen to see who's calling he lets out a long sigh and swallows the rest of his drink.

'Patty,' he mutters, 'why on earth would you be ringing at this late hour?'

As he listens to her, he places the glass back on the desk and runs a finger along the rim.

'I did indeed. Much lower than I thought it would be, but it doesn't matter. It'll go back up.'

He pauses again and his eyebrows lift the tiniest of degrees.

'Does she now? Well, that's your problem. You want to continue this mutually beneficial arrangement we have, then I suggest you uphold your end of the bargain. Get everything in place, and the girl to press the button.'

He puts the phone down.

On the keyboard in front of him he taps a name, and as a satellite map of the City forms on the screen a small red dot appears in a large building towards the outskirts.

He holds down a button and the screen zooms in on the dot, the words 'Gus Evans' next to it. He zooms further and next to the name the words 'City Prison' appear.

'One down,' he says. 'Two, including the Russian woman.'

He presses another few keys, and the words and the dot disappear as the image zooms out again.

Three more dots appear on a different section, and he clicks to make names appear next to them –

Eve Stanton.

Max Stanton.

Thomas Cicero.

He rests his finger on a key and the image zooms in on them, all three together within the walls of Eve's house.

'Good,' he whispers to himself.

He leans forward in his seat, taps at the keyboard again and the map moves downwards, centring on a different point. Slowly it zooms closer, till the caption reads 'Death Row'. He touches the screen with his fingers, measuring the distance from the building to the car-park area within the gates.

'I take your *two birds, one stone*, Jackson Paige, and I raise it to –' he pauses, thinking – 'seven.'

His face cracks into a narrow, malevolent grin and the leather chair creaks as he leans back again. 'One way or another.'

He lifts his arms in the air and stretches in the delight of his own plan, oblivious to the figure hidden in the shadows behind him, and to the long fingers hovering over the record button.

DAY 7

Martha

Hell, I must've fallen asleep.

I was watching him for ages.

From his room, in his house, on his TV.

What time is it now? My eyes are so bleary I can't focus.

The TV's still on. Isaac's TV. Isaac on Isaac's TV.

Nine o'clock. Jeez, twelve hours to go.

The stats say ninety-eight percent guilty as they roll across the bottom of the screen. Back up again. What's all that about?

The last twelve hours of your life, Isaac.

Not if you get him out, my head says.

You mean not if I become a bomber, I reply to it.

I shuffle out of the bed, tiptoe to the window and stare out across the City, waking to a day that to many is just another day, but to me, to you, is . . .

. . . everything.

Isaac

Cell 7.

Day 7.

Here I am, staring out at the room I stood outside a week ago.

'The time is: 9 a.m.,' an electronic voice says. 'You have: twelve hours until your possible execution. The current stats are: 98% in favour, 2% against. We will update you in: one hour.'

Regular updates. I didn't realise they told you. I don't know what I think about that.

At least I'll know, I suppose.

But I think I already do; there's no way I'm getting out of here. I think I've accepted that.

What a terrible thing it is to wait for death.

Will I go to hell because I shot him? It feels like I'm in it already.

Could I go to heaven because I did it to save you, Martha? Because I forfeited my life for yours?

How does God decide?

But I'm not Christian. Not Muslim or Hindu or a practising anything.

Then will it be blackness? Emptiness? Nothing?

Or reincarnated into something I deserve to be.

A beetle?

A cockroach?

I don't know what I believe.

Yes, I do. I believe in people and their humanity.

And I believe in the strength of you, Martha.

Nine o'clock.

Twelve hours. Seven hundred and twenty minutes. Forty-three thousand two hundred seconds.

Less than that now. It's a few minutes past.

What use is being good at maths now?

I'd prefer to die by my own hand than by theirs.

To choose those seconds, minutes and hours myself.

But I won't. I'll keep fighting till the end.

Max

Max steps back into the corner of the shelter as the wind howls down the empty platform at the underpass station.

The first cracks of dawn are lightening the sky on the horizon, but it's still dark and unwelcoming.

The cold of wandering around all night looking for Martha – searching in Bracken Woods, at the underpass, near the crematorium, checking flats and hidden spaces – has eaten through to his bones and he shivers, his face pale, a blue tinge to his hands.

Giving up on her being at the Rises, he stares around looking for signs of life, or the time of the first train of the day, but all he can see is the piles of dying flowers at the tribute to Jackson, and the day-old newspapers, chip wrappers and drinks cans rolling down the gutters or catching in doorways.

Footsteps sound behind him and he turns. A middle-aged man in work trousers, a high-visibility jacket and safety boots, a newspaper under his arm, catches his eye and nods.

'I know who you are,' he says, stuffing his hands in his pockets. 'Max Stanton.'

Max watches him without saying a word.

'Thought so. You looking for Martha? She's not nowhere round here.'

'I've worked that one out now,' he replies. 'Do you know what time the train's due?'

The man, still staring at Max, nods his head, indicating behind him. 'You hear that?'

Max strains his ears against the wind. 'Just,' he replies.

'That'll be it.'

Max looks over the man's shoulder and away down the tracks, and in the distance two pinpricks of light appear through the early-morning gloom. 'Does it go straight back into the City again?' he asks.

'More or less.' Still he doesn't take his eyes from Max. 'If it's any consolation,' he continues, 'I'd've done the same for my wife.'

The headlights are brighter, closer, and the noise of the train is louder. Max frowns at the man. 'Pardon?' he asks.

'To protect her. And so she could be there for the kids. In your mum's case, there for you.'

'I don't know what you're talking about,' Max mutters, and he steps out of the shelter and towards the platform edge, the wind howling and buffeting around him.

'I suppose there'll be an apology issued.'

The white of the train headlights pours over Max, and the noise thunders around him.

'I still don't know what you're talking about!' he shouts.

'What?' the man shouts back. 'You must do. Your mum –' the train quietens as it pulls into the station, but his voice stays loud – 'admitted she was the murderer!'

Max's mouth falls open. 'Wha—?'

'Here.' The man takes the newspaper from under his arm and thrusts it at Max's chest. 'Sorry, mate, I thought . . .' His words disappear on the wind.

Max stares at the newspaper.

'Keep it,' the man says, and he rests a hand on Max's shoulder. 'I meant what I said though. I would've done the same for my wife and kids.'

Max can't look away from the paper in his hands.

'Get on the train,' the man tells him. 'It's an hour till the next one.'

Max shakes his head and walks away.

Martha

Fuck Patty and fuck Patty's plan.

I was sitting in her kitchen, couldn't face food or anything to drink, so I was just sitting there, watching the sun coming up, thinking about stuff, when she comes in, bright as a bloody daisy, hair done, make-up too, and announces she's off to the spa, then going out to lunch after that.

'What?' I asked her. 'But what about . . . ?'

But she didn't even let me finish, just interrupted with something about having loads of time and trotted off. Damn smile on her face too.

So, like I said, fuck Patty and fuck Patty's plan.

I'll do it myself.

What do I need her for anyway?

I'll fill a bag with food and spare clothes, get the bag I need from the garage and head out.

Hide somewhere till it's dark.

Then . . .

Jeez, I feel nervous already.

The Stanton house

The flames in the fireplace have been dead for hours. In the grate something shifts and a pile of ash, in the shape of the log it was, collapses. On the sofa Eve moves in her sleep and the blanket slips from her.

She stirs as the cold hits her skin and slowly blinks her eyes open.

In front of her the television is on with the feed of Isaac, and she reads the stats running across the bottom and sits up.

The light from it sends strange shadows across the room, and as she rubs the confusion from her head she picks up her phone and checks for messages.

Nothing.

Her eyes focus on the time in the corner of the screen.

'How did I sleep until midday?' she mumbles to herself.

On bare feet she pads out of the living room, across the kitchen and down the hallway. At the front door she stops; Max's key is not on the hook. She turns around; his jacket is not on the peg and his shoes are not underneath.

Taking her phone from her pocket, she dials his number, and as she stands there in the gloom it rings and rings, but there is no answer.

Back in the kitchen, her hand hovers over the drinks cupboard for a second, but then she moves away and switches on the kettle. As she waits for it to boil, she flicks the television to the lunchtime news.

'. . . across the east, with chances of showers in the south. In short, if you're going out today, then don't forget your umbrella.' The weatherman smiles into the camera. 'And back to the studio.'

Eve takes a mug from the cupboard and lifts down the jar of instant coffee.

'Thank you,' the newsreader says. 'Before we return to the headlines, let's have a look at today's papers.'

Eve spoons coffee into the mug, turns and takes the milk from the fridge. She unscrews the cap.

'Both *The Daily* and the *National News* are running with the same front-page story today. "The Hypocrisy", states *The Daily*, while the *National News* runs with the headline "I'm So Sorry".

'These both refer to the story that has broken overnight –'

Eve pours milk into the mug and looks up to the television.

'– of Eve Stanton, and a letter she wrote to her son, Max.'

Eve's mouth drops open.

'Stanton, previously designated counsellor to the accused, fought for the instigation of the post following her husband's incarceration and subsequent execution for murder, a case in which he always claimed he acted in self-defence.'

Eve stands stock-still, staring at the screen.

'However, this new development puts the whole case into question, as within the letter she states, and I'll read it for you . . . "I should've told you a long time ago, but there never seemed to be the right time. I feel I owe you the truth, and it's only right that you find out from me and no one else. I'm so sorry, but the truth is that it was me who killed that man –"'

Her hand releases and the milk carton thuds to the ground, spraying her legs and the cupboards and spilling over the floor.

'"– not your father" . . . It goes on to explain further, but –'

Eve stares at the screen, her breath coming in pants, her heart beating out of her chest. Slowly she puts her hand over her mouth and her face pales.

'No,' she whispers. 'No, no, no . . .'

She falls to the ground, crouching on her hands and knees among the spatters of milk, her whole body shaking.

The newsreader continues. 'It's not known where the letter came from, but both newspapers claim the handwriting has been analysed and does indeed match Mrs Stanton's.'

Eve picks herself up off the floor, milk dripping from her hands and running down her legs, and she scurries to the bedroom.

'No,' she says again. 'Please, God, no.' She pulls out drawers, tears through piles of papers, roots through the bin, but can't find what she's looking for.

'Fuck!' she shouts, and her reflection stares back at her from the bedside mirror. 'Fuck!' she shouts again, and she picks up the mirror and throws it at all wall.

At her bare feet the pieces cast back fragments of her face.

Max

The toes of his trainers stretch over the edge of the dock and he stares down into the water below, watches it lapping and splashing up the wall. Out on the river a boat speeds along and he waits for the wave and the spray to wet his jeans.

In his pocket his phone rings and he lifts it out and stares at the screen.

'Mum,' it says.

He waits for it to stop.

'Four missed calls,' it reads. 'One voicemail message.'

He clicks the button and holds it to his ear. The message plays back Eve's voice – '*Max . . . Max, I'm so sorry. Can we talk? Will you call me back? You shouldn't have found out that way. It didn't happen like they're saying. I didn't force your father . . . He . . . I can't talk about it like this. Please, Max, come home. Let's talk. Please.*'

It clicks off and the automated voice takes over.

'Press one to delete, two to replay, three to store.'

Max clicks on one and puts the phone back in his pocket.

For a second he looks out over the river. Then he takes the phone again and dials in a number.

'Yeah, it's me. I need to talk to you. Can you meet me? . . . OK . . . an hour then. See you there.'

He takes a deep breath and exhales slowly. Then, lifting his arm behind him, he launches the phone into the river and walks away.

Martha

I'm so unsure about this.

It's staring at me. That bag with the bomb inside it. Propped up against the wall inside her garage like it's just got sports gear in it or something.

Not explosives.

Makes me feel sick just looking at it.

'If you're not willing to try and save him, I need to know; then I can find someone else.' The memory of Patty's voice echoes in my head. *'Find someone who cares more.'*

Manipulating cow.

'There is near zero chance of anyone being injured,' that man said to me.

What could possibly go wrong?

I stare at it some more.

'Everything,' I say out loud.

But what's the alternative?

He dies.

There's a clock on the wall in here and it reminds me of being in that cell.

Three o'clock.

Six hours till his possible execution.

Patty's still not home.

The bag stares at me some more, the phone – the detonator – next to it.

It's almost as if I can hear them tutting and sighing at me.

Your fingerprints are all over that bag, the voice in my head says.

'Bugger it,' I say, and I grab the bag and snatch up the phone and march out of the garage.

Isaac

How did you feel when you were in here, Martha?

Did you feel as scared as I do now?

Did you long to have someone hold your hand or take you in their arms?

To whisper in your ear that everything will be all right, even though you'd still know, deep in your heart, that it wouldn't be?

Have you worked out the puzzle ring? Is it on your finger now?

I wish you were here with me. I wish we could sit together here on the floor, close our eyes and remember those evenings we spent at Bracken Woods, and live in that moment forever.

There is so much hate in this world and so much fear and so little understanding.

I hope – my God, do I hope – that you can change things, Martha. Wherever you are.

Max

'You need to talk to her.' Cicero lifts the cardboard cup to his mouth and sucks coffee from the hole in the lid.

People buzz around them, pushing through gaps to reach the queue for fries and burgers, loitering for free seats with trays balanced in hands, children clinging to parents, pram wheels spinning on the tiled floor.

Max rubs his head against the noise. 'Did you know?' he asks.

'No,' Cicero whispers.

Max toys with the straw in his cup. 'Aren't you angry?'

Cicero smooths down the sides of his moustache as he thinks. 'No,' he replies.

'But she –' Max leans across the table – 'she killed someone, and she let my dad take the blame.'

'Hmmm.' Cicero nods slowly. 'He *chose* to take the blame. She didn't force him.'

'He died.'

'For her. For you.'

Max scoffs. 'What? Like Jesus or something?'

Cicero leans back in his seat. 'No. Like a man who loved his family.'

'It's fucking shit.'

Cicero winces against his language and at the table opposite a mother with young children tuts and shakes her head.

Cicero folds his fingers together and leans towards Max again. 'Max,' he whispers, 'how did they get the letter? It wasn't you, obviously. Eve thinks they must've broken into the house.'

Max drops his head and stares at the table. His face is stone.

'Max? *Was* it you?'

He shakes his head and a tear falls onto the table. Roughly he wipes his face, sniffs loudly and looks back up at Cicero. 'No, but I took it from her room the day she was arrested. Remember you asked me to go get the phone? I saw this envelope with my name lying on her bed and I picked it up. But I didn't open it. I . . .' He looks away again.

A couple sit down at the table next to them. As the man takes their food from the tray, he turns the cup and a photo of Martha is printed on the side, the words 'Wanted for crimes against the state. Reward offered' stare out.

'She threw it away,' Max whispers.

Cicero frowns at him, confused.

'Martha. I met her. She took the letter from me. Opened it, read it, then ripped it up and threw it in the river.'

'Then . . . how . . . ?'

Max shrugs.

'You met her?' Cicero whispers. 'When?'

Max drops his head into his hands. 'This is so messed up, Judge. Martha . . . she's going to . . .' He closes his eyes and puts his hand over his mouth.

'What?'

Max looks back up, his eyes brimming with tears.

'What, Max?'

He shifts his hand to the side, covering his face from the couple next to them. 'I can't tell you, Judge. Just promise me, promise me that you'll stay away from death row tonight. And keep mum away too.'

'Max, I don't understand. Your mum's going to want to –'

'I've got to go,' Max says, and he stands up to leave. 'There's one more thing I can do.'

Cicero reaches out to grab him but misses. 'Stay out of this. It's too dangerous.'

'Just keep her away from death row,' Max says, jabbing his finger in the air. 'And you stay away too.'

He turns, pushes through the queues of people and disappears among the crowds.

Martha

When the shit hits the fan it really hits, doesn't it?

Divide and conquer, they say.

Guessing that will do it. Max is going to be pretty ticked off with his mum, and with me, and probably with Cicero. Eve's going to be ... well, apart from damn bloody annoyed and upset, probably arrested too.

What to do? Start with putting this bloody newspaper in the bin, that's for sure, and curse whoever wrote the article.

Glad I saw it though. Glad I know.

But how the hell did they get the letter?

They couldn't've had it before I took it from Max, it was sealed.

And when I opened it, I held it, for what? A minute at most. Before I ripped it up and threw it in the dock.

They couldn't've fished it out of there.

Then how ... ?

I look up and my eyes drift to the top of the lamp post next to me; there's a camera up there.

I scan around the area; there's another one about a hundred metres away.

I look back at the newspaper, the image of the letter, the angle of it.

Bloody hell. It's a photograph of the letter. A still from a video ... or a CCTV feed.

A shiver runs down me.

They read it over my shoulder.

Bastards.

But . . . they couldn't've known about that letter before they saw it.

Was it just luck? There was nobody following me. Then how . . . ?

I cut through a passageway between a couple of old buildings. It opens up to a courtyard, some kind of cafe with some benches outside, and I sit down, trying to think.

How . . . ?

I close my eyes. Images of the last week spin and turn through it. Flashes of watching *Death is Justice*, of being near the Old Bailey, outside the TV studios at the Royal Courts of Justice, in Patty's house.

Something, somewhere, will be odd. You just need to find it, I tell myself.

Think, remember . . .

Go back to the beginning . . .

Being on *Death is Justice*.

Then Eve's house, God, it's so hard to remember anything. It's all fuzzy.

Having to leave.

Then Gus's place.

The men outside.

Handing out phones to everyone.

Oh God . . .

The PM's speech. His concession. Giving phones to everyone in the Rises. Of course.

But I didn't get a phone. I've never had one.
I think back again . . .
Jeez . . . Max's phone.
The one he gave me.
They tracked me on it. They're tracking everyone.

Isaac

Will you come, Martha?

Will you watch me die?

Will you speak for me?

Make my plea even though it's futile?

'The time is: 5 p.m. You have –'

Can I walk alongside you when I'm dead?

Will you feel I'm there?

Can I stay with you as you live your life?

Can I whisper in your ear when you sleep and tell you I love you still?

'– four hours until your possible execution. The current stats are –'

Will you find someone new to love?

Will I leave you then?

Will we be together in death when your time comes?

Or will you forget me, forget us and our story after my eyes are closed?

'– 96.4% in favour, 3.6% against. We will update you in –'

I will be dead and there will be nothing.

A plaque or a headstone growing old, turning mossy, left to crumble.

A mark of a life that meant nothing, did nothing.

Who everyone forgot.

'– one hour.'

Max

Max walks from light to shade to light to shade as he heads down the footpath, the day already cut short and the streetlights throwing pools of white on the grey path.

Tall Edwardian houses loom, and as he passes he glances at each number, slowing as he reaches the sixties and stopping at sixty-four.

He stares up the stone steps to the wooden door painted black, a knocker, no lights inside, only darkness.

With his head down he takes the steps, pauses for a second at the top, then raps the knocker and waits.

No reply comes.

He knocks again and after a few minutes a jangling of keys comes from the other side and the door opens.

Joshua stands in the light of the hallway.

'I'm Max Stanton, Eve Stanton's son. I'm friends with Martha Honeydew –'

'I know who you are. I presumed it was some kind of hoax, the phone call, but seems not.'

'I don't know what you're talking about, but I need your help. *She* needs your help. If you don't let me in now to talk, people are going to be killed and everything is going to go to hell.'

For a moment Joshua stares at him, his breathing heavy and a frown on his face. 'I suppose we should drive to the studios,' he says eventually.

Max raises his eyebrows. 'I don't think they'll be welcoming you back after what happened yesterday.'

'I didn't mean for me to present the show,' he says, and he steps aside to let Max in.

The Prime Minister

'This is not organised, and you promised me organised,' he snaps into the phone as he sits in front of the bank of screens. 'She could be anywhere. I've had my team scouring the feeds, but nobody can find her. It would help if you knew what she was wearing . . . Well, your ineptitude is staggering and I will be holding you personally responsible . . . I don't want to hear apologies, we'll talk when this is over. In the meantime, play your part.'

As he puts the phone down, there's a knock on the door behind him and Sofia comes into the room.

'Is everything all right, sir?' she asks.

A thin smile stretches across his face.

'Everything seems to be splendid, thank you.'

Eve and Cicero

'We stay here,' Cicero says, standing beside Eve's kitchen table as she brushes her hair.

'I can't do that. I have to be there. I owe it to that boy.'

'You owe it to your son to do as he asks.'

'He'll understand.'

'No, Eve, I don't think he will. You have to respect his wishes.'

'He's angry with me, I get that, and this is his way of getting back at me. Not letting me give anyone else my attention. I lied to him and I hurt him, but I cannot stay away from death row tonight.'

'Eve –'

'No, Cicero.' She puts the hairbrush down and takes her jacket from the back of the chair.

'The press are going to have a field day. They're going to make it hell for you.'

'I don't care. I'm not going to sit here and watch that boy being killed on live television.' She slips her feet into her shoes.

'Eve . . .' he says.

She turns to him and takes his hand. 'You are my best friend, Cicero. I don't want to do anything to jeopardise that.'

He gives a sad smile.

'But I need to do this.' Her voice is quiet and mild. 'After that article today, it could be me in there next week. They could come for me –'

'They wouldn't do that, not now,' he whispers, squeezing her hand.

'They could, Cicero, and I can't show weakness. I *have* to be there. I *have* to go. Please understand that.'

'OK,' he whispers.

'Thank you,' Eve replies, and she leans forward and kisses him on the cheek.

Martha

Here I am, hood up and hiding.

Rucksack on my back filled with explosive, and the detonator in my pocket.

I'm walking through the streets of the City. I've got time to kill, so I let the crowds pull me this way and that.

It's getting darker again. Long nights of winter, and days when the sun's stuck behind grey clouds and it's just gloom and rain. It matches my mood.

Patty will be doing her nut now.

Or she should be.

I stop now and then. Catch the stats on someone's TV, or hear folks chatting about it. It's all they're talking about round here. It's big news. The way the media treat it, seems it's the only news; no wars going on in other countries, no natural disasters, no political unrest.

No, the only thing happening in the whole world is that a teenage boy has shot his adoptive father and is going to be put to death for it, and anyone linked to him, like Eve or me, is scum.

I turn a corner.

I'm at the Royal Courts of Justice TV studios.

So are hundreds of other people.

For a moment I stand, watching them all with their phones out taking photos, sending messages, videoing the updates on the screen in front of the building.

They want to be here when the decision's made.

In the future folks'll ask, *Where were you when the first teenager was found guilty and sentenced to death?*

And they'll have video mementos or selfies to show.

They all look so excited and pleased to be here.

Misery tourists.

Him over there though, he looks different. He's walked past that side door four times now. He keeps stopping and pausing and looking at something in his hand but I can't see his face. What's he doing?

He turns around and I manage to catch a glimpse of him.

Hell, I know who that is.

But what *is* Max doing? And what's he doing *here*?

I zip across the road between the traffic and fall into step next to him. He glances sideways and catches my eye under my hood, but he doesn't stop pacing.

'Where have you been?' he hisses at me. 'And why are you here?'

'Could ask you the same,' I reply.

He stops walking and glances to the rucksack. 'Is that . . . ?'

I nod.

'Shit, Martha!'

I've never heard him swear before.

'Why . . . ? What . . . ? There are *hundreds* of people here! What are you doing? Where's the . . . the . . . ?'

'The detonator's in my pocket.'

'Shit!' he says again.

'Max, shut up. It's turned off. I'm not about to press it.'

'I can't believe you've brought it here, and what *are* you doing here anyway? Shouldn't you be by the cells? What's your plan? You never –'

I lift my hands up. 'Shhhh,' I say. 'I was just walking. I had to get away from Patty.' I step closer to him 'What are you up to?'

His shoulders drop. He pulls his hands from his pockets, and shows me something cupped between them.

'A key,' he says, 'and a security fob.'

'Where did you get those from?'

He checks over his shoulder. 'Joshua,' he says quietly.

'What?'

'It's gone five,' he says, glancing at his watch. 'Less than four hours to go. He's meeting me in there, if I can find the right room.' He grabs my hands and squeezes them. 'I think I can get the stats down. You won't need to . . . to . . .'

My whole body tingles. My stomach tips like I'm going to be sick but with some kind of excitement or relief.

'But I thought you couldn't get into the system any more.'

'If Joshua can help me from the inside, then hopefully . . . maybe. But let me try, OK? Before you . . . do that . . . give me some time.'

'Course. But . . . when . . . ? What if . . . ?'

'I don't know any of the answers,' he mutters. 'You have to decide.' He looks at his watch again. 'I've got to go now.'

I want to wish him good luck, or grab him and hug him and say how grateful I am and how this could really work, but I just nod, and as he heads back to the side door, I turn away and blend into the crowd.

6.30 p.m. *Death is Justice*

Stage lights flash, the audience applaud. On the screen the words 'An Eye For An Eye For' spin around the iris of the eye. The words stop, the text turns jagged, accompanied by a synthesised sound effect.

From backstage strides Kristina Albright, her tight white dress slightly above the knee and low on the chest, blonde hair loose on her shoulders, and high heels. A slight pause in the applause is followed by whoops and whistles, and she smiles widely, her white teeth and her diamond necklace catching the light.

KRISTINA: Hello and good evening, ladies and gentlemen! Viewers at home all around the world, we welcome you to this fascinating special episode of *Death is Justice!*

The applause is deafening. She tosses her hair back with a laugh and raises her hands with her perfectly manicured nails to quieten the crowd.

KRISTINA: Thank you for such a warm welcome! Unfortunately your regular host, Joshua Decker, has been taken ill and I've had to step in at short notice. Joshua, if you're watching, do take time to recover properly. However, for me personally, it's an honour and a privilege to be back here with you, especially on such an auspicious day.

She pauses, waiting for the applause to die down.

KRISTINA: And what an evening's entertainment we have for you. Of course, top of the bill is the ongoing drama following Jackson Paige's death. What will happen to that miscreant son of his? Will he be put to death as many of you believe is deserved? I cannot wait to find out!

She strides across the studio and takes a seat at her desk, her long legs crossed delicately, one foot swinging in the air.

KRISTINA: I'm sure, just like me, you've all been following this case daily, or even hourly, holding on to every word Isaac mutters, watching every move he makes and building opinions of him in your mind. But, ladies and gentlemen, to me he seems something of a cold fish. Indeed, I've been disappointed with the low levels of emotion we've seen from him. Even yesterday's stunt with the cameras seemed calculated to spoil our viewing pleasure rather than motivated by passion.

On the screen to her right, the eye logo slides to the corner and the centre is filled with the live feed of Isaac in Cell 7.

KRISTINA: Look at him now, no nervous pacing, no biting of nails, no shouting, screaming or banging of fists on the glass. We don't even see any tears. What does this tell us about him? Cold-hearted? Uncaring? Unremorseful? Seems so to me. Surely an innocent person, or someone guilty yet sorry for their actions, would be crying by now. Ladies and gentlemen, teens, children, grandparents, I know how I would be voting; I know how I *have* been voting. I do not want such a monster walking the same streets as me, or as my family.

She pauses, letting her words hang in the air.

KRISTINA: With less than three hours until his possible execution, let's see the stats. Update us, please.

On the screen, the feed of Isaac minimises to the right while on the left two columns appear: Guilty and Not guilty.

KRISTINA: The last update, an hour ago, saw him at 98% guilty. Between you and me, I can't imagine why it fails to be at 100%, but let's see what the update brings.

Red lights run up and down the columns; the tension builds.

KRISTINA: The anticipation is killing me!

The display stops with a bang. Kristina's face falls. The audience are silent.

KRISTINA: My, well, isn't that a surprise? Perhaps we have an electronic fault here, viewers – 84% guilty seems a mighty large drop. Let's refresh again, shall we?

The results disappear from the screen and again the red lights run up and down the two columns. Again they stop with a bang. Kristina sits motionless with her mouth open. Silence hangs over the studio.

KRISTINA: Gosh, 78%, even lower. Seems we are experiencing a turnaround of opinions not seen since the Stanton case. Yet in reverse. How exciting!

Her face strains into a smile. The audience follow her lead and applaud.

KRISTINA: We are on the cusp of something truly special here this evening. What *are* the public thinking? What *do* they know? Something we don't? Surely this young man, who has publicly admitted to killing his father, cannot possibly be acquitted. Surely you, viewers, don't want him walking your streets? Let's recap the voting information. To vote Isaac Paige guilty dial 0909 87 97 77 and add 7 to the end, to vote him not guilty then add a 0. To vote by mobile phone text DIE or LIVE to 7997. You can also vote online by going to our website www.aneyeforaneyeproductions.com, click on the 'Isaac Paige Teen Murderer' tab at the top and log your vote. On the website you can also find up-to-date pricing information and our full Ts and Cs. Join us again after this short message from our sponsor, Cyber Secure.

Max and Joshua

In a small room in the basement of the Royal Courts of Justice, beneath the TV studios, Max and Joshua sit at a computer. The only light in the room is the blue tinge from the screen and a sliver of white under the locked door. Max taps away at a keyboard, while Joshua moves information and boxes around the touchscreen.

'It's still only down to seventy-four percent,' Joshua whispers.

'I can't drop it straight down,' Max says. 'People will be too suspicious. And there are votes coming in all the time. It keeps trying to go back up.'

'Are there still a lot of votes coming in?'

Max nods. 'A *lot*. There are a couple of numbers just on redial, constantly voting guilty. Who'd want Isaac dead so badly?'

'It's not Isaac they want dead,' Joshua explains. 'It's what he stands for. Those numbers will be government numbers. Technically the taxpayer is paying for those votes.'

'And now there's another number doing the same, the same prefix.'

'Government again.'

'But . . . the more I do this, the more they vote against it, the more I'm costing the people.'

'You can't think of it like that. You're fighting for something bigger than money.'

'Nothing's bigger than money.'

'Power,' Joshua says. 'Power is everything to them. What you're doing, your little gang of people –'

'We're not a *gang*.'

'That's how they see you. What you're doing is threatening their hold on power. They will do whatever it takes to stop that.'

'Whatever it takes? Like what?'

'Anything. Murder, bribery, lies, slander, blackmail. But you know this. They've already done it. Isn't it what this is all about? You need to take their power from them.'

'Why are you so interested anyway? I thought you were one of them?'

Joshua looks at him for a moment then looks back to the screen. 'Sixty-nine percent,' he says.

'Thank you,' Max mumbles.

'What for?'

'Doing this.'

'Hmm . . . well, after my speech yesterday, and you turning up, it seemed a case of act now or never. You know what I mean?'

'You think they're going to sack you?'

'Undoubtedly. I'm surprised they haven't already, but at the minute all I am is suspended.' He pauses and looks at Max, his face tired and drawn in the hue from the screen. 'Do something for me in return though,' he continues.

'What?'

'Speak to your mum.'

Footsteps sound from the corridor and they both freeze. Muffled voices talk but they're indistinguishable. In the distance someone shouts and the footsteps move away.

'If they find us in here we're screwed,' Max whispers.

'That we are,' Joshua agrees.

Martha

What's that in the air?

Anger?

Trepidation?

Fear?

Excitement?

It buzzes. Like static.

The people are wired. Edgy.

Flurries of chat, raised voices, fingers pointing.

I see them shaking their heads.

On the outside screen the stats readjust. Why's Kristina there? She looks nervous, worried. Where's Joshua?

Bang. It stops. There it is, in bright red, massive numbers – sixty-seven percent guilty.

People shout and jeer even more. They push and jostle. No smiles, just anger. Anger that someone could be found innocent. Someone could live.

How can they be so callous?

He did it, but it's not as simple as that, is it?

But they don't want complicated.

They want to see justice done. Their version of it.

They need a scapegoat. Someone to point a finger at and to blame.

Who told me that?

Patty.

Patty. Oh God, Patty.

The bomb. It's still on my back. The detonator's still in my pocket.

Jeez.

My face prickles with heat. Sweat on my top lip.

I want to get out of here. Need to. These people are scaring me.

How the hell could they possibly want someone dead so much?

Eve and Cicero

Eve's fingers drum on the steering wheel, her knuckles dry and split in places and her chewed fingernails stubby and broken.

In front of the car the traffic stretches out into the distance and on the windscreen come the first spots of rain. The wipers screech across the glass.

'Why didn't you tell me?' Cicero asks quietly from the passenger seat.

'I don't know,' she mutters in reply. 'Lots of reasons. I didn't know you as well then. I didn't want to put you in a difficult position.'

He nods. 'Whose decision was it? For him to take the blame.'

She turns to him. 'Would it make a difference to you? If I told you that I asked him to die for me, would you suddenly hate me?'

'No, Eve, not at all.'

The rain comes down heavier.

'I tried to talk him out of it. I begged him, but he refused. I didn't . . . couldn't –' She slams her hands onto the steering wheel. 'Why aren't we going anywhere? We're already late.'

Cicero sighs. 'Eve, please, calm down, let's talk about this.'

Ignoring him, she reaches to turn the radio on. Scanning through the channels, she stops as she hears the familiar voice of Kristina Albright.

'. . . quite unbelievable. The stats have dropped by an incredible thirty-three percent in the last two hours and now stand at sixty-five percent . . .'

Eve and Cicero stare at each other.

'. . . utterly unprecedented,' she continues. 'Even when compared to the Stanton case.'

'He could get off,' Cicero whispers.

Kristina's voice carries on: '. . . vocal and agitated crowds outside both the death row building and the Courts of Justice TV studios this evening, with chants claiming votes are rigged.'

'They want blood,' Eve says. 'Even if he's acquitted. What's going to happen if they do let him out? He'll be lynched.'

Cicero's phone sounds and he takes it from his pocket, his eyes squinting through his thick glasses as he reads the message.

'With Joshua. Sorting votes. Should be good. Fingers crossed.'

'We need to get there,' Cicero says, peering through the windscreen at the traffic stretching away into the distance.

'What?' Eve says. 'You've changed –'

'So have circumstances,' he replies, shoving his phone back in his pocket.

Without warning Eve swings the car violently to the side of the road.

'It's double yellows!' Cicero objects. 'You can't leave it here.'

She pulls the keys from the ignition and opens her door.

'Right now,' she says, 'I don't give a damn.'

Isaac

This is all like a dream. A nightmare. I thought when the last stats came in that I must be asleep or hallucinating, that maybe they'd drugged me or were planting images into my brain.

So I hit myself as hard as I could around the face, but nothing changed, and it did hurt, so I think I must be awake.

The clock behind me says 7.58. I'm expecting the next update to be back up in the nineties. I can't let myself be excited or think that perhaps I could get out of here and see Martha again. That I might *live*.

I'm standing in front of the glass, staring out at the seats and the faces watching me and I've looked at every single one and she's not here.

Why?

What was it that caller said yesterday? *Catch her*. I wish someone would explain that to me, but who? I see no one but the guard who moves me, and he doesn't say a word.

I hoped she'd be here; I wanted to see her one last time. But then I didn't want her to see me die. I wanted her memories of me to be good ones, not of my eyes popping out of my head or my hair setting on fire or me screaming in pain.

But what if she is on the run?

And what if I do get out?

Patty's not here. That empty seat in the front row must be hers.

Eve isn't here either. Nor Cicero or Max.

Why?

'The time is: 8 p.m. You have: one hour until your possible execution. The current stats are . . .'

My stomach flips. They've taken to leaving these long, drawn-out pauses. Up the tension or double-check the figures, I'm not sure which.

I breathe in, out, in, out, but too quickly and I'm dizzy.

'63% in favour, 37% against. We will update you in: thirty minutes.'

Hell.

I have to rest a hand on the glass to steady myself.

They need a majority to execute me.

It needs to drop by another 13.1%.

I could get out.

I

could

get

out.

But . . .

Martha, wait for me.

Be there for me.

If . . .

No, don't even dare to think it.

Martha

The City's going mad. It's everywhere.

Every screen, every newspaper, every conversation.

It's all I hear.

'He's a murderer.'

'He deserves to die.'

'Screw the stats, fry him anyway.'

'Get that Honeydew girl back in too! They're both guilty as hell!'

I shudder at the sound of my name.

Crowds are moving through the streets. Some with serious faces pushing past and scuttling home; parents too, some dragging kids at top speed or ramming pushchairs through gaps between bodies, worried. Others clearly don't give a damn and are clothes shopping or eating food as they lean against railings while chaos threatens around them, but most have one thing in mind now and have turned away from the TV studios, have left the cafes and bars and shops and are heading to the death row building.

And so am I.

Less than an hour for stats to drop below fifty.

I want to be there when he gets out.

And if it doesn't drop?

Then I know what I need to do, and I will do it.

In the distance Big Ben strikes quarter past the hour.

Hell.

Get there, Martha.

And be quick about it.

Death is Justice

To the right of the stage, the screen is filled with the live feed of Isaac in Cell 7. Kristina stands to the side of it; a forced smile stretching across her perfect face. In front of her the audience are agitated, commenting among themselves, talking into mobile phones or tapping at the buttons.

KRISTINA: What an evening's entertainment this is proving
to be, as we bring you yet another first on this,
our iconic programme, showing true democracy
and justice in action as –

AUDIENCE MEMBER 1: This isn't justice! He's a murderer!
He deserves to die!

KRISTINA: – as votes are cast and counted. We can tell you
that we've had a record number of votes received
today, a grand total of –

AUDIENCE MEMBER 2: Because everyone wants to see
him die of course!

Kristina's smile falters. A brief loss of control flits over her expression before she rallies and looks back into camera.

KRISTINA: Let's sneak another look at those stats.

The live feed slides away to the right of the screen again as the left is filled with the two columns. The red lights flicker up them.

KRISTINA: I for one cannot wait to see those figures zooming back up the guilty column.

There's the usual bang. Kristina stares at the screen. It reads 55% guilty; the lines on the two columns nearly level. She looks out to the audience who glare at her in silence. She clears her throat, touches her ear and looks into camera.

KRISTINA: With half an hour still left on the clock anything, *anything*, could happen.

AUDIENCE MEMBER 3: It's a fix!

AUDIENCE MEMBER 4: We want him dead! Society deserves justice. *We*, the people, deserve justice.

AUDIENCE MEMBER 5 (shouting): KILL THE KILLERS! NO EXCEPTIONS!

The audience jeer and shout, some standing, some raising fists in the air. Two security guards move onto the stage. Kristina, her plastic smile back in place, but uncertainty in her eyes, steps back to the desk and sits awkwardly on her high stool.

Martha.

Sweat is running down my back.

I'm running through the streets now. Forcing my way between crowds of people who shove me one way then the other.

People are angry.

They frown at each other, sneer, shake their heads.

They're hungry.

They're animals and someone's threatening their kill.

They're vampires desperate for blood.

Frantic.

I keep my hood up.

God knows what they'd do if they knew it was me.

I jostle between a bunch of young men, cans of beer in their hands. 'He gets out, I say we kill the bastard,' one of them says.

'Yeah. An eye for an eye – we shoot *him* in the head.'

'It's a fucking joke. Too many fannies and sympathisers, *that's* the problem with this country. Power for the people is what we want. KILL THE KILLERS!'

They chant it over and over.

It fills the air; rings in my ears.

I move across the road away from them, find a spot near a family, a mother and her two sons, thinking it'll be safer.

'You know why we're going, don't you?' I hear her say.

The children stare at her.

'The Good Lord says in the Bible, "An eye for an eye, a tooth for a tooth." That is what He tells us to do, but some people question the sacred text and see fit to fly in the face of His good word . . .'

What the hell?

'God wants him to die. We need to see God's work is done.'

Just get away from them, I tell myself, and I push and force my way through as best I can, hoping beyond hope that somewhere in this crowd are some who believe in fair and equal justice, who believe in a loving, understanding and forgiving God, if they want to believe in one at all, and who don't believe without question the crap the newspapers spout and who don't follow blindly like sheep, but think about things enough to make up their own minds and form their own opinions.

The crowds get bigger and bigger the closer I get to the death row building.

People are standing on the railings, banners spread between them pleading for Isaac's death, just as I would plead for his survival.

Their hatred rises like warm breath in cold air, seeping into my skin and filtering deep into my bones, but I won't let it infect me.

You are wrong, I want to shout at them. *Open your eyes! Question! Look at why he did it! You ignorant, narrow-minded . . .* Jesus, there is no word to describe them . . . *imbeciles, idiots . . .*

Not insults, Martha. Use your brain, don't sink to their level.

Prejudiced.

Bigoted.

384

Intolerant.

Yeah, fuckwits works pretty well too though.

Strange things come back to you at odd times. Remember school? Remember Mr Shaw, the RE teacher? His favourite saying?

There is nothing more dangerous than the conscience of a bigot.

I don't remember who said it, if it was someone famous or whatever, but I get it now.

The eye logo on top of the building blinks across the darkness; that ice-blue iris lit up neon and reminding us all what happens if we don't do as they want us to. Now and then it fizzes like lightning.

Or electricity.

I'm surrounded by people who want the blood of the man I love, and it hurts like no physical pain I can imagine.

I lean towards a woman watching something on her phone.

'What are the stats?' I ask.

'A bloody joke, that's what.' She turns and points behind me; some journalist has set up a massive screen for updates.

She shakes her head as the numbers come up. 'Only fifty-two percent now. Can't believe it. That's some justice for you, hey? Shoot a man, admit to it, get let off. It's a joke.'

'That's the system we voted for,' I point out, keeping my head down. 'S'pose it works both ways.'

'What?'

I shrug. 'Must be plenty of folks who've lost their lives who were innocent.'

'Better that way than the other,' she replies.

I want to argue with her, but I don't have time. I push towards the railings and peer through. There's the path leading to the entrance for the Cell 7 viewing area, there's the window to what was the counselling room that I stared out of so many times, hoping to be free, and there's the tree where the bird sat, that gave me hope and reminded me of life outside.

The memories stop me for a second. It could've been so different. I could so easily be dead. I'm living in extra time. I need to make it count.

I breathe deep, gather myself.

Come on, girl.

Near the old counselling room, an impromptu car park has been made on the grass, suppose because of all these folks here. But they're not regular folks' cars; they're all big posh ones like Patty's. Yeah, one probably is Patty's.

I scan the registration plates as best I can.

There it is – P P41GE – tucked up close so she doesn't have to walk far and get her hair wet in this rain.

Someone shoves me sideways and I grab the railings to stop myself falling.

'Eleven minutes,' I hear him say. 'Still a majority though, ain't it? Fifty-two percent. They'll still fry him.'

Hell, I think to myself, *I've got to get in there.*

I move on past the railings and towards the turning that runs around the wall to the grounds.

This is it, I think. *Eleven minutes to go.*

And I disappear into the shadows and around the corner.

Isaac

I feel like an animal in a zoo.

Or a cow waiting at the abattoir.

I don't know what to do and I don't know what to think; all I can do is watch them as they watch me. I don't want to turn and see *that chair* waiting, nor think of all the people who've sat in it before me, whether innocent or guilty, and remember this time last week as Martha sat in it and I was out there.

I feel a hypocrite because I am guilty, yet the stats . . .

No, I can't think that. I daren't hope.

I want my three minutes to talk. Explain. Apologise. Just *speak* and know that people are listening.

Patty's in her seat now. She catches my eye and waves. She's smiling. Why is she so happy? I don't wave back.

Eve's at the side talking to a guard, one hand on her hip, the other jabbing in his face. I watch her. Now she's holding three fingers up, then she turns and points at me. What are you saying to him, Eve?

There's a sound behind me. I turn. A small door at the back of the cell is opening. For a moment I think about squeezing through it and trying to escape, but then I see it and I'm rooted to the spot.

Sliding in on the tracks is the machine they introduced for Martha. Automated, no need for an executioner, no chance of human error. I'm certain it's humming. A low electrical purr like it's already plugged in and ready to go. I think it is.

It stops behind the chair, its metal crown waiting for my head.

I feel sick.

I'm shaking.

I can't look away. I step towards it, extending a hand to touch the metal. It is buzzing, and there's a strange smell to it, like Patty's overheating hair straighteners or fireworks. Metallic and burnt. As I lean closer to it I can see marks of charring on the crown, and now I see marks on the straps on the chair too. I rest my hand on the leather.

How many wrists have been held down there?

My legs are weak; suddenly I'm on my knees. Tears falling from my face.

I'm frightened.

I am so frightened.

Martha, I wish you were here with me.

I wish I could hold you.

Martha . . .

I hear a noise, a tapping, knocking, banging, and I turn around.

Eve is at the viewing window and I clamber to my feet and stumble over.

Her palm is on the glass and I lift mine and rest it facing hers. Her eyes are filled with so much care and love. And tears.

I hold three fingers up to her and frown but she shakes her head. Does that mean I won't be able to speak? How can they just change things so quickly and without explanation?

She's mouthing something now but I can't tell what.

One word over and over.

Guards run forward and pull at her, but she stands firm, still mouthing that word.

'Hope.'

That's what she's saying – 'Hope.'

Cicero is with her now, arguing with the guards, but I nod at Eve to tell her I understand, and she nods back, and as she takes her hand from the glass, she wipes her face and walks back to her seat.

Why didn't you do that, Patty? I wonder. So much for being *Proper Parenting*'s Mother of the Year two years running. But I suppose it really doesn't matter now.

Patty won't speak for me when the lines close, I know that. Maybe Eve will. I'd hoped it would be Martha, but . . .

'The time is: 8.50 p.m.'

Hope, I think.

'You have: ten minutes until your possible execution. The current stats are . . .'

Memories lurch into my head –

Hope is the denial of reality.

Hope is the mother of fools.

Hope is the worst of evils, because it prolongs the torments of man.

Hope for me now is ridiculous. Painful. I'm sorry, Eve, but you're wrong.

The pause drags on.

My head is throbbing and my stomach is tipping and turning. I lift a hand up and it's shaking and my legs are trembling.

'. . . 51% in favour, 49% against. The lines will close in: five minutes.'

My head spins. Fifty-one percent.

Oh my God.

I stumble to the floor and put my head between my knees.

Oh God, I can't see properly.

Only 1.1% more needed and I'm . . . I'm . . .

Hope . . .

Dare I?

I close my eyes and in my imagination I reach out a hand and Martha reaches towards me. Our fingertips so close. So close . . .

Hope . . . sees the invisible, feels the intangible and achieves the impossible.

Max and Joshua

'Why can't you just drop it right down now?' Joshua asks.

Max shakes his head, tapping wildly at the keyboard. 'I'm trying, but the lines are going mad. I'm doing the best I can, but there are so many people voting him guilty it's like I'm fighting against them.'

'Block the phone lines.'

'There are the internet votes too, and the texts.'

'Can't you block them all?'

'If we had time!' he shouts.

Joshua puts a finger to his lips and his eyes widen. 'Shhh,' he says. 'If they hear us –'

'OK,' Max hisses. 'Yes, I could block all the lines, but by the time I've done it, the votes will have gone up so much it'll be too late. Understand?'

Joshua looks at his watch. 'Three minutes until the lines close.'

Martha

Over the wall, across the grass, into the shadows of the cars, past Eve's tree and round the back to where no one can see me.

If the CCTV cameras have changed, then I'm screwed.

I can still hear the crowd. I caught the last stats – fifty-one percent – God in heaven, I hope I don't have to detonate this.

I use the lights from the windows above me to find my way, following what that guy said to me, and I run my hands along the wall, counting the windows to make sure I've got it right.

One, two, three, four, five, six and no window for seven.

Past the spiky bush and the drainpipe. Three more paces and stop. Bend down.

Yeah, here it is. Some kind of drain.

'So many prisoners vomit or defecate,' he explained to me, 'that the floors had to be tiled to keep it clean. They put a drain in so all the bodily fluids could be flushed out with a hosepipe. Of course, people around the front of the building don't want to see this, so it was installed at the rear.'

Lovely, I remember thinking.

I force my fingernails into the gap and prise the grille away from the drain. There's a sudden gush of lumpy fluid. It reeks and I gag, glad that I can't see the colour of it properly.

Pull yourself together.

I grab hold of the bag and shove it in the gap.

Then I turn the phone on, make sure it's ready to detonate, and put it in my pocket.

But then I stop.

I don't know why.

Curiosity maybe. Who knows?

I pull it back.

I must have about two minutes until the lines close. Seven until the execution.

If.

Quick. Quick.

My hands are trembling and my fingers are useless and clumsy, but I manage to pull the bag out and force the zip around.

What do explosives look like?

I put my hand inside.

It hits something solid.

Cold, clammy.

I lift it out.

And I stare at it.

What?

What?

That's . . .

My stomach tips again. I turn and throw up.

This is . . . This is . . .

Jesus, do I not understand, but I know and I know damn well that this in my hand is not any kind of explosive.

It's . . . I brush the wrapping with a thumb and squint through the darkness . . . it's . . .

'Modelling clay,' I read.

What? I stand up and chuck it down to the ground.

Modelling clay?

They didn't even try to make it look like explosives!

Jesus . . .

What do I do now?

What are the stats?

Jesus fucking H. Christ, Isaac, I've messed up and I can't do a thing now. I'm sorry. I'm so sorry.

I walk away, round in a circle, back again and I kick the bag.

'Fuck!' I shout. And I kick the bag again.

What if . . . ? What if . . . ? spins through my head. Lights in my vision, throbbing like I've stood up too fast.

Get to where you can hear the stats, Martha, my head says. *Come on, don't fall to pieces now, girl, come on . . .*

Yeah, I think, yeah, come on. Keep your head. Keep sane for when he comes out.

If he comes out.

Death is Justice

A line of security guards stands between the audience and the stage. Kristina is next to the screen again, her fingers fiddling. The audience are rowdy, some talking into phones, some tapping at the keys, some standing and shouting, others up in the face of the security guards, jeering, specks of saliva coming out of angry mouths.

Kristina touches her ear, smiles and looks into the camera.

KRISTINA: Ladies and gentlemen, loyal viewers at home, it seems our groundbreaking, revolutionary show here is, as ever, touching nerves and provoking reactions. We have –

She pauses and turns to the screen and the countdown.

KRISTINA: – thirty seconds until the lines are closed.

Isaac

I watch the audience as they watch me.

Still no Martha.

Is she watching from somewhere else? On TV?

I wish she was here.

Whenever I catch Eve's eye she lifts a hand and places it over her heart.

I thought I'd feel calm now, accepting of my situation, but instead I feel like I'm going to pass out any second, or be sick, or collapse on the floor again. I'm shaking, my head is pounding, my hands are sweaty and I don't know what to do with myself. I sit on the floor and need to stand, I stand and need to walk, I walk and need to sit.

I want time to stretch out ad infinitum so the decision is never reached, and at the same time I want it to stop now and end this torture of waiting.

My brain is confusion, illogic and nonsense.

It's giving up; the stress is too much to bear.

'The time is: 8.55 p.m. and the lines are now closed.'

Oh hell.

My legs won't hold me any more.

'The final stats are ...'

I slump to the floor.

I can't stop crying.

Shaking.

My head spins.

'48.7% in favour, 51.3% against.'

Oh God.

Oh God.

Oh . . .

I look up.

Forty-eight percent in favour? In favour of what? For a moment I panic, I can't remember what is for and what is against.

Then I see Eve standing up.

Smiling. Crying. But smiling.

Nodding her head.

I smile back and tears are pouring down my face.

I'm going home.

I'm going to live.

Martha, I'm going to live. I'm going to be with you soon.

Eve and Cicero

Eve sits back down, closes her eyes in relief and tears slip down her face. She feels Cicero's arm go around her shoulder and she leans into him, his warmth and compassion wrapping around her.

Neither says a word, but they reach out and seek for each other's hands.

Max and Joshua

The light of the computer blinks out and the room is cast into darkness. Joshua takes his jacket from the back of the chair and wraps it around himself.

Zipping his own coat up, Max turns to Joshua.

'I still don't understand why you opened your door to me,' he says. 'Or why you trusted me.'

Joshua pulls his collar up and sighs. 'I had a phone call,' he replies. 'Someone, a female voice, telling me a young man was on his way and I should help him.'

'How did they . . . she . . . ?' His voice trails off.

'I don't know,' he whispers.

Max steps towards the door. 'Who was it?'

'I don't know that either.' Joshua shakes his head. 'A secret supporter? A friend? Who knows? I did wonder if it was a trap. If this was *all* a trap. But I thought, What the hell? Like I said before, it was a case of act now or never. I took a gamble.'

'We're still taking that gamble,' Max says. 'Think we can get out without being seen?'

'Let's hope so,' Joshua replies. 'I know where the fire escape is.'

Death is Justice

The angry audience push against the line of security guards, fists in the air and faces contorted with rage. Kristina stands in the middle of the stage, arms raised and palms exposed.

KRISTINA (shouting): Please be calm!

AUDIENCE (chanting together): JUS-TICE, JUS-TICE, JUS-TICE.

Slowly her smile falters and she backs away.

Martha

I'm blinking and staring, staring and blinking.

I'm looking away, closing my eyes, opening them, looking back again.

But it still keeps saying the same.

I read it out loud off the journalist's display: 'In favour – 48.7%. Against – 51.3%.'

It's real.

It's. Real.

He's coming home.

He's saved.

Oh my God.

I stagger forward and rest a hand on a tree next to me and I remember Eve's tree and the bird.

Some lump in my jacket presses into me and I reach a hand into my pocket.

It's the phone, the detonator, and I laugh out loud.

'Didn't need it anyway, Patty, despite your double cross,' I say to the sky. Our sky, Isaac, with our stars that we are going to stare up at together again.

I can't stop the tears running down my face but I don't care.

I don't give a hoot because the man I love is saved and there is hope for the future.

I head out of the shadows and across the grass.

I see the cars, Patty's parked close, I see the door he'll be coming out of and I see Eve's tree.

I'm smiling and I'm crying at the same time. So excited I can't keep still, my body quivers and my fingers itch with excitement.

I shove my hands in my pockets and absent-mindedly I press a button on the phone . . .

BOOM!

Flash.

White.

Light.

Shock.

Force.

Flame.

Fire.

Heat.

Smoke.

Debris.

Dust.

Quiet.

AFTERMATH

Max and Joshua

'What was that?' Max asks.

They turn around, looking back towards the death row building, to where others are pointing. A cloud of dust is spreading into the air, floating over the eye in the sky. Not so bright now.

'Death row,' Joshua says.

Max shakes his head. 'She did it. Why? Why would she do that?'

'What?' Joshua asks.

'Shit,' he says. 'My mum's in there. I saw her from the computer room.'

And he starts to run.

Death row building

Silence.
  Dust.
  Stillness.
  Rubble.
  A cry.
  A scream.
  A sob.
  Coughing.
  Spluttering.
  A final gasp of breath.
  Bodies.
  Lights through dimness.
  Flashes of blue.
  On off on off on off.
  Wail of sirens.
  Louder.
  Brighter.
  Closer.
  Here.

Martha

Wha . . . ?

Wha . . . what happened?

Oh . . . my head . . . arms . . . back . . .

Throat's thick. Can't breathe. So much dust.

Ow. God.

Sit up, girl, look round, figure it out.

Walls are down.

Cars are on fire.

Alarms.

Sirens.

Some folks are staggering around, some lying still.

Think, think . . .

I was at the death row building.

I saw the stats.

He was free. I was heading around to meet him.

I was excited. So happy.

Look some more, think . . .

I run my hands over me. I'm alive and breathing.

I touch something next to my leg.

The phone.

Oh my God.

No, no, no.

You pressed the button.

This was you.

No. It was modelling clay. Not explosive.

The real bomb was somewhere else.

It was a trick.

It didn't explode around the back.

And it wasn't some small explosion like the guy said. It was a fucking huge blow-the-roof-off blast.

You detonated it. It was you.

My stomach tips.

My chest is tight.

I can't breathe.

I'm confused.

I suck in a difficult breath and look up. Look around.

Carnage.

But . . . where was the explosion?

The car park.

The new car park. Right next to the entrance.

They tricked you.

They played you the whole way.

You were never setting off a bomb to help Isaac escape. You were setting off a bomb for –

'Put your hands in the air,' some voice shouts at me.

– them to frame you.

Fuck.

I look up, but there are stars in front of my eyes and I can't see properly. I'm going to pass out.

'Hands in the air. Now.'

I do as I'm told.

You played right into their hands.

A light shines in my eyes. I flinch against it.

'I didn't do it!' I shout to the air . . . but actually, I realise, I did.

They drag me to my feet. I can barely stand. My head lolls forward and I see one of them grab the phone and put it in a plastic bag.

'No,' I cry. 'No, it's not my fault. I didn't mean to. They set me up!'

I look up. Flashes of cameras in my eyes, blue lights of police and ambulances, orange of streetlights, white dots of people filming on phones.

Through it all I see someone run towards me.

Be Isaac, I think, *please, please* . . .

It comes closer, dark shape against light.

'Martha!' it screams.

Eve.

'Oh God, Eve,' I say, straining against some police officer as my legs shake. 'It wasn't my fault. It was a trick. They tricked me. Patty. It was Patty.'

Eve tries to come to me, but the officers pull her back.

'It can't have been,' she says. 'Patty was in there.'

I shake my head. I don't understand. 'But, Patty, she told me . . .' But she's right. Why would Patty be in there if she knew this was going to happen? 'I promise you, Eve, this wasn't me. You have to believe me.'

But was it Patty? And if not, then who?

Eve nods her head and Cicero appears behind her.

I stumble again as I see he's alive too, and the police yank

409

my arms backwards and I feel the cold of the handcuffs on my wrists.

Eve lurches forward and takes me in her arms and this time they let her. 'I believe you,' she murmurs into my ear.

I stare at her.

'Isaac?' I whisper.

She doesn't reply. There are tears in her eyes.

I shake my head. 'No,' I say. 'Don't tell me that. No. Not after all this.'

'I don't –' she begins, but the police interrupt.

'Martha Elizabeth Honeydew, we are arresting you . . .'

I stop listening.

Who cares any more?

The Stanton house

In the dim light, Eve, Cicero, Max and Joshua sit around the kitchen table, cradling mugs of coffee, glasses of wine or a tumbler of whisky, while in the background the news chatters away on the television.

Plates of half-eaten bacon buns and sausage rolls sit in front of them, slowly congealing in their own fat, and strewn between them are photographs and pieces of paper.

Max picks one of the photographs up. 'They have us right where they want us,' he says, staring at the image of himself and Joshua sitting at the computer, tapping away at the keyboard to forge the stats.

'Where did this all come from?' Joshua asks.

'It was put through the door while we were out,' Eve replies.

Cicero slugs back the whisky and sucks at the bottom of his moustache.

He looks at Eve, but she's turned to the television. Frowning, she takes the remote and turns up the volume.

'Following the tragic explosion at the death row building a few hours ago, police now believe it to have been masterminded by a group trying to bring about the collapse of the government. It is believed this group is made up of dissenters already known to police – Thomas Cicero, Eve Stanton, Joshua Decker, Max Stanton, Martha Honeydew,

411

Isaac Paige and the late Lydia Barkova. Police are referring to them as the Rises 7.

'Following the attack, Paige is still missing, presumed dead, and Honeydew is in police custody. We are waiting to hear updates as to the status of the others and will bring you news as soon as we know.'

'What do we do?' Cicero asks.

'We go where we'll be welcomed and looked after,' Max replies. 'We go to the Rises.'

There's a knock at the door. They all freeze, looking from one to the other.

'Eve Stanton!' a voice shouts from the other side. 'Open the door. We know you're in there.'

Nobody moves.

'Mrs Eve Stanton! You are under arrest for murder and for perverting the course of justice.'

Eve shakes her head. 'Go,' she says to them all. 'Head to the Rises. I'll deal with this.'

'But, Mum –'

'This is your last warning. Open this door or we will break it down.'

'Go now,' she says. She leans across to Max. 'I love you,' she says.

He mutely nods his reply.

As Eve stands up, Cicero takes her hand. She pauses for a second, and something unsaid passes between them.

'Go,' she says again, and she walks to the door.

1.30 a.m. Credits roll for
Buzz for Justice

Slow, sad music. Lights spin above the studio then focus down on Kristina, standing next to the black witness box dressed in a deep green dress with black lace around the waist, black patent shoes and an emerald necklace.

Her hair is scraped up into a bun with well-placed strands falling over her face, and her dark lipstick glistens in the light as she smiles weakly.

KRISTINA: Welcome to our very special early-morning – in fact middle-of-the-night – episode of *Buzz for Justice*.

The audience applaud, but they are subdued; there is a seriousness in the air.

KRISTINA: This emergency episode is being brought to you live following the tragic events at the death row building yesterday evening, and our thoughts and prayers go out to those affected by the heartless attack.

She pauses for effect and drops her head for a moment. The audience are quiet. She looks back up.

KRISTINA: However, we are very pleased, and somewhat relieved, to share the news with you that the suspect was promptly arrested at the scene, and as with all our models of justice, her sentence will be passed promptly and thoroughly.

She turns slightly.

KRISTINA: Please bring out the accused – Martha Honeydew.

With her arms cuffed behind her back, her clothes caked in dust, and with blood on her knees and elbows, Martha is steered out across the stage and put into the witness box. Her face is scratched, bruised and bloodied, and she wobbles unsteadily on her feet. Boos and jeers sound around the audience.

KRISTINA: Moving this case speedily along as we all wish to see justice served in this, the most odious of attacks, let's go straight to the board. Please tell us – what is the crime, or crimes, which former death row inmate, Martha Honeydew, is accused of this time?

On the left-hand side, under 'CRIME', LEDs flash and flicker before the display settles. The list extends down the whole height of the screen – 'DAMAGE TO PUBLIC BUILDINGS, TRESPASS, DAMAGE TO PERSONAL PROPERTY, PLANNING AN ATTACK, PURCHASE OF A CONTROLLED SUBSTANCE, INSTIGATING AN EXPLOSION, CAUSING SERIOUS BODILY HARM, ENDANGERING LIFE, DETONATING A VEHICLE-BORNE IMPROVISED EXPLOSIVE DEVICE . . .'

MARTHA (shouting): A car bomb? What? I didn't do any of those. I swear I didn't!

Kristina mimes sliding a finger across her throat, and the sound from the witness box is cut. Martha's hands lift in exasperation.

KRISTINA: What a list. And tell us, what is the sentence for those crimes?

Next to 'TOTAL' the lights flicker and stop. Instead of numbers it reads 'LIFE'. A gasp comes from the audience.

AUDIENCE MEMBER: The bitch should fry! Why no death penalty?

KRISTINA: Yes, I feel I should explain here, that as there is currently no *verified* loss of life, the death penalty is not able to be imposed, although I must point out that should the bodies of Patty Paige or Isaac Paige, who are still missing, be found, or should

415

any of the eight of those currently in intensive care not survive, Honeydew will again be placed on death row.

AUDIENCE MEMBER: How? She blew it up, remember.

With a confident air, Kristina turns to the audience.

KRISTINA: We do have alternatives, sir. I can guarantee death row will continue. But right now we all need to see some closure here, so – to our panellists. Panellist number one, Robbi, how do you find the accused? You have thirty seconds.

The timer begins.

ROBBI: I don't need thirty seconds.

She slams on the button, and the eye shines down from above.

KRISTINA: My, my. Strong emotions here tonight. Let's not be too speedy. Our audience do like a bit of drama, you know! Panellist number two, Ishaan, let's move to you. Your time starts . . . now.

ISHAAN: Why didn't she get her thirty seconds to speak?

KRISTINA: It was felt insensitive to the families of those still in hospital. Twenty-five seconds left on the timer.

ISHAAN: I don't see what good locking her up would do.

KRISTINA: Do you want her let loose on our streets, Ishaan?

ISHAAN: But –

AUDIENCE (chanting): SEND HER DOWN, SEND HER DOWN, SEND HER DOWN.

KRISTINA: Fifteen seconds.

Panellist number one, Robbi, shakes her head at Ishaan.

ROBBI: Are you a fucking sympathiser or something? Do your duty. Press the bloody button!

Robbi shoves Ishaan on the shoulder. He shies away from her.

KRISTINA: You need to make a decision, Ishaan. Seven seconds . . .

The audience chant louder. Ishaan shakes his head, lifts a hand and gently presses the buzzer. The second eye lights up.

Cheers erupt across the studio. Kristina smiles.

KRISTINA: Well, decision made, ladies and gentlemen. We do only need two votes to convict, however for democracy's sake let's give our third panellist the opportunity to vote, and let's see if the vote will be unanimous! Sid, your timer starts . . . now.

Sid looks to the others, then to Martha, whose head is down and who is silent.

KRISTINA: Is there anything you want to say quickly, Sid?

Shouts and jeers come from the audience.

SID (nodding): Yeah, actually, there is. Teenagers nowadays are a bloody disgrace. In my day, this never would've happened. She should be made an example of.

KRISTINA: Twenty, nineteen, eighteen . . .

Sid stands and jabs a finger into the air as he speaks.

SID: She led us a right merry dance last week, made fools of us and the press. God knows how much that cost us taxpayers. She shouldn't be costing us any more –

KRISTINA: Nine, eight, seven . . .

SID: Put her back on death row, I say!

The audience roar.

KRISTINA: Five, four, three . . .

Sid slams a fist on the final buzzer and all three eyes shine their blue hue across the studio and onto Martha's injured face.

Kristina's smile spreads wide and bright.

The Prime Minister

In front of his bank of screens in the blue room, the PM leans back in his chair.

On one of the screens walk three figures – Cicero, Max and Joshua – bags in hands, as they step from the train at the underpass and walk towards the grass and the Rises in the distance.

He glances to a screen on the left – the feed from a police station. He presses a button and zooms in on Eve's face as she looks at a form on the table in front of her, the words 'Entry onto Death Row, Terms and Conditions' visible across the top. He watches as she lifts a pen and signs her name across the bottom.

Next he looks right – sees Martha being led across the front of the stage on *Buzz for Justice*, flinching as eggs and rotten fruit are thrown at her.

Finally he focuses on the screen above. The largest, it shows the carnage of the death row building. The ambulances and police have gone and the dust has settled. Yellow police tape stretches across it, keeping people out as it flaps in the wind.

He smiles, leans forward and switches off the screens.

'I'm done for the night, Sofia,' he says. 'We've done an outstanding job between us. You have been a remarkable help.'

No answer comes, but he fails to register that and as he stands and takes his jacket from the hook, he speaks to himself.

'One stone,' he says, '*all* the birds.'

Martha

They took my clothes. Put me back in white prison garb.

Took the ring Isaac gave me too.

And they've made me stand outside in this *pen* thing.

Said they didn't want trash like me in the police station. Said it was bad enough having me in their yard. They did take the handcuffs off though.

Freezing.

But what's it matter?

White headlights swing in and near blind me.

This is it then.

My last few minutes of freedom as they drive me to prison.

Freedom? What is that? Was I ever free? Were any of us?

The rear passenger door opens. There's a buzz and the metal gate in front of me opens too.

Hands grab my arm and I'm shoved into the car.

At least it's warm.

The doors thud.

The engine revs and we pull away.

I keep my head down, don't want to see anything.

Death row building

Everywhere is empty, the crowds all gone.

A man sits in a stolen car in the shadows, waiting.

His tears have come and gone and his face is dry now.

He steadies himself, steps out of the car and closes the door softly behind him. With a quick glance behind he walks calmly across the road and ducks underneath the flapping police tape. Keeping to the shadows, he pushes past the broken walls and railings and into the grounds of the death row building.

He passes the tree, now on its side, roots exposed and branches splayed and broken. He pauses to touch it as if hoping to offer it some comfort, before he carries on and disappears into the chaos of the rubble.

Half an hour later, he reappears. His hands are cut and bleeding, his face grazed and his whole body covered in dust. But in his arms he carries something.

Martha

The streetlights flash intermittently through the car windows.

White to dark, white to dark – but too quickly for me to see who's driving.

The journey to whatever prison I'm being sent to is longer than I expected, but I don't care.

I'm done.

So much pain and loss. Injustice, unfairness.

I've had it.

They win.

'Drink something.' It's a woman's voice; the driver. A plastic bottle hits me as she throws it back.

I open my mouth to make some quip about it being poisoned, but I change my mind. Just unscrew the lid and drink it down gratefully.

'Thank you,' I mumble.

I turn now, stare out the window at a city that's been my home for sixteen years and that I will never see again.

You've not been kind, I want to tell it, but the City's a victim just as we are.

I don't know where we're going, but I recognise these streets.

There's the eye in the sky, a little broken, its blue flickering, but still hovering over us all. I cry. Quietly and alone, watching as the eye gets bigger as we get closer to it.

Right near it.

Right next to it.

The driver, the woman, flicks the indicator and pulls over.

'What . . . ? Where . . . ?' I mutter, but she doesn't reply.

We sit, engine rumbling, waiting.

I can't help but look out. At the carnage they say I caused. The rubble, the remnants of the building, Eve's tree on its side, the bird probably dead. The explosion didn't go off where I left the bag; it was at the front, in the car park. A car bomb. Someone must've planted a car bomb, given me the detonator, told me it was for the bag they gave me. Lied. Caused this. Killed Isaac when all I wanted to do was save him.

Who?

Patty?

Then why would she have gone inside?

Still the same questions are going round my head and still I have no idea of the answers.

And I don't know what I'm doing in this car, or what the hell is happening, or who the woman driving is, or even what we're doing here.

I don't know anything.

I open my mouth to ask her, but suddenly she shuffles in her seat and flashes the headlights into the darkness.

'Move across,' she mutters to me.

I do as I'm told and I hear the clunk as she unlocks the doors.

'Stay here,' she says. 'Try to run and I can have you removed from the face of this earth in half an hour. Understand?'

I nod.

She climbs out of the car and I see her run in front of it and disappear. But I still don't see her face.

I could take off now, couldn't I?

She'd never find me, would she?

I could try.

Holy . . .

I freeze.

Blink.

Try to focus.

A man's walking towards the car, his body silhouetted in the headlights.

Something long and heavy in his arms, held carefully to his chest.

The driver woman's next to him, guiding him.

He's struggling with every step. His legs look like they're shaking. He's a skinny guy, doesn't look strong. Messy hair, scruffy clothes . . .

Oh . . .

The car door opens.

'Martha, help me.'

Gus.

Jesus Christ. Gus.

'How . . . ?' I say. 'What . . . ?' But I stop because next thing he's leaning in from the dark . . .

And he's . . . and he's . . .

A body . . .

He was a carrying a body.

He was carrying . . .

Gus lays him down next to me. I take his head in my hands

426

and rest it on my lap. 'Is he . . . ? Is he . . . ?' But I can't say the last word. Too scared of hearing a reply I don't want.

The door shuts.

Darkness again.

I rest a hand on his neck, feel for a pulse.

Please.

Can't. Oh God, I can't.

Gus inside now. The woman back in the driver's seat. Engine revs. Car pulls away.

'How?' I say between sobs, and I touch his hand. So cold.

'This lady here,' Gus says, peering through the darkness at me. 'That's how.'

'Who are you?' I ask.

She catches my eye in the rear-view mirror. Hers shine with mischief or excitement or . . . *something*.

'I'm Sofia,' she says. 'I think we can work together. Finish what you've started. But first . . .' She nods her head towards Isaac sprawled across me, unconscious.

Isaac.

Isaac?

My heart smiles with hope and thuds with fear, but as I lean over his bloodied and battered body and move close to his face, I swear I feel a whisper of breath.

Turn the page to read
an extract from

FINAL 7

the exciting conclusion
to the trilogy,
coming in 2018.

PROLOGUE

Martha

Was that a heartbeat?

I don't know. Can't find it now.

Can't feel it.

I move my hand, try again.

Nothing.

Try again.

Fuck, still nothing.

'He's . . .' I mumble, shaking my head. Can't say the word.

Can't end it.

Tears drip from me.

Can't see for blur.

I wipe my eyes. My hands feel sticky.

I look at them.

Looks like blood.

Isaac's.

The car tears down the road.

Streetlights flash through the window.

Light

dark

light

dark . . .

across Gus's face as he turns around in the front seat.

He's staring at Isaac; he stretches and puts a hand on his chest.

So calm.

Then he looks at me.

I'm shaking.

Don't know what to do.

I watch Isaac's face as light hits it.

Wish his eyes would open.

I close mine.

Stay with me, Isaac, I say in my head.

Something, a truck or lorry, flies past us so fast and heavy it rocks the car and I open my eyes.

The car slows.

'What the –' the woman driving says.

I open my mouth to ask who she is, but as I turn to look out the window, I stop.

Not far ahead, at the boundary of the Rises, under a barrage of floodlights, are rows and rows of lorries and trucks.

I squint through the windows and the darkness, blinking to try to make sense of what I'm seeing.

Cranes in the sky. Orange flashing lights. Workmen all over.

And massive ugly concrete panels, stacked up to make a huge wall.

For what? To keep us out?

Stop our influence? Control us?

What?

'Berlin,' I whisper. 'Israel, Belfast. Korea.'
'Now London,' Gus replies.
What the hell?
What the actual hell?

TV STUDIO

11 p.m. The programme – *Death is Justice: Late-Night Round-Up* – is beginning

The screen fills with an image of the outside of the death row building – recorded footage from a CCTV camera. Throngs of people. Half-light. The blue of the eye logo above it all.

The image shakes, distorts, blurs. A massive boom rocks the area and clouds of smoke rise into the sky.

GEROME SHARP (off-screen): This is Gerome Sharp, new roving reporter for *Death is Justice*, reporting live from the death row building. Viewers are warned that footage contains flashing images and scenes of an upsetting nature.

In the recording, clouds of dust plume towards the camera and the blue from the eye logo flashes and flickers.

GEROME (off-screen): As an earth-shaking explosion rocks death row we ask, did terrorists bring this carnage to the City?

The screen changes to a shaky image from a hand-held camera. People are screaming and running, some with blood pouring from them. Others stagger. The camera zooms in on the building. Bodies can be seen on the ground close by.

GEROME (off-screen): Countless injured as panic rips through the streets in what many are calling 'justice's blackest day'.

Blue lights flash over the scene. The wail of sirens and crying. The camera focuses on Martha on the ground with her hands in the air. Eyes wide and mouth open. Blood on her face. Police pointing guns at her as they approach.

GEROME: Fugitive, and prime suspect, Martha Honeydew is arrested at the scene. What may be a detonator is found nearby.

The footage fades and is replaced by live feed of Gerome Sharp at the scene: chiselled jaw, long dark coat and neatly tied check scarf. Running along the bottom of the screen are the words 'Terrorism in the heart of the City'.

GEROME: This important symbol of justice was brought crashing down earlier today in a targeted and bloody attack. Only minutes after the final verdict had been cast in the Isaac Paige case, an explosion rocked central London, threatening to bring the justice system to its knees.

At present the cause of the explosion is unknown, although many onlookers claim it was a bomb. We are also waiting for confirmation on the number of dead, however it's feared that the amount of people injured when the building crashed to the ground in clouds of smoke and dust, throwing the entire area into chaos, may well reach into the thousands due to the crowds the case attracted. Martha Honeydew, who has been the focus of a nationwide manhunt since her acquittal from death row a week ago, was arrested at the scene. While the exact nature of her involvement in the attack is unclear, CCTV footage shows Honeydew approaching the building wearing a backpack, leading to suspicions this could have been a suicide bomb attack gone wrong. We'll go to the Prime Minister now for a live statement on the events.

Acknowledgements

A big thank you to the whole gang at Hot Key Books – Emma Matthewson, Tina Mories, Charlotte Norris, Talya Baker, Melissa Hyder, Monique Meledje, Ruth Logan, Emily Burns, Emily Cox and Carla Hutchinson.

Special and MASSIVE thanks as always to my fab agent, Jane Willis, and the rest of the team at UA. And to Poppy for her enthusiastic reading!

Thanks to readers and librarians – Bobbie Quinn, Eammon Griffin, Melanie Wheeler, Katherine Jago, Lawrence Dunn, Robin Garland, Tarnia Roberts, Jo Smedley.

And to the LTC readers too – Gail Castledine, Michelle Cooper, Laura Peach, Laura Stott-Allworthy, Ros and Phil, Mags and Sean, Steve and Jo. Steve, I feel very honoured that *Cell 7* was the first book you've read since leaving school!

To the LAC gang, and Mick and Debbie – because I do remember the conversation while running through the cow field!

For so many laughs and sweary discussions, thanks to Kate and Richard Conway, Tracey Wilkinson, Chris Giles and Jac Hall – sorry neither c***w****e nor l**pd**k made it!

To authors Keris Stainton, Rhian Ivory, Jo Nadin, Zoe Marriott, Sheena Wilkinson, Paula Rawsthorne, Vanessa Lafaye, Rachael Lucas, Beth Miller, Emma Curtis, Sarah Todd Taylor,

Liz Kessler, Eve Ainsworth, Liz de Jager, Antonia Honeywell, Essie Fox, Louisa Treger and Rae Earl. To Chris Callaghan for always making me laugh, especially with the selfies! And thanks to The Prime Writers for your help and support – you guys are fab!

Massive thanks go to my writing pals, fellow sci-fi fans and sanity rocks Rebecca Mascull and Emma Pass, who offer sound advice, listen patiently when I moan and are always ready with the cake.

To Martin and Mim's Book Club – your discussions push me to think more and write better.

Thanks to family for everything – Russ, Jess, Danny, Bowen, my dad – Richard Gage – Ann Gage and Colin Gage; Meghan Holden and David Smith; Janet, Jack, and Paul Baron; Helen and Patrick Megginson; Pat Sheard; and Dan Hill (you've snuck in under 'family thanks', Dan!)

And finally thanks to you, the reader. Without you, there would be no books, no libraries, no bookshops, and the world would be a poorer place.

Kerry Drewery

Kerry Drewery is the author of CELL 7, the first book in this exciting trilogy which has been translated into more than a dozen languages, as well as two highly acclaimed, more literary YA novels: A BRIGHTER FEAR, 2012 (which was Love Reading 4 Kids Book of the Month and shortlisted for the Leeds Book Award) and A DREAM OF LIGHTS, 2013 (which was nominated for the CILIP Carnegie Medal, awarded Highly Commended at the North East Teen Book Awards and shortlisted for the Hampshire Independent Schools Book Awards). Both were published by HarperCollins in the UK and Callenbach in The Netherlands.

HOT KEY BOOKS

Thank you for choosing a Hot Key book.

If you want to know more about our authors
and what we publish, you can find us online.

You can start at our website

www.hotkeybooks.com

And you can also find us on:

We hope to see you soon!